AN ISLAND IN THE SUN

KATE FROST

Boldwood

First published in Great Britain in 2023 by Boldwood Books Ltd.

Cover Design by Alexandra Allden

Cover Photography: Shutterstock

A CIP catalogue record for this book is available from the British Library.

Paperback ISBN 978-1-80280-462-1

Large Print ISBN 978-1-80280-461-4

Hardback ISBN 978-1-80280-460-7

Ebook ISBN 978-1-80280-463-8

Kindle ISBN 978-1-80280-464-5

Audio CD ISBN 978-1-80280-455-3

MP3 CD ISBN 978-1-80280-456-0

Digital audio download ISBN 978-1-80280-458-4

Boldwood Books Ltd
23 Bowerdean Street
London SW6 3TN
www.boldwoodbooks.com

In memory of Frodo, our scrumptious Cavalier King Charles spaniel and the best writing companion I could have asked for.
Miss you, buddy.

1

Saying goodbye was always hard, but Tabitha Callahan was used to it. Most of her life had been spent moving from one country to another, making new friends, attempting to learn a new language, trying to fit in, only to move again and start over. The one and only time she'd decided to put down roots, it had gone horribly wrong. And the pain... She was trying her hardest to forget how it had all ended.

Twenty house sits and eleven countries in nearly a year. She'd lost count of how many animals she'd looked after: lots of dogs, a fair few cats, three lizards, a dozen chickens, two sheep and a Shetland pony called Comet. Not all at once, obviously. She'd fallen in love with every pet she'd met, but she had her favourites – a poodle called Midnight and Chester the boxer. There were a handful of locations she'd felt the tug of regret leaving too, but never strong enough to consider living there permanently. Not that she'd be able to afford the equivalent of a luxurious log cabin in Canada or a houseboat in Singapore. She was making new, happier memories, even if it was mainly animals who kept her company on a daily basis. What Tabitha loved the most was the ability to reset her life every few weeks. Starting from scratch in a new place where no one knew her was appealing.

Adjusting her rucksack, Tabitha gazed up at the flight information board. It was the tail end of summer, a warm afternoon at the beginning of September and Humberto Delgado Airport in Lisbon was filled with families and couples, along with a fair few single travellers like her. With no gate number yet and time to kill, Tabitha went in search of coffee.

It's going to be a long day, she thought as she settled herself in a corner of a coffee shop with a latte; it already had been. She'd said goodbye the day before to Lola, the tortoiseshell cat she'd been pet sitting in an apartment in Barcelona. The forty-something owner had returned after two weeks, and Tabitha had handed back the keys, spent a pleasant enough couple of hours over lunch with them before staying at a hotel near the airport ready for an early flight. She was now waiting in Lisbon for her second flight of the day to her final destination, the Portuguese island of Madeira, her home for the next three weeks, housesitting two dogs and a cat.

Tabitha snapped a selfie and posted it on her Instagram feed. A summer spent in Barcelona, and before that Provence, had left her naturally pale skin gently sun-kissed, the freckles across her cheeks more prominent. A mass of loose auburn curls framed her face where they'd escaped from a messy bun.

Clasping her latte, and listening to music through her AirPods, she watched the world go by. She didn't mind sitting on her own. Given the choice, she was perfectly happy to go for days without seeing another person; over the last year, she'd always had at least one pet for company – they were easy to talk to and excellent listeners. Tabitha smiled wryly. She never went days without talking to someone, though. Being part of a large and happy family, and the youngest of five, she was rarely out of contact with them. They had a Callahan family WhatsApp group chat where she kept up with her older brothers and sisters, Elspeth, Jack, Iona and Lorcan, and her mum and dad.

Elspeth regularly called – she stressed that it wasn't to check up on her, but Tabitha knew she wanted to make sure she was okay. Tabitha and Elspeth were best friends and closest in age, with only four years between them, compared to twelve with her eldest brother Lorcan. Even though Tabitha was thirty-two, Elspeth still felt the need to look out for her. Tabitha secretly liked it and loved talking to her. And it wasn't as if she never talked to anyone else. She spoke to her parents every week, plus wherever she'd stayed, people tried to strike up a conversation: a friendly neighbour in the apartment building; the barista in the local coffee shop; or a guy would hit on her, usually if she was having a quiet drink on her own. Her hair was often an opening topic of conversation. Long gone were the days of being teased for being a curly redhead; she'd grown into her looks, which were often described as 'striking'. The only trouble was, she didn't want the attention, particularly from men. Getting over heartache was easier on her own; after all, she'd wanted to escape. She was perfectly happy with the company of a dog or two.

The flight information board flashed with the gate number. Tabitha drained the rest of her coffee, slung her rucksack on her back and set off for her flight to Madeira.

* * *

It was unusual to be picked up by the house owners, but Rufus and Cordelia, a British expat couple, were adamant that it was no trouble. The flight was less than two hours, landing in Funchal early in the evening, so at least it meant that Tabitha didn't have to spend all day with them. She felt rather mean and unsociable thinking like that, but the personal questions were inevitable when having dinner with strangers – why she was travelling from place to place on her own for months on end being the obvious one...

Tabitha was a pro at this travelling lark, though. Not only was it in her blood, with her family having moved about since she was little with her dad's job as a water engineer, but she'd had plenty of experience navigating airports, train and coach stations over the last year as a pet sitter, finding house sits around the world as a member of a pet-sitting website. She'd been to countless places, but as the plane flew over the grey-blue Atlantic, she relished the idea of being somewhere far from anywhere. A beautifully green and mountainous island in the Atlantic Ocean took a bit of effort to get to. She liked that.

The flight landed on time and, as Tabitha waited for her luggage, she glanced at the other passengers. They were mostly tourists, young and old couples enjoying the relative peace that September brought, along with the added bonus of Madeira's subtropical climate. There were young families too with pre-schoolers, making the most of the cheaper post-summer holiday flights. Her suitcase, covered in stickers depicting her travels, was easy to spot and, with relief, her guitar had arrived safely too. She dragged them off, readjusted her rucksack, slung her guitar across her shoulder and set off.

Rufus, holding a neatly written sign with her name on it, was the spitting image of his pet-sitting profile picture. He looked relaxed in sunglasses, cream-coloured trousers and a linen shirt, his skin a leathery bronze colour. Tabitha's immediate impression was that he spent a lot of time outdoors, probably playing golf and sunbathing shirtless in the garden. He must be somewhere in his mid-sixties – she sensed he knew how handsome he was.

Over the last year, she'd got quite good at guessing not only people's ages but their personality and hobbies through their first brief meeting. Then, during the house sit, she'd discover if her first impression was close to the truth or not, coming to a conclusion through their pets, their house, the décor and the photos on the walls. It was fascinating to find out about people without having to make the effort of getting to know them in real life. She knew how that sounded, but she'd chosen to cut herself off as much as she could. It had been good for her, even if her family had questioned it.

Recognition crossed Rufus's face as he clocked her. With her red hair and distinctive style, Tabitha knew she was instantly recognisable.

Rufus lowered the sign as she reached him, offering his free hand. 'Tabitha?'

'Hi there, Rufus.' She shook his hand firmly.

'It's great to meet you at last. Here, let me take that.' He grabbed the suitcase handle and manoeuvred them out of the way of the continuing stream of arrivals, towards the exit. 'We're thrilled you applied to house sit for us. It will really help to put my wife's mind at rest while we're away.'

'Good, I'm glad.' Tabitha blinked as they emerged into bright sunshine. 'It's a win-win for everyone having a sitter.'

'You're a musician if I remember correctly?' He motioned to the guitar slung across her shoulder.

'A songwriter mainly, yes.'

'Have you written anything I might know?'

'Oh, I'm not sure. Depends if you're into upbeat pop.'

'Hmm, does Depeche Mode or Tears for Fears count?' His laugh boomed into the fresh, sunny day.

Tabitha couldn't help but smile. 'They're a little before my time.'

She'd got good at making small talk with the people she was house sitting for – that she could cope with; it was the questions that delved deeper she feared. Even though she craved being alone, she could manage brief pockets of time with new people. What she loved the most was the insight into other peoples' lives, which, she hoped, was slowly helping her to figure out her own.

* * *

Within a couple of minutes of driving away from the airport, Tabitha got her first glimpse of the ocean and a swathe of green-clad hills dotted with white houses with red-tiled roofs, before they plunged into the first of many tunnels as the road cut through the hillside above Funchal. The view of the forested interior on one side and the glittering ocean beyond the gleaming city disappeared and reappeared, making Tabitha blink in the brightness of the sunny evening as they re-emerged.

'That's the botanical gardens on your right,' Rufus said as they whizzed along the road, with the city of Funchal spread out to their left, its predominately white buildings carpeting the hillside down to the sparkling Atlantic. 'It's well worth a visit if you get the chance.'

Tabitha gazed at the landscape as it dropped away from the road, a lush valley rising up into jagged green hills, the shadow of a solitary cloud the only thing to taint the sun-drenched hillside. As they powered along the fast road, in and out of tunnels, Rufus chatted about the island, suggesting that Tabitha take Funchal's cable car up to the gardens at Monte Palace and telling her which levada trails – the system of channels built to carry water to different parts of the island – had the best waterfalls.

Eventually, they made it through the sprawling metropolis of Funchal and its outskirts. The tunnels continued where the mountainous island rolled right down to the ocean, the road cutting through the hillside and back out again to a village of cream and pink villas with banana plants and palm trees in gardens. Even after a year, the novelty of travelling hadn't got old. She could already see what a wild and special place Madeira was.

Rufus seemed more than happy to dominate the conversation, which was fine by Tabitha – although at times his constant chatter felt as if he couldn't bear for there to be even a few seconds of awkward silence. She found it interesting, though, listening to him talk about the island and the towns they passed as the volcanic interior loomed on their right, offset by the vastness of the Atlantic Ocean to the left.

The pets that she'd be looking after was another easy topic. After all, it was the reason she was here.

'My wife Cordelia has been so worried about leaving the dogs again.' Rufus glanced at her before turning his attention back to the road. 'They pined so much for us last time, Bailey in particular. They went to a pet sitter's house before, but Bailey is rather nervous, a real homebody. It's just not fair on him, nor Fudge. Misty's not fussed either way, you know how aloof cats can be, but we think the dogs will be much happier being looked after at home.'

'It's good to have that peace of mind,' Tabitha said.

'And you're it.' Rufus nodded. 'Particularly as we're going away for longer than usual.'

'You're going on safari, is that right?'

'Oh yes, a holiday of a lifetime to celebrate our fortieth wedding anniversary – starting in Cape Town, then exploring Stellenbosch winelands, on to Tanzania for the safari, then Zanzibar for a relaxing last few days.'

Tabitha happily listened as Rufus described what they had planned. It was a good fifty-minute drive from the airport to the house in the southwest of the island and the sun was beginning to set, a wash of gold spreading across the horizon. After what felt like an endless day of travelling, Tabitha was eager to reach their destination and meet Bailey, Fudge and Misty. She was relieved when Rufus eventually announced, 'We're nearly there.'

They turned off the fast main road onto a single-track lane that finished at the gated entrance of a large driveway edged by palm trees and bushes fringed with pink flowers.

Tabitha had learned not to go by first impressions and she got the sense that it would be the same with this place, the unassuming stone exterior cleverly hiding the luxurious and chic interior she'd seen in pictures.

'Well, we just made it back in daylight,' Rufus said as he parked next to a white BMW.

They got out into the still evening air, which was pleasantly warm and scented by the flowers filling the borders. Rufus took her suitcase and rucksack out of the boot and Tabitha pulled her guitar off the back seat and followed him towards the villa.

The front door opened and a woman appeared with a beaming smile.

'Tabitha, welcome!' She greeted her with a kiss on each cheek and ushered her inside. 'I'm Cordelia.'

Cordelia was also in her sixties, elegant and well-dressed for spending an evening at home. She had a deep tan, bright pink manicured nails, lots of rings, and her make-up was flawless. Long flowing baby-blue trousers were paired with a delicate floral blouse. Tabitha had opted for comfort in black cotton dungarees with a simple white T-shirt and she was wearing little make-up beyond mascara and her trademark red lipstick.

Leaving her bags in the entrance hall as instructed, Tabitha followed Cordelia and Rufus through to the large living and dining area at the heart of the villa. Despite the view through open bifold doors onto a terrace with an oblong pool, Tabitha's eyes were immediately drawn to the two Cavalier King Charles spaniels rushing towards her.

'The tricolour is Bailey,' Cordelia said with a smile as a black, tan and white Cavalier reached Tabitha.

Tabitha knelt down and offered the back of her hand. Bailey sniffed, his damp nose connecting with it.

'The tan and white is Fudge. They're brothers and seven years old. Our cat Misty is a law unto herself – she spends most of her time outside, but I'm sure she'll show herself later.'

Fudge was as eager as Bailey for Tabitha's attention. She stroked their soft heads and tickled beneath their long drooping ears. She'd looked after a Cavalier before and knew them to be the friendliest dogs with a lovely nature.

'They're absolutely gorgeous,' Tabitha said, thinking what good company they'd be.

Her attention flicked from them to outside. The tropical garden was bathed in the golden light of dusk and the sun was low on the horizon, retreating into the distant ocean. She breathed a satisfied sigh, knowing how, despite craving travel, she was more than happy to have this place and its four-legged inhabitants to herself for the next three weeks.

2

Cordelia was as affable and chatty as her husband and Tabitha began to relax. It wasn't always this way; not everyone she'd met over the last year was as easy to talk to. Cordelia took charge, showing Tabitha around, the dogs following them. The main living area had direct access to the pool and garden, plus stairs going up to a mezzanine level with two en suite guest rooms. At the back of the house was a swish kitchen filled with the delicious smell of something roasting. Rufus pulled on oven gloves and ushered them out.

'I chose well,' Cordelia commented as they returned to the living room. 'A husband who's a sublime cook.'

Misty, their velvety soft, grey-haired cat, silently appeared, smoothing herself around the furniture while eyeing Tabitha.

'I told you she was aloof – just until she gets used to you.' Cordelia led the way from the living room along a hallway with a bathroom and utility room off it. She pushed open a door on the garden side of the house. 'You'll be staying in our room. As we discussed via email, the dogs always sleep in here, Bailey in his basket, Fudge usually on the bed. As Bailey can be quite nervous, we thought it best to keep things as much the same for them as possible. It's also the best bedroom.' She smiled and wafted her hand around the space.

Everything was spotless with not a speck of dog hair visible. The wall behind the king-size bed, painted a deep peppermint green, echoed the outside. The dressing table was empty apart from a box of tissues and an unused scented candle. It looked like a show home, not that there was anything wrong with that, but Tabitha felt the pressure of having to be on her best behaviour.

'I've cleared space in the wardrobe and the chest of drawers for you to use. The en suite's through there.' Cordelia gestured to a closed door. 'There's also air con in here and the living room.' With wagging tails, Bailey and Fudge clattered across the polished wooden floor to the huge sliding door that opened onto a terrace that overlooked the garden.

Tabitha wandered further into the room. From the bed, she could see past the room's private terrace, to the edge of the pool. Apart from the solar lights marking the stone paving that dotted the sloping grass, the expanse of garden with its palm trees and tropical plants was now shrouded in darkness.

Cordelia joined Tabitha by the wall of glass. 'It's a view I'll never tire of. Leave the curtains open and wake up to this, it's magical. You'll be very comfortable.'

'I'm sure I will be,' Tabitha said, tearing her eyes away from the garden.

'Our cleaner Dolores comes once a week on Thursday mornings and she'll continue to do so while we're away, but please do tidy up after yourself and the dogs.'

'Of course.'

'Hopefully all the information you'll need is in the welcome pack. We're going to sleep in one of the guest rooms for the night. It's no trouble,' she said before Tabitha could protest. 'We thought it would be a good idea for Fudge and Bailey to get used to you in their usual environment while we're still here. I'll let you settle in. Dinner will be ready in twenty minutes.'

'Thank you,' Tabitha said as Cordelia left with the dogs on her heels.

She had a good feeling about this place. A wild and mountainous island with year-round sunshine and a subtropical climate appealed to her, plus Madeira had long been a place she'd wanted to come to, not least because she'd heard lots about it through an old friend. Being here was the perfect chance to heal old wounds and reconnect with him, despite the idea leaving her on edge. But she wouldn't think about that now; she turned her focus to unpacking.

Over the last year, Tabitha had got used to being blown away by some of the places she'd stayed. Not all were as large or luxurious as this. A tiny apartment in the artistic Saint-Germain-des-Prés area of Paris looking after a toy poodle had been memorable because of its stunning oak parquet flooring and exposed stone walls, plus a cafe with the most incredible coffee, pastries and macarons just a thirty-second stroll away. Then she'd spent three weeks on a houseboat in one of Singapore's marinas with a friendly bichon frise. What she loved most was being immersed in the culture of a place, staying in someone's home and getting to know their particular neighbourhood. She was looking forward to discovering Madeira and staying put in a place for a little longer than she had all summer.

* * *

With the front of the villa completely open to the garden, light from the living area pooled onto the terrace. Misty stalked across the grass, her eyes glinting in the darkness, while the dogs settled themselves on the paving. Tabitha sat with Rufus and Cordelia at the table to the side of the pool, beneath a pergola strung with lights and sheltered by leafy palms. Tabitha imagined it would be lovely to sit there during the heat of the day.

Cordelia hadn't been lying about Rufus being a good cook. Dinner was *carne de vinha d'alhos*, tender pieces of pork that Rufus had marinated in garlic and wine for two days before slowly roasting them in the oven, served with salad and *milho frito*, a fried cornbread. The setting was idyllic and a perfect temperature despite the sun having set.

'Thank you so much,' Tabitha said as Rufus offered her the bowl of pork and she spooned more onto her plate. 'This is very kind of you.'

'We're just grateful you'll be here to look after our babies.' Cordelia smiled sweetly.

Tabitha understood that pets were part of the family, but she was put off by the sickly sweet 'ooh my little cutie-pie' way some people doted on them. Perhaps it stemmed from not having had a pet growing up. Being the youngest, she'd never had a baby brother or sister to help look after either and she'd never believed herself to be maternal... A dull pain ricocheted from the pit of her stomach to her heart. Catching her upset before it spilled over, she quashed the thought, shifted uncomfortably in her seat and skewered a piece of pork.

Misty curled herself around Tabitha's leg with a satisfied purr.

'Well, that's a good sign,' Cordelia said. 'Misty doesn't much like strangers, does she, Rufus?'

With his mouth full, Rufus nodded in agreement.

'You're obviously good with animals and have lots of experience house sitting from your profile,' Cordelia continued, 'but you've never had a pet of your own. Is that right?' She popped a forkful of salad into her mouth.

Tabitha nodded and swallowed her mouthful of the unbelievably tender pork. She got asked this question frequently. 'We moved around a lot when I was growing up so we weren't able to have a pet. There's never been a chance since being an adult either, but I love animals and have looked after friends' pets. Pet sitting seemed like the perfect solution.' She held off from saying that she preferred them to most humans.

Cordelia clasped her wine glass and nodded. 'But you're obviously in a position workwise to travel?'

'Yeah, I toured as a musician with bands a few years ago, but I've been focusing on songwriting more recently, mainly as a topliner, which means I write the melody and lyrics over a beat I get sent by a producer. Working remotely is great.'

'And there's no partner to miss...?'

Tabitha caught Rufus's raised eyebrow as he shot a look at his wife.

'No, there's no one,' Tabitha said firmly. 'Lots of friends and family scattered all over the place, but no, um, boyfriend... not any longer.'

'Oh dear,' Cordelia said. 'I did wonder if heartbreak was the reason you were house sitting on your own.'

Tabitha's cheeks flushed and Rufus coughed, blustering through the awkward silence by topping up their wine glasses. 'So, tell us, Tabitha. Why Madeira?'

'I tend to go wherever fits in with the house-sitting dates I already have scheduled and, honestly, it depends on who says yes to me.'

'Yes, we were amazed by just how many applications we received,' Cordelia said. 'We didn't realise that there would be so many more sitters than there are sits!'

'It is rather competitive from a sitter's point of view, that's why I try to be as flexible as possible and never too fussed about where I end up. I've discovered some incredible places that way and have been pleasantly surprised by locations that I wouldn't necessarily have chosen.'

Cordelia sat back in her chair and smoothed out a crease in her trousers. 'Anywhere in particular?'

'Ghent springs to mind because it's not somewhere I knew much about. Often, it's the places I would never have considered that have surprised me the most in terms of how much I love them.'

'The places or the pets?' Cordelia's eyes twinkled as she looked at Tabitha over her glass of wine.

'Oh, both.' Tabitha smiled. 'I haven't yet met a pet I haven't liked, and everywhere has something appealing about it. Sometimes I hit the jackpot with everything: perfect pet, amazing location and a fabulous home. Much like I imagine your place will be.' She leaned down and tickled the top of Fudge's head.

'He'll be the first to sit next to you hoping you'll drop some food, won't he, Rufus?'

'He certainly will, although we refrain from feeding them anything from the table.'

'Oh, don't worry about that,' Tabitha said. 'I'll follow exactly what you've set out in your welcome pack.'

'And I'm sure you'll love Madeira,' Rufus said with confidence. 'We certainly do.'

'Have you lived here long?'

'Twenty-two years,' Cordelia said with a satisfied smile. 'We lived in Surrey and Rufus worked in finance in the City so he was forever commuting and he wanted to do more, didn't you, love? He was full of business ideas – a proper entrepreneur.'

'I worked sixty hours a week and brought home a lot of money, but I knew I'd burn out if I carried on at that sort of pace. And Cordelia was a marketing whizz, driving companies to commercial success, which made us think why couldn't we do it for ourselves. We started our luxury travel company, Sun & Stars, from our spare room, both of us working all the hours we could to get it off the ground. When it felt like a permanent and viable business, we took the plunge, sold up and moved out here.'

Folding her arms and clasping her wine glass, Cordelia looked at Tabitha. 'Friends and family did question why Madeira rather than somewhere like the south of France, but it was an island we'd both fallen in love with on a holiday in our twenties. The subtropical climate appealed, didn't it, love. We both adore walking and the levada trails across the island are wonderful.'

'Not to mention there's a world-renowned golf course, which made me rather happy.' Rufus grinned. 'Back in Surrey we craved the outdoor life, but England doesn't exactly have the right climate.'

Cordelia placed a manicured hand on her husband's arm and laughed. 'When he says "outdoor life", we're not talking about hiking in winter or camping in the rain – we love walking, but we are rather partial to home comforts.' Tabitha could easily believe that. 'No, we wanted a large garden, somewhere to invite friends over and enjoy barbecues with an ocean view.' She swept her hand towards the Atlantic Ocean glinting in the moonlight beyond the sloping garden.

Tabitha could certainly see the appeal. 'Do you still work from home then?'

Rufus nodded. 'We run our business from our home office at the bottom of the garden, but we've grown over the years, so we have an office in London too where most of our employees are based – we're there a couple of times a year, aren't we, love.'

'It's good to touch base, but really we can work from anywhere, so being here is perfect. We have the best of everything.'

'The location too,' Rufus added. 'We're just outside the village with walks on the doorstep and nothing's too far away. Even Funchal is only forty-five minutes.'

'It's really peaceful,' Tabitha said. 'And no neighbours?'

Rufus and Cordelia glanced at each other.

Cordelia picked up her wine glass and leaned back in her chair. 'Julie and Anton are next door – well, when I say next door, they're a couple of minutes' walk away, but they're our closest neighbours. We're all spread out here, which is a dream, but the bottom of their garden butts onto the side of ours.' Cordelia gave Tabitha what she assumed was a knowing look and wrinkled her nose. 'The wife is rather nosy, so I do apologise in advance. If, however, you know you're going to be out for the whole day, then please do ask Julie to check on the dogs. The only good thing about her is she has time on her hands and is always happy to walk them, isn't she, love?' She looked at her husband.

'They have their uses.' He chuckled.

Feeling a little uncomfortable about the downbeat tone over a couple she hadn't yet met, Tabitha smiled weakly.

'They're aware you're staying and have a spare key if ever needed,' Cordelia added.

'Just duck behind a bush if you're out in the garden and Julie pops her head over!' Rufus laughed.

One of the greatest appeals about house sitting, beyond the initial meeting with the owners and handing over the keys on their return, was generally only having animals to deal with. From the short time she'd been in Rufus and Cordelia's company, they were beginning to come across as the sort of couple who could become overwhelming. One evening was probably enough, not that it had been unpleasant in the slightest, but she knew she'd be far happier when she was finally on her own.

With Rufus and Cordelia leaving reasonably early in the morning, the evening drew to a close. Tabitha helped clear the table, and once Cordelia had stacked the dishwasher and Rufus had locked up, they said goodnight.

It felt a little like a test: Tabitha having their room with the dogs, while they stayed in the guest room. Not that they could kick her out when they had a holiday of a lifetime to go on.

The dogs seemed confused when it was Tabitha who headed down the hallway towards the bedroom. She paused outside the door and watched them padding around, both of them glancing back as if trying to work out where their owners had gone. Then, without further hesitation, they trotted down the hallway and followed her into the room.

'Good boys,' she said, crouching down and tickling them beneath their chins. They looked up at her with big brown eyes and she knew in her heart that they'd be another two pets who she'd find it hard to say goodbye to. But there was no need to think about that yet. Her time on Madeira was just beginning.

3

Tabitha woke with a jolt to Fudge walking up her legs. He lay on her stomach and rested his head on his paws, making her laugh and need a wee at the same time. She reached out and stroked his ears.

'Well, good morning to you,' she said, pleased that he seemed to be fine about her temporarily replacing his owners. 'I suppose you want food.'

At the mere mention of the word, Bailey leapt from his basket and trotted round to the side of the bed.

Tabitha glanced at her watch. Just gone seven. Exactly the time Cordelia had said the animals got fed.

'Come on then, you two.' Tabitha wriggled out from under Fudge and pulled a hoodie on over her vest top and pyjama shorts.

They followed after her along the hallway, the mouth-watering smell of coffee enticing as they reached the kitchen.

Rufus was already up and dressed, leaning against the worktop clasping a mug of coffee.

'Morning,' Tabitha said, searching around for the dog bowls.

Rufus greeted her with a smile and glanced at his watch. 'Right on time.' He gestured at Bailey and Fudge at her feet. 'Hungry tummies wake them like clockwork. Their food is in the cupboard next to the sink and there's a pot of coffee on; help yourself.'

Rufus left Tabitha alone with the dogs scampering around her feet. She measured the dried kibble into two bowls and got them both to sit before placing the bowls on the floor. Fudge dived straight in, gulping down his food, while Bailey was a little more sedate. Tabitha grabbed a mug and poured herself a coffee.

'Morning, Tabitha.' Cordelia breezed into the kitchen dressed in white linen trousers and a capped-sleeved top, fully made up, her choppy blonde hair perfectly tousled. The stack of bangles on her arms clinked as she topped up her coffee. 'I hope you slept well?'

'I did indeed, thank you.'

Cordelia smiled and glanced down at Bailey and Fudge finishing off their food. 'And I didn't hear a peep out of you two. That bodes well, doesn't it.' She smiled warmly at Tabitha. 'You're a star for staying here and keeping our minds at rest. It will be lovely to not have to constantly worry about them while we're away this time.' She headed towards the open door with her mug but turned back. 'By the way, you'll find Misty curled up on the armchair. She's not as interested in food as these two. I'll let you get up, but we'll be leaving in half an hour.'

After letting the dogs outside for a wee and feeding Misty, Tabitha went back to the bedroom for a quick shower. As she was getting dried, she glanced at her phone and realised she had a missed call and message from Elspeth.

Did you get there safely? No idea what I'd do if you didn't. Just let me know you're okey-dokey. Pretty please. Xxxx

It had slipped Tabitha's mind to let Elspeth know that she'd arrived safely. After spending a good chunk of their life travelling and working all over the world, their parents were unconcerned about Tabitha continuing the travel bug, but Elspeth had always taken it upon herself to look after her baby sister, even more so now she had children of her own. As Tabitha thumbed a reply, she felt horribly guilty for making her worry.

So sorry, E. Got swept up in everything last night and totally forgot to message. I'm here, I'm fine. Saying goodbye to the owners this morning so will have a chance to speak to you later. Hope you, Gethin and the girls are all good. Xxxx

By the time Tabitha had dressed, Elspeth had replied.

Looking forward to catching up. Need pics of the dogs. Cavs are Olivia's favourite ever dog (she told me to tell you that!), she's already begging us to get one. Cute pics needed to pacify her please! Xxxx

Tabitha smiled and replied with a thumbs up and a kiss emoji. Elspeth had her hands full with a three- and four-year-old. There was no way she'd want to add a dog into the mix, even one as chilled out as a Cavalier. Rather than pacify Olivia, Tabitha was certain that photos of the dogs would just fuel her longing for one.

Dressed in relaxed boy-fit jeans and a cropped T-shirt, Tabitha ran mousse through her hair in an attempt to tame her curls before drying it, then followed the sound of voices to the living room, where Cordelia was ordering Rufus around while she checked their hand luggage.

Cordelia turned to Tabitha. 'I think that's it. There's always so much to think about when we go away. I don't quite know how you manage to spend your whole time travelling around.'

'I've got used to it. And staying in people's houses rather than a hotel makes life easier. There are very few things I need beyond clothes, a couple of personal items and what I need to work, which isn't much: my phone, laptop, guitar, microphone for recording, internet access and my imagination.'

'Well, I hope you feel at home here while we're away,' Cordelia said, trailing after Rufus, who was dragging their suitcases to the door. 'Any problems, just let us know. As long as everyone's fed, watered and groomed, they'll be fine. The most important thing is to always keep the driveway gate closed. Bailey's a homebody, but Fudge likes to explore and has absolutely no road sense; given the chance, he'd be out of the gate like a shot.'

'They'll be fine, Cordelia,' Rufus said, gently nudging her out of the door.

'I know they will.' Cordelia sighed and beamed a smile in Tabitha's direction. 'But if you could please update us at least twice a week on WhatsApp, I'd be ever so grateful, make sure my babies are all okay.'

'Which we're sure they will be,' Rufus stressed, hooking his arm in his wife's. 'Tabitha's a pro.'

'I am indeed. Please don't worry and enjoy your holiday,' Tabitha said, walking out with them and closing the door on Fudge and Bailey so they couldn't escape. That was always her greatest worry.

A taxi was waiting and, while the driver loaded the suitcases and Rufus and Cordelia got in with a wave, Tabitha bristled with excitement at her returning freedom. She understood how difficult it must be to entrust their house and beloved pets to a stranger, but she hoped she'd put them at ease. She was certain that they would return to happy pets and a well-looked after home.

Tabitha watched the taxi until it was out of sight. Silence. She breathed easy. She closed the gate – one of the many clear instructions from Cordelia – and turned back to the house. Bailey and

Fudge were sitting patiently looking out of the front door's glass panel. Tabitha was looking forward to having their company for the next three weeks.

* * *

After finishing the unpacking from the night before, Tabitha wandered down the sloping lawn with a coffee. The garden was bathed in sunshine and the peace was absolute. The ocean view was framed by palm trees and the only sound besides birdsong was the hush of the breeze through the trees.

It was quite easy to lose track of time while house sitting. The routine of her day changed depending on the country she was in and the animals she was looking after. Generally it didn't matter what day it was, unless she had a Zoom call planned. Each change of location usually meant she had to take a couple of days off – easy enough to do when she was freelance and able to organise her own schedule – plus the change of scene and inspiration was worth it. She had no doubt that it would be the same here.

After a refreshing swim in the pool and updating her social media – a selfie with the tropical garden and the Atlantic Ocean as a backdrop – Tabitha planned out her work for the following week, messaged friends, posted the selfie in the Callahan family group chat and phoned her parents in Devon before grabbing an early lunch.

At least being on Madeira there was no time difference with the UK, but a Friday afternoon for Elspeth with two young children to look after was not a good time to call, so Tabitha went shopping in the local village to stock up on the few extra things she needed. She took the dogs for a walk before making a simple dinner of tuna salad and curling up on the sofa with the bifold doors wide open, Bailey lying on the rug and Fudge curled up next to her. A sense of utter contentment swept through her as she stroked Fudge and gazed out past the pool to the birds fluttering between the trees.

She called Elspeth and, as the phone rang, Tabitha couldn't help but compare the peace and ease of her current life with the madness of Elspeth and her husband juggling two young children alongside a relatively new business.

'Hey, there.' Elspeth sounded flustered as she answered.

'Is now a good time?'

'Yes, the girls are finally in bed,' she said with a sigh. Tabitha imagined her flopping down on the sofa.

'They've been difficult?'

'It's the end of a long week, and Nancy, well, let's just say three can be the most adorable age, but three-year-olds can be right little shits too. Pardon my French.'

'I hope you're having a large glass of wine tonight.'

'Already poured.' Tabitha could hear the smile in Elspeth's voice. 'Now, tell me what blissful place you're staying in this time.'

Tabitha described the villa and its location, trying not to lay it on too thick about how luxurious and perfect it was with its pool and ocean view. Not that Elspeth's life wasn't idyllic too. They lived in the foothills of the Brecon Beacons running a glamping retreat for eight months of the year. Although a new business venture and lifestyle move from chaotic Camberwell to the Welsh countryside hadn't been easy with young children, the girls now had wildflower meadows to run wild in, fresh air and space. They also had stability and a permanent home.

Tabitha tuned back into what her sister was saying.

'What are the pets like this time?'

'The two Cavaliers are just scrumptious; the cat's shy but has her moments of being friendly and lovable.'

'I'm trying my hardest not to be jealous...'

'Fudge is with me now. He's been following me around like a

shadow.' She took her hand away to scratch her knee and Fudge batted it back with his paw. 'Bless him, every time I stop stroking him he whacks my hand.'

'Getting a dog is all the girls talk about at the moment. They're always asking "why can't we look after dogs like Auntie Tabitha?"'

'Sorry.'

'Ah, don't be. If it wasn't tantrums about not getting a dog, it would be a tantrum about something else. It's never ending.' She sighed.

'Hey, are you sure you're okay?'

'Just tired, that's all. Secretly I want a dog as much as them, Gethin too. This place is perfect for one, but the girls need to be a little bit older to appreciate it and to understand they take up a lot of time and can be hard work. With the glamping being so new, plus the first wedding in two weeks in the barn we've not yet finished, well, there's too much going on to add a dog into the mix.'

'You can always do a pet sit. Before you say anything,' Tabitha rushed on, imagining her sister rolling her eyes, 'I don't mean travelling all over the place like I do, just combining a holiday while looking after someone's house and pet. There are loads of sits in the UK. I'm sure you'd find something.'

'Perhaps, but I'm worried that would fuel their desire even more. I'm fed up of them asking and having to say no. So, for the time being, we'll continue to enjoy the pics you send of the animals you're looking after. Talking of which, I'm losing track of where you've been and where you're going next.'

'I'm here until 26 September, then I might stay in Lisbon for a few days. After that, I'm not sure. I love moving around, but after a summer of travelling loads, it's nice to be in one place for a bit.'

'And you're on Madeira too...' There was a pause. Tabitha pre-empted Elspeth's next question, but didn't try and interject. 'Are you going to see Ollie while you're there?'

Tabitha gazed through the open doorway, down the garden to the banana trees framing the view of the ocean. She absently stroked Fudge. 'I don't know. I'm torn. I'm not sure if it's a good idea or not.'

'He's your friend, Tabs.'

'You mean he was my friend.'

'It's not too late to salvage your friendship, is it?'

Tabitha sighed. 'It's not as straightforward as that.'

'I know it's not, but I also know how much you miss him. And, regardless of your friendship, think of your career. He owes you big time.'

'I'm just worried about reopening old wounds. I'm trying to get my head into a good place and seeing him again could undo all the positives of the past few years.' Tabitha's insides tightened at the mere thought of Ollie. And yet, if she really had no intention of contacting him again, wouldn't she have steered clear of Madeira altogether? 'It's a big island, it's not as if I'm in Funchal and likely to bump into him. I've got time to decide if I want to see him or not.'

'Good; just think on it is all I'm saying.' Elspeth paused. 'My next question is, when are you going to come and stay with us? We all miss you terribly. You can't keep travelling forever, you know.'

'Why not? It's what Mum and Dad did.'

'Yes, well, sort of. But it was with all of us, not just one of them on their own. And wherever we went we did at least stay for a year or two at a time. I mean, this year alone, how many different places have you been?'

'I don't know; I've lost track.'

'Exactly.'

Tabitha could imagine the worried expression on Elspeth's face.

'Come for Christmas, or before if you can manage it. You can always stay in one of the cabins rather than bunking in the crazy house with all of us. That way you can stay for as long as you like.'

Tabitha continued stroking Fudge, a feeling of homesickness washing over her despite not having anywhere she thought of as home to go back to. 'You know I'd love to see you.'

'I know you would, so make time and fit us in.' A muffled voice sounded in the background. 'Gethin's saying dinner's ready. I'd better go. Talk again soon, yeah? Love you, Tabs.'

'Love you, E.'

They said goodbye and silence descended. Tabitha imagined Elspeth being swept back into her busy life, crashing on the sofa for an hour or so with Tabitha's brother-in-law before one of the kids woke up. For Tabitha, there was simply stillness with only the occasional fluttering snore from the dogs.

Ollie played on her mind, though. She opened Instagram and went to his feed. She didn't allow herself to look at it often, because she'd tried hard over the years to bury the envy she felt at his success, despite her own. She was a silent stalker looking at the images, but not liking or commenting on them. Being on Madeira, though, gave her the perfect opportunity to reach out. It wasn't as if he'd never tried to make contact; she'd been the one to snub him, although she'd had good reason to. Platinum-selling, award-winning Ollie Pereira with his twenty million Instagram followers.

She scrolled past image after image of the friend she once knew so well – on stage and at parties, living the ultimate pop star lifestyle ever since he'd won *The Star*, the biggest show on TV, seven years ago.

Tabitha sighed and put down her phone, wanting to forget all about him and the feelings he stirred.

4

With the arrival of the weekend, Tabitha relaxed into her temporary home. It was as if she was able to reinvent herself with each house sit, slotting into a different way of life influenced by the pets she was looking after and the type of home she was staying in. The Madeira villa leant itself nicely to chilling out while soaking up the view and that was what she'd planned for the weekend. Proper work could wait until the following week.

Bailey and Fudge needed a walk, so, with the use of Cordelia's sleek white BMW, Tabitha decided to explore. After securing the dogs in the boot, she navigated her way through Prazeres to the top of the village. It was reasonably early on the Saturday before the day heated up and the walk followed one of Madeira's many levadas. The dogs trotted in front of her along the narrow path next to the levada, stopping to sniff the grasses and ferns growing beneath the shady trees. It was places like these where Tabitha was able to switch off and push her worries away. Rather than thinking back on the past or ahead to the future – which she knew she was avoiding doing, even if travelling was supposed to be helping her with that – focusing on the moment was refreshingly stress-free. Just the dogs for company and sunshine on her shoulders.

She cleared her mind and concentrated on the sounds of the forest and the sun glinting between the leaf-laden branches. Birds twittered and the water flowing along the levada was a constant murmur. The surrounding countryside switched from woodland to open farmland with ploughed fields and farm buildings, the vivid blue ocean the backdrop before they returned to the patchy shade of the trees.

Tabitha was itching to explore more of the island, and although she liked the idea of staying somewhere peaceful, she did want to experience Funchal and be in a place that pulsed with life. Funchal, however, would put her closer to Ollie. Although she'd never visited, she knew where his Madeira villa was and had seen the pictures on Instagram. She knew he had a pool that overlooked the ocean; there were plenty of bare-chested images of him in and out of the pool sprinkling his Instagram feed. There were plenty of photos of his London pad too. He'd upgraded from the poky flat he used to have, where they'd spent many an evening together putting the world to rights, to something far larger and swankier. She sounded bitter, she knew. It was pointless dwelling on the past, when there was nothing she could do to change it. Focusing on the here and now was all she needed to do. Funchal and Ollie could wait.

* * *

The rest of Saturday was filled with sunshine and the outdoors. Apart from a couple of walks, Tabitha didn't venture far, not that there was any reason to with the garden to enjoy, the pool to swim in and the dogs for company.

As promised, Tabitha sent a couple of photos of Bailey and

Fudge on a walk and Misty curled up on her favourite armchair to Cordelia and Rufus along with an update.

All good here and everyone's happy and settled – they're a dream to look after. Hope you're enjoying your time away.

Cordelia replied with a load of heart emojis, followed by:

I can't tell you what a relief it is to hear that. I can relax at my spa afternoon now, thank you.

* * *

On Sunday afternoon, Tabitha took her guitar to the sunny spot two-thirds of the way down the garden. She sat cross-legged on the cushioned rattan sofa and strummed the chords of the song she was working on. A fragment of a melody was lodged in her head and had been for some time. The tentative notes joined the birdsong and Tabitha sighed with satisfaction. This was what she loved, spending time on her own, pursuing her passion without the drama of being around other people. Occasionally, she missed gigging and the endless merry-go-round of touring and the thrill of being on stage playing to thousands of people, but she didn't miss the non-stop travel from one hotel room to another, the lack of sleep, too much drink and the temptation of drugs. This was better. It was easier, however much she knew she couldn't continue like this forever, not if she was serious about her songwriting career.

A faint voice tugged Tabitha from her thoughts. She looked up, assuming she'd misheard.

'Hello.'

There it was again, a little louder this time.

Tabitha glanced around. A woman, with a large sun hat, was smiling at her from over the fence in the gap between the bushes.

'Hi there,' Tabitha said as the woman gave her a little wave.

'Cordelia said they had someone staying while they...' Her voice trailed off, masked by the rustle of a lizard in the undergrowth. She had a gentle way of speaking, one of those people you had to really listen to otherwise every few words were missing, not someone Tabitha could easily hold a conversation with from where she was sitting.

Tabitha rested her guitar against the side of the sofa and wandered over to the one bit of neighbouring fence that wasn't screened by bushes and trees.

'Oh, I'm sorry, I didn't mean to disturb you. I'm Julie.'

The neighbour Cordelia warned me about, Tabitha thought.

'That's okay. It's good to meet you. I'm Tabitha.' She stuck her hand through the wilderness on her side of the fence, which was so unlike the rest of Rufus and Cordelia's manicured garden. Tabitha wondered if they'd intentionally left this bit wild in an attempt to deter the neighbours from seeing in quite so much.

'I was just doing some gardening and spotted you,' Julie said, shaking her hand. 'I hope you don't mind me saying hello.'

'Of course not,' Tabitha said almost truthfully. Cordelia and Rufus's less than flattering comments about the neighbours had left Tabitha intrigued. Julie was younger than she'd imagined. Cordelia had certainly made her sound older than the fifty-something woman standing across the fence. Her features were as delicate as her voice and the sun hat shaded her pale skin. Her wispy dark-blonde hair was tied into a low ponytail. On first impressions alone, Tabitha wouldn't have been at all surprised if Cordelia walked all over Julie. Tabitha decided to continue the conversation rather than making an excuse and walking away. 'You have a lovely garden,' she said, looking beyond Julie to the large and immaculate lawn edged by flower-filled borders and well-spaced shady spots beneath palms and custard apple trees.

'Oh, thank you; it was the main reason we bought the place.' Her voice filled with pride. 'The house itself isn't huge – although with it being just the two of us, it's not really a problem, but the garden makes up for it.'

'Have you been here long?'

'Nearly thirty years on the island, but twenty-two here. I'm English and my husband Anton is half Portuguese; his grandparents are Madeiran. We met while doing our teacher training in London but moved out here. What about you? You must have Celtic heritage with that lovely red hair?'

'My dad's Irish and my mum's Welsh.'

'You don't have an accent, though.'

'I've travelled around too much to ever really pick one up.'

Julie nodded, looking as if she wanted to say more, but was unsure. 'I didn't mean to disturb you before.' Her cheeks flushed as she motioned towards Tabitha's guitar.

'I'm a songwriter,' Tabitha said by way of explanation.

'That must be a fascinating job.'

'It has its perks.'

Julie smiled softly, fine lines crinkling the edges of her eyes. 'Well, I'll let you get back to your writing. If you need anything, just let us know.'

'I will, thank you.'

'It's nice to meet you.'

'You too.'

Tabitha wandered back over to the rattan sofa and picked up her notebook. She sensed that Julie would have liked to have talked for longer but was probably conscious of taking up too much of her time. She liked her, though, her quiet and unassuming demeanour quite a contrast to Cordelia's confidence.

Tabitha decided she'd make a conscious effort to chat with her if she saw her across the fence.

* * *

What was left of Sunday afternoon rolled by at a leisurely pace, the dogs keeping Tabitha company as she pottered about and lazed by the pool before taking a dip, the evening sun deliciously warm on her bare shoulders.

When Elspeth messaged asking how her first couple of days had gone, Tabitha replied with a selfie of her in the pool clasping a glass of G&T. Elspeth's reply was swift.

You make me sick...

Quickly followed by:

Love you though. Xxxx

Tabitha smiled and sent a kiss emoji back. She spent another twenty minutes in the pool watching the sun slide towards the horizon before padding wet footprints across the paving to her room.

After an evening spent in front of the TV with Bailey sleeping by her feet and Fudge curled on the sofa next to her, she went to bed with a sense of calm contentment.

5

Tabitha had barely nodded off when she thought she heard something. She opened her eyes. The room was blindingly dark. She lay still, listening. On the end of the bed, Fudge stretched and yawned, shifting over until his head and paws were resting on her feet.

It was probably nothing. It always took a few days to get used to somewhere new, its sounds and the feel of a place, particularly at night. She was glad the curtains were closed across the French doors. The view into the garden was spectacular, but at night, the darkness was suffocating and her overactive imagination fixated on thoughts of ghostly figures peering in.

As she rolled onto her side in an attempt to get back to sleep, she heard a thud, as if something had been dropped on the floor.

Now wide awake, she held her breath and listened harder. Nothing beyond Bailey and Fudge snoring. Perhaps she'd been mistaken? Although two cute Cavalier King Charles spaniels were hardly the best guard dogs.

Through the open bedroom door, a faint light suddenly filtered in. Tabitha swallowed. She gently manoeuvred her feet out from beneath Fudge. He briefly raised his head before flopping back down again.

Footsteps.

Tabitha's heart raced. She slipped from under the covers and silently crossed the room.

Fudge jumped off the bed and landed with a thud. Tabitha froze. The footsteps paused too. Fudge sat on the floor and started licking himself.

With sweaty palms, Tabitha crept from the room, along the hallway towards the faint glow of lamplight, *bad idea, bad idea* repeating over and over in her head. She wished she was holding something she could bash over an intruder's head if it came to it...

A shadowy figure loomed in the doorway of the living room.

Tabitha screamed.

'Shit!' the deep-voiced shadowy figure exclaimed. 'Who the hell are you?'

'Who the hell am I?' Tabitha managed to catch her breath enough to speak. 'Who the hell are you?'

'I asked first,' the deep voice said, far more calmly than Tabitha was feeling.

She stared wide-eyed at the shadowy intruder. 'You need to get out!'

He moved further into the hallway.

'I'll call the police,' she said forcefully. Not that she had her phone on her or knew the number.

'I'm just going to turn on the light,' he said gently as if she was a frightened animal. He reached his hand to the light switch.

Tabitha blinked in the sudden brightness. Standing in the hallway with a bemused look was a man around the same age as her, wearing snug-fitting jeans and a Foo Fighters T-shirt. He was tall, with the build of Chris Hemsworth and not dissimilar to Tom

Hardy with dark hair and thick stubble, tattooed arms and brooding good looks.

Holy moly was he hot.

Their eyes locked, neither of them saying anything for a moment, both seemingly confused.

Fudge broke the spell, emerging from the bedroom, clattering past Tabitha and running straight up to the stranger.

The man dropped his gaze from her and turned his attention to Fudge. He crouched down and tickled him beneath his chin. 'Hey there, buddy.'

Perhaps she was still asleep and dreaming; this was beyond weird.

The man looked up. 'I'm Raff,' he said in a way that sounded as if it should mean something to her.

'Okay,' she said slowly, 'but *who* are you?'

'Rufus and Cordelia, they're my parents.'

Tabitha frowned. Now she was properly confused. She opened her mouth to say something, then closed it again.

Raff sighed. 'Let me guess, they failed to mention me.'

Tabitha folded her arms, suddenly conscious that she was in just a vest top and pyjama shorts. 'Not a word,' she said. Despite having spent an evening with them, they hadn't once mentioned having a son and she hadn't thought to ask if they had children. They'd come across as a wealthy, childless couple, enjoying life to the full. 'But, regardless of that, you've just waltzed in in the middle of the night, and I'm 100 per cent certain you shouldn't be here. So, you need to either leave, or explain to me what the hell's going on and then leave.'

Raff stroked Fudge's head and stood up. 'I will, but I'm parched. I'm going to put the kettle on. You want something?'

She looked at him in a way that she hoped conveyed she

thought he was mad. 'Um, no. I'll say it again. It's the middle of the night!'

Raff shrugged. 'Suit yourself.'

He walked purposefully towards the kitchen. Fudge looked wide-eyed at Tabitha, then turned and trotted after him.

In a daze, with her heart still thudding, she retreated to the bedroom, chucked a hoodie on over her pyjama vest and pulled on some socks. Bailey was still in his basket snoring, oblivious to the intruder. She left him sleeping – wishing that was exactly what she was doing – and walked with trepidation to the living room.

The lamps were on and through the wall of glass the silver-white glimmer of the moon broke up the darkness. The kettle was boiling and the sound of rummaging drifted from the kitchen. A large khaki rucksack, pinned with badges from different countries, had been dumped next to the front door. Whoever Raff was, he seemed to be well travelled.

Tabitha twisted her hands, unsure what to do. She felt lost in a place that she'd just begun to feel at home in. *Screw this*, she thought. Regardless of who he claimed he was, she was in the right. With her mind made up and ready to demand that he leave, she marched across the living room towards the kitchen, just as Raff entered with a mug of steaming tea, Fudge trotting happily after him.

Unnerved by just how at home he seemed, Tabitha stopped in her tracks.

'So much for a guard dog...' she muttered as Raff brushed past, along with a waft of spiced aftershave that reminded her of her ex-boyfriend Lewis.

'They're Cavaliers, they love everyone,' Raff said, sitting down on the sofa. Fudge jumped up next to him and looked at him lovingly. 'Seriously, if I was an axe-wielding murderer, he'd still come up to me wagging his tail.'

'You're so not helping.' Tabitha folded her arms. She'd lost any sense of control and Raff looked as comfortable as Fudge did.

'So,' Raff said, switching his attention from Fudge to her. 'I've told you who I am, but who are you?'

Tabitha's nostrils flared. The feeling that she was in any real danger had begun to ebb away, but her discomfort remained and she was mightily pissed off to be questioned like this in the middle of the night.

She opened her mouth to say something, then closed it again. With annoyance, she realised the sooner she explained why she was here, the sooner she could get rid of him.

'I'm house sitting and looking after Fudge, Bailey and Misty while your... while Rufus and Cordelia are away.'

'And your name is...?' He looked at her expectantly, a slight smile twitching his lips as if he was finding the whole situation amusing.

'Tabitha.'

Raff leaned forward, placed his mug on the coffee table, stood up and held out his hand. 'Well, it's good to meet you, Tabitha.'

Tabitha kept her arms firmly folded. 'If they're your parents, how do you not know that they're away and I was staying?'

Raff grunted and glanced at Fudge. 'I knew they were going away; I just didn't know about you. Last time they went on holiday, they took Misty to a cattery and the dogs got looked after somewhere else. I thought they'd be doing the same thing this time.'

'But why are you here when they're away? They certainly didn't mention anything about you.'

Tabitha noticed his jaw clench as if she'd hit a nerve.

'I don't see them often,' he muttered.

Or speak to them apparently, Tabitha thought. She shook her head. 'How do I even know you're telling the truth?'

He pulled a set of keys from the back pocket of his jeans and dangled them in front of her. 'I didn't break in for starters.'

'That doesn't prove anything. You could have stolen them.'

Shooting her a withering look, he crossed the living room to the shelving unit along the back wall. He riffled through one of the drawers and pulled out a photo album. He paced back to the sofa, put the album on the table and flicked through it almost to the end. Turning it around, he jabbed a finger at a tall, dark-haired lad of about eighteen. 'There,' he said. 'Me.'

Tabitha moved closer and squinted, trying to work out if the lad in the picture resembled the thirty-something man in front of her.

'How long ago was that taken?' she asked.

'You need more proof?' He seemed annoyed and flustered now, which was very much how Tabitha was feeling standing at gone midnight with a total stranger in the house she was looking after. He closed the album. 'My mother, Cordelia, will have definitely been wearing pink nail varnish and too much jewellery. My father, Rufus, has got such a tan that it looks fake and he will certainly have bored you to death about golf. They will also have been rude about the neighbours and told you never to feed the dogs anything other than their usual food. Am I right?'

There was a look of defiance on his face and she had to admit he'd got Rufus and Cordelia spot on. The more she looked at him, the more she realised there was a family resemblance too. Cordelia and Rufus were a good-looking couple and Raff certainly shared their good genes. However bizarre the situation, Tabitha realised that she was going to have to accept that he was their son.

'Why are there no family photos out?' she asked, not wanting to fully agree he was who he said he was.

'Because my parents like the uncluttered look and we're not exactly a big happy family.'

Tabitha thought of the clutter in her parents' house. For years, they'd lived all over the place, but photos would always be one of the first things to be unpacked. And where they lived now, finally retired and settled in a cottage in Devon, there wasn't a room without a picture of Tabitha and her siblings in it, and every weekend at least one of her brothers or sisters, plus their children, would visit.

'What I don't get, though, is why you're even here, if you knew your parents weren't?'

He remained silent for a moment, his defiance morphing into discomfort. 'Because I was planning on crashing here while they were away.'

'So you really were sneaking in?'

'Yeah, except I wasn't expecting, well, you.'

'Well, I'm sorry, but here I am.'

Tabitha had remained standing, while Raff was sitting with Fudge snuggled against him. They both eyed each other. This was certainly one of the strangest situations Tabitha had found herself in while house sitting. She'd had to take a cat to the vets during one house sit and dealt with a leaking pipe during another, but she'd never been confronted by an intruder, which Raff technically was, even if he was Rufus and Cordelia's son.

'Look, it's late…' Raff finally broke their silence.

Tabitha raised an eyebrow. 'I know it is.'

'Yeah, sorry about that. Honestly, I didn't think there'd be anyone here. But it is late,' he stressed again, 'and I've got nowhere to go tonight, so if I can just stay in the spare room I'll be out of your way in the morning.'

Tabitha rubbed her fingers across her forehead, weighing up how bad an idea it was. 'How about I phone your parents first…'

Raff reached out, as if to touch her arm, but stopped himself.

'Please don't. I honestly didn't mean to cause any trouble, but you phoning them will cause me a shitload, so I'm begging you.'

Tabitha didn't understand what on earth was going on, but his pleading eyes and serious expression spoke volumes. She always noticed how animals were around people and Fudge seemed filled with nothing but love for him. She glanced at Fudge now, with his head on his paws resting on Raff's thigh, which filled his jeans in a considerably attractive way.

Raff caught her looking and smiled. 'What can I say.' He smoothed his hand over Fudge's head.

Fudge was obviously happy in his company. She knew she shouldn't let a Cavalier, the soppiest, least guard-dog-like of canines, sway her, but the one thing she felt she could put her trust in was an animal. Didn't they have some kind of sixth sense when it came to danger? Above all, she was tired and wanted this bizarre stand-off to be over. Her only other option was to kick him out in the middle of the night. Even though he was in the wrong and she shouldn't be worried about him, she couldn't do that.

'Fine,' Tabitha said, with a resigned sigh, 'you can stay, but you leave first thing in the morning.'

'Thank you.'

It sounded heartfelt, but he'd left her with so many questions, not least the small matter of Rufus and Cordelia failing to mention they even had a son. It was almost as if they'd erased him from their life.

Raff gulped a mouthful of tea and manoeuvred Fudge's paws off his thigh.

'I assume you know where the guest bedrooms are?' Tabitha asked.

'Of course.'

'Your, um, parents slept in one the night before they left as I'm in their room, but I think the other one is made up.'

'I'll sort myself out, don't you worry.'

Tabitha frowned, wanting to say 'great, but I'm not worried' but let it slide.

Raff picked up his rucksack and, with the mug of tea in the other hand, headed towards the stairs that led to the guest rooms on the mezzanine level, calling, 'See you in the morning,' over his shoulder.

Tabitha waited until she heard the first bedroom door open and close. She breathed a sigh of relief, but the unsettled feeling she'd been rudely awoken with remained. Her private haven had been intruded upon.

Tiredness mixed with further annoyance washed over her. She glanced at Fudge sitting on the sofa looking put out that the lap he'd been resting on had gone.

'Come on,' she whispered. 'Let's get to bed.'

Fudge padded after her to her room. Rufus and Cordelia's room. That's why Fudge was following her, because it was where he usually slept, but at least he hadn't deserted her completely. Tabitha couldn't help but smile at Bailey curled up in his bed, dead to the world, having missed out on all the excitement. Excitement she could have done without. She crouched down and gently stroked his head. He barely responded, one eye flickering slightly open before closing again.

Fudge jumped onto the bed and Tabitha left Bailey alone. She went back to the door and listened. All was peaceful again, but it was weird knowing that there was someone else in the villa. She closed the door and slid the lock across it, just in case.

6

Scratch, scratch. Scratch, scratch.

Tabitha groaned and rolled over, trying to ignore the noise.

Scratch, scratch, scratch, scratch, getting faster and faster.

Tabitha sat bolt upright, realisation stealing through her at what the sound was. Through sleepy eyes, she clocked Bailey scrabbling at the closed door. With everything that had happened in the night, she'd completely forgotten Cordelia's rule about leaving the bedroom door open so the dogs could get out. She swore and jumped out of bed, jolting poor Fudge awake. He thumped down on to the floor after her. She stopped Bailey's continuous scratching and opened the door for him. Even without kneeling down, the scratch marks were obvious.

Arse, Tabitha thought. *Now I'm going to have to explain that to Cordelia and get it fixed.* Annoyance flared within her.

With Fudge on her heels, she headed after Bailey along the hallway and into the kitchen. All was quiet and it was easy to believe that the events of last night had never happened.

With the dogs around her feet, she fed them both and, rubbing her tired eyes, wandered back into the living room to look for

Misty, who wasn't asleep on her chair. Perhaps she'd been scared off by Raff's intrusion.

Tabitha stood at the bottom of the stairs. The bedroom door was closed and it was quiet, so she presumed he was still asleep. After all, it was early. If it wasn't for the animals, she wouldn't choose to be up at this time, particularly after being rudely awoken in the night. She faltered, unsure what to do about Raff. She decided nothing. When he got up, she would ask him to leave.

Tabitha scooped Misty's dried food into a bowl and went outside to find her. Early-morning sun bathed the garden in golden light and the bright orange flowers of the birds of paradise were vibrant. Still in her pyjama shorts and vest top, she walked down the garden, the short grass tickling her bare feet.

'Misty,' she called gently as she searched for movement in the bushes dotted between the tropical trees and plants.

A flash of grey and Misty emerged from fronds of green, stalking towards her and rubbing her soft fur against Tabitha's bare leg.

At least she had one less thing to worry about knowing Misty was fine. Just Rufus and Cordelia's son still asleep in the house now.

* * *

The annoyance that Tabitha had woken up with began to turn into anger as the morning marched on and there was no sign of Raff. By eleven, unable to fully concentrate on work, she'd had enough. Raff was still here in the place she was responsible for and it grated on her nerves. She didn't care if he was jet lagged or simply lazy; she wanted him gone and the villa to herself again.

Tabitha took the stairs two at a time, no longer attempting to keep quiet. She faltered on the landing outside the first bedroom, considering if she should give him a little longer but decided he'd overstayed his welcome. Without further hesitation, she knocked on the door.

It felt like an inordinately long wait. Then, just as she was about to bang on the door again, there was the sound of fumbling, followed by footsteps and the door swung open. Raff, with bed hair and wearing only pants, filled the doorway. He yawned and rubbed his eyes. Without meaning to, her eyes drifted downwards, taking in the black ink decorating his arms, right shoulder and edging across his muscled chest. She snapped her attention back to his face and met his cool blue, smiling eyes.

'Morning.' His voice was gravelly in a just-woken-up sort of way and she suddenly felt rude having disturbed him. 'What time is it?'

'Um, just gone eleven...'

'Ah, sorry,' he said, tucking his hands beneath his armpits, which showcased his muscled arms, tattoos and six-pack all the more. 'I was dead to the world.'

Tabitha's annoyance dissolved. 'I, um, just wondered if you wanted some, um, brunch...' And now her guilt had spoken before she'd thought her words through.

'Yeah,' he said, looking a little more awake, his eyes trailing her face as if properly taking her in for the first time. 'But I'll make it; my treat for disturbing you last night. Just let me shower first.' He gestured at his state of undress.

'Sure,' Tabitha said lamely, keeping her eyes firmly fixed on his face. She walked away thinking that she'd now made the situation even more awkward – for her at least. Raff seemed quite at home.

As she returned downstairs, she silently cursed how fit he was, distractingly so. For the last twelve months, it had been just her. It wasn't that she hadn't received any male attention or that no one had caught her eye, she just wasn't interested, wanting instead to focus on herself and needing the time to heal without the complication of another person, even in the form of a short-lived fling. Raff was very much a complication. Tabitha tried to erase the image of his chiselled chest from her mind.

She opened the bifold doors, letting Bailey and Fudge out and a waft of warm air in, the buzz of a bee and the rustle of grasses the only sound. Fudge barked and started chasing a butterfly unsuccessfully as it spiralled higher to safety.

Tabitha stood on the shadowed patio in front of the pool, watching the dogs but feeling increasingly as if her day was revolving around Raff. Ignoring him wouldn't make him go away, but it felt simpler to escape with the dogs into the garden. She'd have brunch with him, he would leave and she'd be able to concentrate on work again. Simple. But as she strolled in the shade of the banana plants, Tabitha realised she was annoyed with herself because she was intrigued by Raff.

She wandered to the end of the garden, relishing the sun's gentle warmth. She stood for a while gazing beyond the rocky coastline at the endless ocean, its presence both calming and unsettling, nothing beyond her but water for hundreds of miles.

Escaping was what she was good at, she reflected as she scuffed her foot on a patch of dry earth. Wasn't that what she'd been doing for the last year? Running away felt a hell of a lot easier than facing up to and reconciling her feelings.

Misty slunk past, disappearing into the undergrowth to hunt for lizards, while the dogs were happy sniffing about. Tabitha wandered up to the rattan sofa, sat down and breathed in the fresh ocean air.

Elspeth had messaged Tabitha earlier in the morning with a photo of the girls sitting in their glamping wildflower meadow with daisies threaded in their hair. It looked utterly idyllic, as if the picture had been lifted from a glossy magazine, the girls' cherub faces so perfect and squashable. Tabitha fought back a wave of upset as she thumbed a reply.

You should use this on the website. They're both so lush. I miss them loads. x

She really did miss them, both her nieces and her sister. Her other siblings too, and her parents, along with the menagerie of extended family that was now filled with husbands, wives, partners and lots of other nieces and nephews. The family seemed to have exploded over the past decade as her older brothers and sisters had started families of their own. Thinking about her family inevitably led her to thinking about the what-ifs with her and Lewis, had things been different. No, not things, if they had both been different. She wasn't right for him – exactly as he hadn't been right for her. A relationship equivalent to forcing a square peg into a round hole was doomed from the start. It didn't mean that she hadn't loved him, but it did mean she'd made the right decision leaving, even if she was still trying to make herself believe that.

After sitting and contemplating her failed relationship for a good twenty minutes, Tabitha pocketed her phone and wandered slowly back up the garden, her senses alive with the honey-like fragrance of phlox and the pop of colour breaking up the green tones. As she neared the villa, she got a waft of something delicious. The dogs raced ahead, enticed by the smell.

Raff, dressed in jeans and a snug-fitting T-shirt, his hair still damp, emerged from the kitchen into the living room holding two plates.

'Perfect timing,' he said, placing the plates on the dining table in front of the open doors. 'I've made us a *prego* sandwich – a Madeiran staple. I hope you're not vegetarian?'

'Nope. I eat pretty much anything.' Tabitha followed his lead, sitting down opposite him, her eyes widening at the sizeable sandwich made from the *bolo do caco* bread she'd bought, filled with a thin beef steak, lettuce, cheese and tomato.

It was oddly civilised and incredibly unexpected to be sharing breakfast with someone. She hadn't done this since... well, the last time had been with Lewis. The last thing she'd craved was anyone's company, but she had to admit, as she took a bite of the sandwich, that it was oddly welcome.

'This is seriously good,' Tabitha said, after swallowing a delicious mouthful of tender beef with a kick of garlic.

'I worked in a Michelin-starred restaurant for a year. I picked up a few things.'

Tabitha frowned. 'You're a chef?'

Raff shook his head. 'No.'

'Then what do you do?'

He took a bite of his sandwich and sat back in his chair. 'Lots of things.'

That explained absolutely nothing and only made her wonder more about why he'd rocked up to his parents' house in the middle of the night without them knowing.

'Do you know,' he said, tapping his finger on the Denby plate, 'my folks always used to reserve the good china for special occasions; now it seems to be their everyday stuff.'

It was hard to ignore the underlying bitterness. Tabitha didn't comment; the last thing she wanted was to emotionally invest in whatever was going on with him and his parents. Best to ignore, because she certainly didn't want to pry into Rufus and Cordelia's lives.

'If you don't live on the island, where do you live?' Tabitha asked instead, while watching him carefully.

'I'm between places.'

Huh, another non-committal answer. Tabitha pursed her lips

and covered her discomfort of a conversation that kept hitting a brick wall with another mouthful of food. But, then again, the more she asked and found out about him, the more involved she became and vice versa. Keeping a distance could only be a good thing.

'But home for me, at least, has always been the UK,' Raff eventually said, breaking the uncomfortable silence. 'London, to be more specific, although I've travelled a lot. I've got itchy feet.'

Tabitha met his gaze across the table. 'You and me both.'

Raff finished his last bit of sandwich and folded his arms. 'You're a professional pet sitter?'

Tabitha noticed the underlying smirk. She also noticed how he seemed happy to turn the conversation from himself to her.

'No, I'm a professional songwriter who house sits pets. There's a difference.'

'Have you written anything I'd know?'

Tabitha thought back to the Foo Fighters T-shirt he'd been wearing the night before and wrinkled her nose. 'I've written songs for well-known pop stars, but it might not be the sort of music you listen to.'

'Huh.' His nod suggested he thought she might be right. 'But it's how you earn a living?'

'It is.'

'Seems a sweet gig, travelling around and working while looking after pets. I take it there's nothing keeping you in one place?'

She met his steady gaze. 'No, nothing.'

Tabitha stopped herself from asking the same question. She could guess the answer and, once again, she didn't want to get drawn in, to him or his life, whatever was going on. House and pet sitting was straightforward because beyond the pets there were no attachment issues. It was an easy, clean break after a short stay somewhere. In Paris, she'd flirted with an attractive barista in a local coffee shop and when she'd been writing music with a young up-and-coming pop star in LA earlier in the year, there'd been occasional hellos with the handsome neighbour in the swanky apartment building she'd stayed in, but an uninvited visitor, albeit an incredibly good-looking one, was on a whole other level.

Tabitha was aware of the silence that had grown between them. 'The songs I write for myself are different to the songs I write commercially,' she said to fill the silence. 'I think of it as two different strands. One satisfies me creatively, the other is my bread and butter and enables me to live my life.'

'Which you want to spend travelling around house sitting for other people and their pets...'

'For the time being, yes.' The same way he seemed reluctant to go into great depth about his life, she was as reluctant to share too much with him. Tabitha popped the last bit of bread into her mouth and wiped her fingers on a napkin. 'Thank you, that was lush. It's been a long time since someone else cooked for me.'

The look of interest on his face made her wish she'd swallowed her words. The last person to cook for her, beyond Christmas spent at her parents', was Lewis. She hadn't meant to compare Raff to him.

Raff nodded but didn't comment. 'I'll clear away; the least I can do. I'm sure you've got work to get on with.' He scooped up their plates and was off towards the kitchen before she could say, 'no, it's okay, you should really get going...' or something along those lines.

Raff was one of those guys, much like his dad, who were aware of their good looks and oozed confidence. He seemed at ease turning an awkward situation into one he was comfortably in control of – at least on the outside. He filled the place with his presence and he was noticeable for both his looks and attitude. As she remained sitting at the table, staring in the direction he'd gone, it didn't feel right to ask him to leave, and yet wasn't the alternative worse? She'd floundered all morning knowing that he was in the villa, that the space wasn't hers and hers alone; she hadn't been able to concentrate and she didn't feel able to get on and work. Somehow he'd managed to infiltrate her quiet time on Madeira and she was at a loss for how to deal with the situation. Or him.

7

Tabitha did what she did best and escaped. With Raff tidying the kitchen, she took the opportunity to grab her guitar and head down the garden. Not dealing with the situation felt like the easiest option for the time being. Perhaps Raff would see her working and be more inclined to leave of his own accord.

She sat cross-legged on the rattan sofa, her fingers hovering over the guitar strings. It was as if her mind had been emptied of everything except for one thing. Or, rather, one person. When she thought about it, of course Raff was in her thoughts. His arrival had been dramatic and his presence dominated her refuge. She strummed a chord, the sound blending with the drone of a bee. Maybe she could use the emotion of the last few hours and turn it into a positive. Not that she wanted to write a song about Raff, but there was a hidden story there, she was sure.

Thinking time was as helpful as actual writing time, allowing the space for melodies to take shape, for words to form, ideas to develop and blend into something coherent. Travelling had helped with all of that. Constantly being in different places kept the ideas flowing; nothing felt stale and she was free to play around with ideas as she explored. And then she'd move on and new ideas would capture her imagination. Sitting outside a pavement cafe on a street in Paris or Barcelona had been one of her favourite things. People-watching was pure joy and she always found inspiration, whether it was by watching a young couple attempting to contain a whispered argument, or the twenty-something on her own, head down reading a book trying to hide the tears trickling down her cheeks. Tabitha was fascinated by strangers and their stories, which was why, she reasoned, she was intrigued by Raff.

Bailey and Fudge jumping up from their slumber at her feet brought Tabitha back to the present. They rushed towards Raff as he strolled into sight.

'You've found a good spot to work then,' he said, glancing at her guitar.

'Yes. It's about time I did some,' she said pointedly. Now would be a good time to say goodbye... but the words faltered on her lips.

He rammed his hands in his jeans pockets, which accentuated his muscles. The ink on his bicep was bold in the sunshine, an intricate pattern that Tabitha couldn't quite make out. She failed miserably at tearing her eyes away from him.

Raff gazed down the garden. 'There used to be a hammock down there between those trees; would be a good place for you to write. Wonder why they took it down?' There it was again, that bitter tone. 'Maybe they still have it.'

Before Tabitha had a chance to say anything, he turned and paced back up the garden.

Tabitha sighed and shook her head as she looked into Fudge's big brown eyes. She scratched him under the chin. 'This is a bit of a pickle, isn't it,' she muttered as Fudge pawed her hand for more attention. 'Yeah, yeah, I know. You're much easier to deal with. Food and cuddles are all you want.' Although, when she thought about it, would a bloke really be any different?

With Fudge pawing at her and her head fizzing with thoughts of Raff, Tabitha knew she couldn't concentrate on writing or playing the guitar. She was tempted to give up for the day, but with a deadline looming to deliver the lyrics for the song she was working on, plus a Zoom catch-up scheduled the next day with her producer at the record company, she couldn't simply do nothing. The one advantage of travelling around on her own was that if she didn't get work done during the day, she could always make up for it in the evening. Being by herself, that was the time of day she found the most difficult. She did occasionally go out to eat but didn't like sitting alone. There were times when company would be good.

Raff returned with a blue and white hammock tucked under his arm and a grin that lit up his face. 'Follow me.'

Despite herself, she did, with Fudge and Bailey at her heels.

'Morning, Tabitha.'

Julie's soft voice seemingly came out of nowhere.

Raff dived to the side until he, along with the hammock, were hidden from view by the pampas grass screening the two gardens. With his free hand, he held a finger to his lips.

Tabitha stifled a laugh and shaded her eyes with her hand. 'Hi, Julie.'

'Beautiful day, isn't it.' She stopped deadheading flowers and came over to the gap by the fence. 'It must help to inspire you with your writing.'

'It does, although not today. Not had much chance to work.' She aimed the comment at Raff, who she could just see out of the corner of her eye.

'You'll have to wait until inspiration hits.'

'Unfortunately, it doesn't really work like that. Sometimes I just have to work through it even if it feels like I'm wading through treacle. Particularly if I have a deadline to meet,' she said firmly, in the hope that Raff would get the hint.

'Well, I hope the creative juices flow. By the way, if you're wondering where Misty is, she's sunning herself on our patio. We don't feed her or anything like that, she just seems to enjoy that spot.'

'I did wonder where she goes to during the day, so thanks for letting me know.'

'You're welcome.' Julie smiled, faltered and then said, 'I'll leave you to it, but you must come over one day and have coffee. If you can spare the time, of course.'

'Sure, that would be lovely.'

Tabitha waited until Julie had wandered away to retrieve her secateurs and was out of earshot.

Raff emerged from between the pampas grass with the hammock, a grin lighting up his face.

Tabitha shook her head but couldn't help returning a smile. 'You were seriously planning on staying here and sneaking around like that?'

'Yep, and I see you've already made friends with the neighbours.'

'What's the deal with your parents not liking Julie and Anton?'

'Fuck knows.'

There it was again, him deflecting. She knew he knew the reason why. Even in the short time she'd known his parents, she could see how different they were to Julie; it was obvious there was a clash of personalities and she sensed it came from Cordelia and Rufus rather than the other way round.

Raff paced ahead, obviously not wanting to continue the conversation. At the bottom of the garden, to the side of the wood-clad office, were two palm trees, hammock distance apart. She watched as Raff started to tie the hammock securely between them. She couldn't help but compare him to Lewis. Lewis certainly hadn't had Raff's confidence or his swagger. Raff had erupted into her life, while Lewis had crept in, the two of them introduced by mutual friends. Lewis, her clean-cut financial advisor ex-boyfriend. He and Tabitha couldn't have been more different – had their relationship really been doomed from the start? Tabitha had been the wild one, a songwriter and musician who at the time had been used to late-night gigging and spending more time in a hotel than at home, wherever that was. Lewis had changed her, she knew. Perhaps that was what she resented the most.

Raff finished securing the hammock and turned to her with a grin. 'Go on, try it.'

'You want *me* to test it out?' She folded her arms in mock indignation.

He pushed his weight down on the centre of the hammock to prove it was secure, yet all it really did was showcase his biceps. He turned back to her. 'It's perfectly safe, I promise.'

Rather than focusing on Raff, Tabitha contemplated the hammock and how to gracefully get into it. At least she was wearing shorts and not a skirt. Bailey had settled himself beneath one of the palm trees, while Fudge was racing around between the trees, probably wondering what his temporary human was about to do. She tentatively leaned her hands on the middle of the hammock, causing it to wobble.

'You need some help?' Raff said with laughter in his voice.

'Just a bit concerned I'm going to topple out the other side.'

With both of her hands firmly gripping the material on either side, she tried to push herself up. The hammock swung wildly.

'It'll be easier if you go in bottom first,' Raff said with an amused snort. 'It's like you've never been in a hammock before.'

Sensing her cheeks reddening, Tabitha turned to face him. 'Well, I haven't for a long time.'

Raff folded his arms and, with a look of amusement, watched as she backed into it. She took a deep breath and sat back, her legs flying into the air.

'There you go.' Raff gently pushed her legs and she swung them inwards until she was in the supportive depths of the hammock.

Feeling giggles rising, she adjusted herself and came face to face with Raff. His stubbled cheeks were dimpled with a cheeky grin.

She held his gaze. 'I would have got up here by myself, you know.'

'I'm sure you would have. Eventually. But that was a lot more fun, watching you floundering around like a beached whale.'

'A beached whale – seriously?' She raised her eyebrows and shook her head, but the glint in his eyes suggested he was teasing.

'Shuffle over,' he said.

Once again, she found herself doing as he asked. Perhaps after pushing people away for so long, it was refreshing to be around someone like Raff, someone who didn't know her or her history.

Raff leant against the centre of the hammock, shuffling back until he was just touching her. He swung his legs up and over in a far less whale-like way, expertly manoeuvring himself until he was lying next to her.

'You've done that before,' she said.

'I went backpacking in Thailand; slept in a hammock for a while.'

Tabitha gazed ahead, incredibly aware of how close they were to each other, the hammock enclosing them and pushing them together. The day was turning out nothing like she'd imagined. The view was magnificent and she tried to concentrate on it rather than Raff pressed tight against her. On a slight angle between the two palms, she could see over the shrubs edging the garden to the vast blue ocean glinting diamond-like in the sun.

'For the record,' Raff's deep voice filled the quietness, 'you look nothing like a beached whale. It was just the helpless floundering that made me think that, not anything else, I promise.'

'You should really stop talking.'

They returned to silence and gazing at the view, the hammock swaying gently. Fudge had stopped running around and was sitting on the grass, his head cocked, looking at them. Tabitha tried to not overthink the situation, but it was hard not to. And it was a situation. A right old pickle, just as she'd said to Fudge. She'd been avoiding human company as much as possible, yet Raff had gatecrashed her peaceful life with his easy-going nature and appealing looks. And, it occurred to her, if he didn't look the way he did, wouldn't she have sent him packing by now?

In such close proximity, it wasn't only Raff's looks that were having an effect. He smelt delicious too, a citrusy yet manly smell. It unsettled her how good it felt pressed against him, their bare arms touching. It was so peaceful, she was conscious of their breathing syncing as they gently rocked. The way in which he had infiltrated her quiet slice of Madeira should have been off-putting and yet she realised she was enjoying his company.

'Aren't you worried about Julie finding out that you're here?' she asked.

'Nah, I'm not worried about her. She's a good 'un. And even if she did, she wouldn't tell on me.'

'But you hid from her.'

'I don't want to put her in a difficult position and have to lie to my parents.'

Tabitha stole a glance at him. 'And yet you're okay with me lying to them...'

'Yeah, about that. I really would appreciate it if you didn't say anything.' His fingers brushing her arm sent a jolt through her. 'I know it's a lot to ask...'

She turned her head just enough to see him. He really was gorgeous. Up close, thick stubble coated his chin and jaw and his cornflower blue eyes implored her to keep his secret.

'Don't worry, I won't say anything.'

'Thank you. I appreciate it.'

They held each other's gaze for a moment longer before Raff broke the growing silence.

'You know what,' he said, 'it's been good having your unexpected company. I know you're supposed to be working and I know I need to go, but, er, how about we take the dogs out first. I can show you one of the levada walks.'

This was her chance to say no, for Raff to leave and for things to go back to normal. As normal as they could for someone bouncing from place to place trying to avoid dealing with her emotions.

'That sounds great,' Tabitha said, realising she meant it. 'It's just I think I might be stuck in here.'

Raff snorted. 'It's a piece of piss getting out. Watch me.'

Tabitha did, her eyes unwavering as he swung his legs out and planted his feet on the grass. He stood, his bum in snug jeans coming into view as she was left swinging back and forth.

She followed his lead, lifting her legs out and releasing herself from the depths of the hammock with Bailey and Fudge at her feet.

Tabitha used to have Raff's confidence, until life had ground her down. Not life; a relationship. Trying to please someone else, compromising but ending up being the only one to make sacrifices. Of course, Raff's blustery assuredness could all be a front; she couldn't tell without talking to him properly. A stranger's company was the last thing she'd craved, yet a part of her wanted to get to know him better.

8

Raff offered to drive, but there was no way that Tabitha was going to allow him near the driving seat of Cordelia's spotless white BMW. Driving somewhere new didn't bother her; she was used to it, with many of the places she'd been staying being inaccessible by public transport.

They drove along the road that hugged the coast. It was more comfortable with Raff; he didn't feel the need to fill the silence like his dad had. Tabitha was relieved to be able to concentrate on driving, in and out of tunnels and through the villages that clung to the edge of the island and overlooked the Atlantic. After twenty-five minutes, they reached the village of Ponta Do Sol and Raff directed her up the heart-stoppingly narrow and winding roads past houses nestled between pockets of banana plantations, to park by the Church of the Lombada and the start of the Levada do Moinho.

With one dog each, they set off, Tabitha taking in their surroundings as they followed the levada up through the valley which was studded with a mix of cultivated and uncultivated terraces. Clouds clustered, drifting across the distant shadowed peaks. Raff was good company and they chatted easily about the dogs and the other places on the island that were worth a visit. Tabitha gleaned a little more about him, discovering that although he no longer lived on the island and hadn't done for quite some time, he had when he was younger. His love for the outdoors was evident, and there was an ease about him as they walked that made Tabitha think he was in his happy place.

They navigated the narrow walkway, with the levada running on one side and a steep, fenced-off drop into the sun-flooded valley on the other side, where a narrow river was visible. Tabitha relished the parts of the trail where the dirt path plunged beneath the acacia and eucalyptus trees, the dry leaf and twig-covered ground speckled with sunlight. They let the dogs off their leads to race ahead, both of them stopping every so often to sniff clumps of grass or the fronds of a fern glowing luminous green in a patch of sunlight. The path emerged back into bright sunshine to sweeping valley views edged with sugar cane.

The climb up to the waterfall was a scramble and hard on the thigh muscles, but it was worth it for the welcome shade of the trees and the soothing trickle of water.

'This is one of the quieter levada trails,' Raff said, as they walked alongside the ice-clear stream. 'What do you think?'

'It's lush.'

The different trills and calls of birds filled the wooded glade as they neared the waterfall. Water plummeted between curved rocks, as if, over thousands of years, the constant pressure had worn it away, shaping and smoothing it into a vertical tunnel. The path cut through the rock, so they were able to walk behind the waterfall. Fine mist dampened their skin as they gazed through the curtain of water back the way they'd come, the view distorted by the constant flow so it was just a blur of fresh greens and russet. With Bailey and Fudge running ahead to lap up the cool water of the stream, Tabitha and Raff continued along the path curving out from beneath the grey rock, its damp surface flecked with moss.

On the return walk, they were rewarded with the view back down the valley. A patchwork of green, the hillsides studded with trees and bushes swept all the way to the red roofs of Ponta Do Sol and the ocean, a darker shade of blue than the sky.

By the time they reached the car, the dogs were panting in the afternoon heat. They eagerly drank from their bowls of water, while Tabitha and Raff swigged the remainder of their water bottles.

'I've lived in London for too long,' Raff said, cutting through the sound of the dogs' lapping.

'Oh?' Tabitha screwed on the lid of her bottle.

'I miss all this.' He swept his hand in the direction they'd just walked. 'I don't mean being here exactly, but the space... It's good for the soul.'

'You don't like London?' Tabitha asked tentatively, aware that he'd opened up slightly and she wanted to encourage it.

'Oh, I like it. A bit too much, that's the problem. At least I used to.' He gave her what she assumed was a knowing look. 'Too much temptation.'

'And by temptation you mean...'

'Ah.' He shook his head. 'The wrong crowd.' He suddenly pushed away from the car door, disturbing Fudge. 'I'm flipping starving. You fancy grabbing something to eat?'

And just like that the start of an interesting conversation was shut down. Whatever troubles he'd been dealing with back in London, Tabitha wondered if coming to Madeira had partly been to escape them. She wanted to continue the conversation, but the most pressing thing after their hike was that she was hungry too, even after the generous brunch Raff had made. The day had raced by. Food and the chance to talk further sounded rather appealing.

* * *

The ocean glimmered, ripples of waves forming far out but kept from the pebble beach by the stones sheltering the lagoon. The village of Ponta Do Sol was enclosed by cliffs, one with a hotel perched on the edge, the opposite one covered by a banana plantation. The air tasted of sea salt, the smell of grilling fish drifted towards them and a sultry afternoon heat permeated everything. Fudge and Bailey's noses twitched as Tabitha and Raff wound their way to a free table at a beachside restaurant and tied the dogs' leads to the table legs. Even surrounded by people tucking into plates of seafood, both dogs lay panting in the shade.

'This is on me,' Tabitha said after a waiter had taken their order. 'A thank you for taking me on the walk; I'd probably never have done it otherwise.'

'I should be the one thanking you,' Raff said, folding the edge of a napkin between his fingers. 'I appreciate you being so cool about the situation last night.'

'I'm just relieved you really didn't end up being some psycho murderer...'

'Ha, yes! And I'm just glad that you ended up being, well, you.'

He was utterly gorgeous when he smiled and his comment left her feeling appreciated. A warm fuzzy feeling spread inside, stirring something she hadn't felt for quite a while, along with a desire to spend more time with him.

Raff's beer and Tabitha's lemonade arrived with their food and Tabitha was grateful to switch her attention away from how Raff made her feel. Fudge half-heartedly lifted his head from his paws, sniffed the air, then immediately flopped back down again.

Tabitha's grilled cuttlefish, prawns and peppers on skewers was so good, all she could do was make 'mmm' noises for a moment, while Raff tucked into a huge bowl of *lapas*, limpets drenched in butter, garlic and lemon served with *bolo do caco* bread.

It was good for the soul, as Raff had pointed out earlier, being somewhere like this. Tabitha always found being by the sea soothing. Not that she was averse to city living, having lived in London for years. Some of her favourite places had been cities, but they were brief stops, and she understood how different it would be to permanently live somewhere such as Paris or Barcelona. Although perhaps living in a city by the ocean would be ideal.

'Do you like travelling?' she asked once she'd finished chewing a lemony prawn.

'Yeah, I do. I haven't had the chance to travel as much as I'd like over the past couple of years, though.' He sipped his beer and looked at her over the top of the glass. 'I definitely crave the freedom of being able to do what I want when I want.'

'Is that a money thing, or being held back by someone thing?' Tabitha braved an attempt to dig a little deeper into his life.

'It's both.' Raff laughed and skewered a limpet. 'But for you, bouncing from place to place, doing all this pet sitting, is because of itchy feet?'

Tabitha shrugged. 'After growing up with a nomadic sort of life, moving countries every couple of years, I've struggled with the idea of settling down in one spot.'

'But why do you feel the need to?' Raff asked. 'You obviously do a job where it's possible to work from anywhere. And it must involve the opportunity to travel too? Am I right?'

'Yeah, you're right.'

'Then why has it been an issue feeling stuck somewhere?' Raff took another sip of his beer. 'It was because of someone, right?'

Tabitha shifted in her seat. 'Yep.'

'Isn't it always.'

'It's the same for you? What you said before about doing what you want when you want – you were held back by someone?' Tabitha had noticed how quickly he'd turned the conversation back on her, but she didn't want to be the only one to open up, particularly when it came to revealing past heartache.

'Yeah,' Raff said, relaxing back in his chair and resting his foot on his knee. 'I made the mistake of buying a place with my ex-girlfriend. We shouldn't have moved in together, let alone made a commitment like that. The crazy thing is, deep down we both knew we wanted different things, yet we went ahead and did that anyway.' He shook his head. 'I don't know, I figured it was the next natural step because at the time I wanted to be with her, and in hindsight I know it was because she wanted that sort of commitment and more. Well, a lot more actually, which was the root of the problem.'

'Because you didn't want to commit?'

'Uh-huh. Story of my life.'

While he seemed willing to talk, Tabitha decided to go with it. 'What's the deal, though, with you and your parents? If you have a strained relationship with them – which I presume you do—'

'I do, yeah.'

'Then why come back?'

'Because they're not here and I've been going from one place to another for the last few months because of the whole break-up situation. I figured I'd make the most of them being away, except I hadn't factored you into the equation.'

Tabitha looked across the table at him and smiled. She liked the way he said that, as if she was a good thing. It was foolish to think that way about someone she'd only just met, but she liked the effect she seemed to be having on him.

'I used to wish that my parents had bought a place in Funchal, you know, where something actually happens, but in their wisdom,' he said in a tone that suggested the complete opposite, 'they thought it would be a good idea to buy a place out this way, where lots of other Brits live – great for parties, lots of space and suited their lifestyle – if they'd been a childless couple. For people who like to socialise, they like to do it on their own terms. And when they do go out in Funchal, they have the money to get a taxi there and back. It's a pretty sweet life they've made for themselves.'

Tabitha frowned, wondering how to go about unpicking the animosity coating his words. He was an adult, yet his comment about them being a childless couple must have stemmed from way back. For Raff to effectively be breaking into and creeping around his parents' house while they were away, there were probably an awful lot of skeletons in the closet. Considering that she was taking care of their house and pets and they didn't know their son was here, perhaps it would be for the best if they remained locked away.

They finished their meal and sat in comfortable silence, soaking up the sun. The ocean bubbled gently onto the shore and a buzzard soared high overhead. Tabitha paid and, with effort, they woke Fudge and Bailey, encouraging them to leave the shade of the table and walk back to the car.

Fudge jumped into the boot, but Bailey refused to. Raff and Tabitha laughed as she scooped him up and secured him safely inside.

'Hey,' Raff said, his fingers brushing her arm, stilling her breath momentarily. 'I know this is a lot to ask, but if I could just stay another night while I try to sort something out. You won't even know I'm here.' His smile showcased his perfect white teeth, his eyes crinkling at the corners in a way that at least looked genuine.

Tabitha was certain that she'd notice him, because she already had, in a way that made her insides go mushy and her thoughts fixate on just how noticeable he was. And the way he'd been looking at her and the things he'd said...

Tabitha stopped her thoughts in their tracks. It wasn't that he was interested in her; of course he had an ulterior motive. He wanted to stay in the house, that was his game and he was undoubtably playing on her good nature and his good looks to get exactly what he'd set out to get. He was distracting and everything she didn't need, and yet...

'Of course,' she heard herself saying, 'you can stay another night.'

With little faith, she hoped that she wouldn't end up regretting her decision.

9

They got back to the villa a little before dusk. Worn out after their hike, Bailey and Fudge pattered inside and wolfed down their food before settling themselves on the cool tiled floor. Tabitha eased her feet out of her walking boots, peeled off her socks and walked past the dogs to open the bifold doors and let in the gentle warmth of the evening. Pink and gold streaked the horizon as the glimmering sun melted into the ocean.

With Raff raiding the drinks' cupboard, Tabitha gave up on the idea of work; she would make up for it the rest of the week and work on the weekend if needed. After a shaky start, the day had turned out surprisingly well. It had been a long time since she'd felt relaxed in anyone's company besides her family, particularly with someone new. Her fallout with Ollie seven years ago had made her wary of getting too close to anyone, fearful of disappointment and being let down again. As for romantic feelings, even though she and Lewis had only split a year ago, hindsight had shown that the strain on their relationship long preceded that. The idea of being attracted to Raff had taken her by surprise; she wasn't ready, her emotions and heart still in a muddle.

Misty appeared in the living room, meowing for food. Tabitha fed her, then freshened up in the bathroom, splashing her face with water. She gazed in the mirror at her wayward curls. The freckles scattered across her cheeks were more pronounced after a good dose of sunshine. As she dried her hands, she contemplated the day. Allowing Raff to stay wasn't because she was a wallflower – she was quite capable of standing up to him and telling him where to go, yet she knew she wanted him to stay. Perhaps she saw something of herself in him, someone who didn't understand their place in the world; a drifter.

Tabitha switched off the bathroom light, returned to the living room and put music on. Raff was outside with his jeans rolled up, sitting with his feet in the pool, clasping a bottle of lager.

'I was thinking that perhaps we should start over,' he said as she joined him. 'You know, after me gate-crashing last night.'

She sat down next to him and swung her legs into the pool, relishing the cool water on her skin.

He handed her a lager and knocked his bottle against hers. 'I'm Raff, short for Rafferty, but no one's called me that for years.'

'Well, as you know, I'm Tabitha.'

'So, Tabitha, do you prefer being called that or is there a shortened version?'

'My brothers and sisters call me Tabs, but I'm known as Tabitha to everyone else. It's my songwriting name too – Tabitha Callahan.'

'That's a good name.'

'Yeah, I like it.'

Raff took a swig of lager. 'How many brothers and sisters do you have?'

'I'm the youngest of five – two brothers and two sisters.'

'Wow, your parents were busy.'

Tabitha raised an eyebrow.

'It must be nice, though, having all that company.'

'You're an only child?'

'Yep.' He downed the rest of his lager and stood up. 'Want another?'

She waggled her nearly full bottle. 'Need to catch up first.'

Raff retreated inside, padding water across the stone paving, returning a minute later clutching another two bottles.

Tabitha shook her head. 'You're going to be a bad influence, I can tell.'

He sat back down and dunked his feet in the pool with a splash. 'I'll try my best.' He grinned and knocked his new bottle of lager against hers.

Without hesitating, Tabitha downed her first bottle, hard to do in one, but she drained it as fast as she could, smacking her lips once she finished. 'Thought I'd better at least try to catch up.'

'That's what I like to see.' Raff handed her another lager. 'So, tell me, with so many siblings, I bet you had a nickname?'

'My eldest brother – who knew exactly what he was doing – turned Tabs into Tabby cat, which in turn changed to Pussy.'

Raff nearly spat out his lager.

'So between the ages of four and ten that's what he called me.'

'As in referring to you as a pussy, scared about doing stuff?' He held her gaze, almost as if he was challenging her.

Tabitha laughed and shook her head. 'No chance. I was a bit of a bruiser as a kid, so that term definitely didn't fit.' She gave him a sly grin. 'The joys of having an older more worldly-wise brother. I should point out he doesn't call me that any longer. No one does.'

'If you say so, P—'

'Don't even think about it.' She playfully whacked him, the back of her hand connecting with his muscled arm. She turned her attention to the darkness that had now descended beyond the pool and took a large swig of lager. Of all the things she could have told him, why on earth had she thought sharing that story was a good idea?

'So, next question,' Raff said, thankfully steering the conversation away from her embarrassing nickname. 'How old are you?'

'Thirty-two. You?'

'Thirty-one.' So she hadn't been far off in her estimation.

'What makes someone your age spend their life travelling from one place to another?'

'Someone my age?' Tabitha narrowed her eyes and pursed her lips.

'Okay, someone our age.' Raff nudged her shoulder with his.

'The short version is I was in a place in my life I wanted to escape from and I thankfully have a career that enabled me to work pretty much anywhere for a while.'

'And the long version...?'

Tabitha sensed him watching her. She felt a familiar knot in her chest; finding the words to explain her reasons for leaving still felt impossible. It was hard enough thinking back on that time. She'd even struggled to talk to Elspeth about it, let alone someone she'd only just met. Dwelling on events, she felt the panic crawling up her chest. Breaking up with Lewis had been hard but right; getting pregnant by accident, then suffering a miscarriage had left her devastated. Fighting to control her emotions, she kicked her legs out, sending ripples across the water and splashing onto the paving.

'I don't really want to go into the long version, but let's just say I needed to take time out... from everything. I took six months off, didn't work, just moved from place to place looking after pets while trying to get my shit together.' She turned and met his gaze, hoping he'd understand there was pain in her past that she wasn't ready to share. Not that she wanted there to be any awkwardness. He may have instigated them spending time together, but ultimately she was in charge of where they went from here. 'Travelling's in my blood, though. Our family moved around loads. By the time I was eighteen, we'd moved seven times, so it feels normal to go from place to place, even if I move a lot more frequently house sitting than I did when I was a kid.'

'Sounds like a character-building way of growing up. I imagine it takes a fair amount of confidence to travel and slot yourself into a new place all the time.'

'Yeah, I guess so.' She took a swig of her drink. 'With four older siblings, I learnt to stick up for myself and moving around so much I got used to constantly having to make new friends and trying to fit into a new school. Confidence came with that.'

Raff nodded and polished off his lager. 'But the house sitting came about because you wanted to escape your life back home?' he asked tentatively. 'Wherever home is?'

'Yeah, I was living in Wimbledon. Not that it ever felt like home.'

'Was it the place you were escaping from or someone?'

'Are you trying to ask if I've had my heart broken?'

'Have you?'

Tabitha gently kicked her legs back and forth, relishing the now-warm sensation of the water. 'Not exactly,' she eventually said. 'Although I certainly broke his heart.'

'Your ex?'

Tabitha nodded. 'Perhaps it's a similar story for you?'

'Yeah, I was definitely the one doing the heart breaking.'

Did she really want them to unravel their messy pasts and divulge the relationships that had gone wrong?

She swigged more lager, put the bottle down and turned to him. 'This is beginning to be a rather serious conversation after a very enjoyable day.'

'I can be less serious.'

'Good. Let's try that.'

His grinning face betrayed little as he leant closer. It crossed Tabitha's mind that he was about to kiss her, when his hands landed on her back and, with one gentle shove, she went sprawling forwards. With a shriek and an almighty splash, she plummeted into the actually-not-so-warm water of the pool.

Although muffled beneath the water, Raff's laughter filled the night as she broke through the surface.

'You bastard!' she shrieked.

He held his hand to his chest, hardly containing himself as he wracked with laughter. 'I'm so sorry, I couldn't help it.'

Finding her footing on the base of the pool, she flicked water in his direction before surging forward. She grabbed a handful of his T-shirt, tugging him in with her. She was submerged again, the tepid water bubbling around them. Raff reached out and grabbed her waist, pulling her up with him as they surfaced together, water spraying into the night. The noises that had been muffled underwater screamed back into surround sound, Bailey and Fudge's barks overpowering the gentle chatter of night-time insects as they ran up and down the length of the pool, their long ears flapping.

Raff removed his hands from her waist, although his grin remained. 'Was that less serious?'

'It wasn't quite what I had in mind,' Tabitha said, laughing. She pointed at the dogs. 'We're so going to disturb the neighbours.'

'They'll just think you're having a party.'

'That's the problem.'

'They won't tell on you, I promise.'

'Hmm...' Tabitha huffed, unconvinced, but she couldn't contain her smile. She gestured to her soaked T-shirt. 'What now?'

Raff's eyes travelled downwards. Submerged to his waist, his T-shirt was pretty much see-through and the way his eyes lingered suggested hers was in a similar state.

'We could play a game?' His attention drifted from her wet T-shirt upwards.

She met his gaze. 'Like what?'

'Maybe strip poker.'

Tabitha snorted. 'That's wishful thinking.'

'Was worth a try.'

He swam to the edge of the pool and heaved himself onto the paving, water pouring from his jeans. Turning back, he offered her his hand. She took it and clambered out.

He ran a hand through his soaking hair. 'To be honest, it's just been good to drink and chat.'

'I couldn't agree more,' Tabitha said as she squeezed the excess water from her hair. Droplets splashed onto the stone, as well as on Fudge and Bailey, who were skittering around their feet.

Although tempting, Tabitha refrained from changing her mind about playing strip poker. She hadn't had quite enough to drink yet to say yes to that, although thinking back on her mid-twenties when she'd toured with bands and hung out with rock stars, it wasn't as if she'd never done anything like that before. Not that Raff needed to know...

With the dogs on their heels and dripping water across Cordelia and Rufus's spotless living room floor, Tabitha grabbed towels from the bathroom and threw one to Raff before they separated: Raff to the guest bedroom and Tabitha to hers.

Fudge followed her into the room and she closed the door. She took a deep breath. Every part of her tingled. *Every* part of her. She bit her lip and looked down at Fudge gazing up at her.

'This is another right pickle.' Fudge cocked his head to one side and Tabitha shook hers. 'You wouldn't understand, buddy.'

Peeling off her soaking shorts, T-shirt and underwear, she left them in the shower to deal with later and got dried and redressed in a skirt and top. She towel-dried her hair, spritzed product in it and scrunched her curls. With Fudge following like a shadow, she returned to the living room to find Raff already there in a dry T-shirt and jeans, pouring tequila into two shot glasses.

'This bottle's been in the cupboard unopened for years.' He handed her one of the glasses. 'Thought we'd forgo the lemon and salt.'

Tabitha wondered if this was a good idea, but as Raff raised his glass to hers there wasn't time to dwell. They clinked glasses and downed the tequila in one. Tabitha pulled a face as the liquid slid down her throat.

'Tequila is one of the few spirits I can still drink,' Raff said, raising an eyebrow as he poured another shot. With little hesitation, they downed them too.

Raff poured them a third shot and placed the bottle on the coffee table. With Bailey and Fudge both settled on the sofa, Tabitha and Raff sat together on the rug. Along with Florence and the Machine's 'Dog Days Are Over' playing in the background, night-time noises floated in through the open doors – a distant bark, a rustle in the undergrowth – giving a sense of the inside and outside converging. Moths fluttered around the patio, drawn to the blue-lit pool. Beyond that, there was star-speckled darkness. The moon cast a silvery glow over the Atlantic Ocean.

'I have a fair few drinks I can't stomach any longer.' Tabitha swirled the clear liquid around the shot glass.

'Yup, me too. I remember at school me and my mates sneaking bottles of WKD Blue into the dorm. I was seriously sick that night and seriously bollocked by the Housemaster the next day.'

'You went to boarding school?'

'Uh-huh.' He downed the third shot. 'What can't you stomach?'

'More like what can I?' Tabitha downed her shot too. She grimaced and stuck her tongue out. 'Quite a few things: cider and vodka among others. All due to a fair bit of late-night partying when I toured with One Love. Massive stadium tours back in the day, the UK and European leg.'

'Seriously? You toured with them? I mean, they're not my kinda music, but I bet it was pretty mental.'

'Yeah, it was a big deal. A whirlwind couple of years. Playing to a hundred thousand screaming fans – even if they weren't my fans – was such a buzz. There's nothing quite like it. I co-wrote a few songs with them too.'

'Shit; that's serious.'

'Yeah, I think back on the places I went, the people I met, the things we got up to...' She raised an eyebrow. 'I was in my twenties, having the time of my life. It was easy to say yes to things and that whole lifestyle, you know being a part of a mega machine like that: the parties, the craziness, the gigs. It was epic, if unsustainable.'

'What made you stop?'

Tabitha reached for the tequila bottle and topped up their glasses. She downed hers and turned to Raff. 'The conversation is getting serious again.'

His eyes traced her face before locking on hers. 'I'm still up for strip poker.'

Tabitha snorted. 'Not a chance.'

Even though she was definitely feeling the effect of the tequila, she still wasn't prepared to play that with him.

'Fair enough.' He shrugged. 'But if serious conversation and strip poker are ruled out, this'll make you giggle.' He lifted up his T-shirt and pulled down the top of his jeans, revealing his toned abs. 'I lost a bet at uni.'

She sat upright and leant forward, squinting at the area he was showing. 'Is that a Smurf?'

'Yep.'

'Is it doing what I think it's doing?'

'Yep.'

Tabitha ran her fingers over the ink, tracing the contours of his firm stomach as much as the regrettably bad tattoo of a Smurf mooning.

She laughed and looked up into Raff's face just a heartbeat away. Her fingers remained against his hot skin. Tequila-scented breath, come-to-bed eyes and exceedingly kissable lips made her heart thud.

Things were moving fast, making her wonder how the rest of the night might play out...

'You know what we need,' she said, removing her fingers, 'more tequila!' She turned away a little too fast, the few tequila shots making her head spin. At least concentrating on pouring took her attention away from his abs and the thought of kissing him.

After another couple of shots, Tabitha's worries about the neighbours overhearing and thinking she was having a party evaporated. Raff stressed that they were far enough away and even if they did hear something, neither of them was likely to go blabbing to his parents – they weren't that sort of people.

She hadn't laughed this much in a long time. Raff was surprisingly easy to get along with and, as they got increasingly drunk, they chatted about everything, bar their personal lives, from politics and city living to travelling and food, putting the world to rights over excessive amounts of tequila.

Over the last year, she'd strongly believed that she didn't want company, but after the last day with Raff, it wasn't so much company she'd been avoiding, as the fear of committing to someone again and feeling as trapped and uncertain as she had done with Lewis.

The conversation moved on from the jobs they'd had over the years – from how Raff had travelled the world and ended up doing a stint in the marines before getting into video game design, to their most drunken mishaps, including Tabitha toppling off stage with her guitar at a London gig. Tabitha began to relax, opening up a little about how studying music at the Royal Welsh College of Music & Drama in Cardiff and playing guitar in a band with Ollie, who'd been studying drama, led her to working as a session musician when she and Ollie had moved to London. She left out much about Ollie, though, focusing instead on her work in the recording studio with One Love, which was how she had ended up touring with them, rather than Ollie's path of singing with two short-lived bands before getting his big break on *The Star*.

As they laughed and joked together, the idea that it was irresponsible to be in someone else's house getting this drunk on their booze kept hijacking her thoughts. Even if she was with their son. The son they'd never mentioned. The son who wasn't supposed to be here... Although it was just as well he was staying another night; she would hardly have been able to kick him out while he was wasted.

Wasted... In her head, it sounded incredibly high-pitched. She giggled.

'What's so funny?'

Tabitha shook her head, which made the swirling wooziness even worse. 'I have no idea.' She giggled harder and hiccupped. 'It's been a long time since I drank like this.'

'I can tell.' He tapped his glass against hers. 'I'm going to have to keep an eye on you.'

Tabitha held his gaze, as much as she could with her head spinning the way it was. She liked the idea of him keeping an eye on her. She liked the idea of him.

That's a foolish thing to think. And yet, here she was, spending the evening with him, drinking a copious amount of booze, when there was no reason why they couldn't have spent the evening separately. After all, it was only a place to crash that he needed.

Raff picked up the nearly empty bottle of tequila.

Tabitha held her hand over the shot glass. 'Uh-uh. No more.' She scrambled unsteadily to her feet, disturbing Fudge as she did. 'So need a wee.'

She made her way across the living room to the bathroom, feeling as if she was zigzagging across the bow of a ship in a stormy sea.

After the longest wee in the world, Tabitha washed her hands and leant on the sink. Her face was flushed, her semi-dried curls a wayward mass, her features distorted in the mirror as if she was still on that rocking boat.

She switched off the light and staggered from the bathroom, promising herself to slow down on the drinking, although the damage was already done. She was going to have a raging hangover in the morning. However, even in her drunken state, she acknowledged how much she'd enjoyed herself with Raff. He was exceedingly good-looking too, making her feel all kinds of delicious things that she hadn't felt in a long time.

Talking of the devil, he was heading towards her, a tall, muscled figure, shadowed in the dimly lit hallway, reminding her of their first unexpected encounter. From an intruder last night to sharing an evening laughing and flirting together…

'Hey,' he said as he reached her. 'Just wanted to make sure you weren't passed out somewhere.'

'It may be a long time since I've drunk like this, but I can hold my drink.' She tried to contain a hiccup.

Raff smirked. 'If you say so.'

Up close, she could just make out the cool blue of his eyes, half closed from drunkenness, and dark stubble shading his defined jaw.

'You need a little help walking back?' Raff slid his arm around her waist and she leaned into him, except they didn't move. She heard the clack of the dogs' nails on the polished wood floor as they joined them in the hallway.

With her head whirling, Tabitha gazed up. He leaned closer, tequila breath tickling her skin, not in an unpleasant way. Her heart raced. On tiptoes, she faltered momentarily, then pressed her lips to his, kissing him gently until he responded and kissed her back. Their tongues toyed with each other. He tasted of tequila and lager.

Dipping her hands beneath his T-shirt, she smoothed them across his firm chest. He did the same, connecting with her bare skin and sending a jolt of excitement through her. She closed her eyes and everything spun. Her senses were overloaded, a mish-mash of desire and drunkenness, coupled with the taste of him and his touch, firm and enticing. He backed her against the wall, his body pressed against hers as their kiss intensified.

Tabitha opened her eyes and pulled away, the sensation of being spun on a fairground ride overwhelming, the only difference being Raff's strong arms contained her, instead of hard metal sides. She grabbed the bottom of his T-shirt and tugged it up and over his head. She caught his drunken grin as she discarded it on the floor. She trailed her fingers across his sculpted chest before taking his hand. They staggered along the hallway together, crashing into each other in a fit of giggles at the bedroom door.

10

Tabitha woke with a groan, nausea rising into her throat. Sunlight filtered between half-drawn curtains, forcing her to squint, her pounding head unable to cope with even a hint of daylight. Images from the night before flashed through her mind: downing shots of tequila, tumbling into the pool, revealing tattoos, snogging Raff...

Tabitha forced her thumping head to turn. Squinting through tired, hungover eyes, she took in Raff, sprawled next to her on the bed in just his jeans. His arms were curled around a pillow, his shoulder muscles tense, his broad back shapely.

Thank goodness he's wearing something, Tabitha thought.

With a start, she pulled down the sheet covering her. She was just in her bra and knickers, her skirt and top crumpled on the floor.

'Oh God,' she mumbled, her thoughts spilling out loud.

Raff groaned. 'Ugh, what time is it?'

Tabitha glanced to the bottom of the bed and Fudge looking expectantly at her. 'I guess, seven.' Her voice sounded gravelly. The excesses of last night pounded her head like she'd fought ten rounds with Tyson Fury.

Raff groaned again and rolled onto his back. The buttons of his jeans were undone, his ripped chest in her eyeline. All the feelings from last night came flooding back in a wave. Not to mention nausea. God, did she feel rough.

Tabitha's eyes drifted over Raff's enticing form. She'd had no qualms about kissing him last night. She frowned, her memory hazy as she tried to remember who had made the first move. Whoever it was, she'd been party to the flirting. Her eyes lingered on his toned stomach, traced across his regrettable Smurf tattoo before drifting to where his unbuttoned jeans revealed a smattering of hair...

She tore her eyes away. This was wrong on so many levels. Even if nothing had happened beyond a snog, which she was completely unsure about, she'd betrayed Rufus and Cordelia's trust. Tabitha breathed deeply at the thought that she was in *their* bed with their son who wasn't supposed to be there.

In desperate need of fresh air and feeling as if she was about to be sick, Tabitha forced herself out of bed. Her throat felt hoarse as if she'd been in a club all night, her mouth furred with that morning-after-the-night-before feeling. She pulled on her top and staggered from the room, Fudge and Bailey following, while Raff gave another sleepy groan.

Raff's T-shirt was discarded on the hallway floor, and her heart dropped when she reached the living room. The doors were wide open, the coffee table and terrace littered with empty bottles of lager, shot glasses and the tequila bottle from Rufus and Cordelia's drinks' cupboard. With her heart pounding, Tabitha glanced around, checking that everything was still there. How could she have been so stupid? The dogs could have ended up outside during the night; anything could have happened to them. She'd been completely irresponsible, behaving in a way she'd never done while house sitting.

Fudge and Bailey were padding round her feet, trying to get her attention, spinning round in circles.

'Yes, yes,' she muttered. 'I'm going to feed you now.'

They raced after her to the kitchen. The sunshine pouring through the window was way too bright. She closed the blind, dimming the light a little. She was mightily relieved that the dogs had dried food, yet even the smell sent her racing to the bathroom off the hallway.

As she leaned over the toilet, retching up the acidic contents of last night's drinking, she wished she'd made different choices. She hadn't drunk like that for a long time and she was feeling horribly sorry for herself, as well as confused about the feelings Raff had ignited in her. She downed a glass of water, rinsed her mouth with mouthwash she found in the cupboard and grimaced when she caught sight of her washed-out face in the mirror.

After letting Fudge and Bailey out and with Misty curled up on the armchair ignoring Tabitha's enticement of breakfast, she pulled the bifold doors closed. While the dogs settled in the living room, she stumbled back to the bedroom. She was too tired and groggy to even contemplate staying up. Raff was still fast asleep, so she slipped into bed and turned her back on him, closing her eyes and tucking her hands beneath the pillow.

* * *

Tabitha woke for a second time that morning with a groan. The sun had fully risen, flooding the bedroom with warmth. The pounding in her head had lessened, but she still felt groggy. She stretched and yawned before realising that the other side of the bed was empty.

She shuffled upright, groaned again and swung her legs out of bed. She sat for a moment, her elbows resting on her knees, her head in her hands. The bedroom door was wedged open and Raff's deep voice floated in. She frowned, confused that there was someone else in the villa before it dawned on her that Raff must be talking on the phone.

Forcing herself to stand, Tabitha rummaged through the chest of drawers for a pair of shorts, pulled them on and wandered down the hall to the living room. Raff was on his mobile, perched on the arm of the sofa looking much fresher than when she'd first laid eyes on him that morning. She noticed he'd also cleared away the empty bottles, although she still needed to tidy up before Cordelia's cleaner turned up later in the week. She also made a mental note to replace the tequila.

'Yeah, great, I'll give you a call later to arrange. See ya.' He clicked end call and tucked the phone in the back pocket of his jeans. He looked over at Tabitha. 'Morning.'

'Morning.' Her throat was raspy and still felt like sandpaper.

'I realised you must have been up earlier to feed the dogs. If you want to get a shower, I'll make breakfast – figure we could both do with a pick-me-up.'

Tabitha was relieved he was acting normally with no obvious awkwardness, although she was happy to escape back to her room for a much-needed shower. The hot water pummelled Tabitha awake, giving her a sense of washing away the excesses of the night before. Not that she could remember anything after kissing Raff in the hallway. That was the bit of the night she wanted to piece together. Surely she would remember if they'd done more than just kiss?

She stepped from the shower smelling much sweeter and wrapped herself in a large fluffy towel. It felt rather domestic, Raff making breakfast again, as if they were a couple... Her heart skipped as she glanced in the bin next to the dressing table. No condom or empty packet. Was that a good or bad thing? Muddled emotions surged through her as she got dried and dressed in relaxed cargo trousers and a fitted white T-shirt. These feelings were partly the reason she'd escaped from everything she'd been dealing with back home.

Rather than it turning her stomach, the smell of something sweet frying made her mouth water as she walked towards the kitchen. She wasn't much of a cook and having lived by herself for the last year, it was a novelty having someone else cook for her.

Tabitha leaned against the open kitchen door and watched Raff looking at ease as he shook the contents of the frying pan while humming a tune under his breath. She couldn't help but smile.

He caught sight of her and stopped humming. 'Coffee's on if you want to grab a couple of mugs.'

The smell of the coffee was even better as she poured it and took the mugs out to the patio table. The sunshine made her squint and her head began to pound again, but the gentle warmth and a whisper of breeze was a tonic.

Raff joined her and placed two plates on the table. 'French toast to kick our hangovers to the kerb.'

Neither of them hesitated, tucking in greedily.

'This is so good,' Tabitha mumbled with a mouth full of the sweet and delicious eggy bread drizzled with maple syrup and topped with juicy blueberries, tart passion fruit and sweet chunks of banana.

Raff nodded in agreement and they continued eating in silence, with the dogs padding around the patio and a blackbird hopping on the grass.

As she polished off her breakfast, Tabitha felt less hungover and more like herself. She clasped her hands around her mug of coffee and looked across the table at Raff. She didn't want to have to ask the question, but she didn't want the uncertainty any longer.

'About last night. I take it we didn't, um... you know.'

'Have sex?' Raff laughed. 'I could barely stand, let alone do anything else, plus you were too far gone to even begin to know what you were saying yes to.'

Huh. Tabitha was impressed. Despite breaking in and confusing the hell out of her, he was seemingly a gentleman. He was right too; with only a hazy recollection of the night before, she'd been too drunk to fully know what she was doing and he hadn't taken advantage of that. If he had, she was pretty certain that she wouldn't have been able to say no, even if she'd wanted to. Although, last night, saying no was the last thing on her mind. And it sounded as though Raff had wanted to, if the circumstances had been different.

What she was most impressed by, though, was how unfazed he was about the situation. And she would have been too, a long time ago. She'd spent years as part of a couple. It had been a long time since she'd been intimate with anyone. It had been a long time since she'd had this much fun with anyone, which made what she was about to say all the harder.

'About you staying…' she said tentatively.

He waved his hand and downed the remainder of his coffee. 'Don't worry. I've arranged to meet a friend; I'll sort something out.'

So that was who he was talking to earlier.

'It's just I need to work.' Tabitha felt she should explain. 'Even though I travel around, it doesn't mean I can have this much, um, downtime…'

'I get it, I do. I'll clear up and be out of your way.'

That had been surprisingly easy, yet, as she watched Raff retreat to the kitchen with their breakfast plates, she acknowledged the pang of disappointment that their time together would soon be over.

11

It was nearly the middle of the week and already much later in the morning than Tabitha had intended to start working. Leaving Raff to wash up the breakfast things, she took her guitar and laptop onto the shaded terrace at the side of the pool. Being in a new place, it was easy to lose track of time, the days rolling into one with no distinction between the weekend or weekdays, but today she had a Zoom call scheduled with her producer at the record company and the lyrics to finish for the track she'd been working on. As she'd explained to Julie, sometimes she just had to write even if her creativity felt stifled.

Tabitha was so focused on the melody she was listening to that she didn't notice Raff until he placed a hand on her shoulder. Startled, she looked up.

'Hey,' he said as she paused the track on the laptop and took out her AirPods. 'I didn't mean to disturb you, but I'm off.'

Tabitha stood, a wave of disappointment inching through her at the idea of saying goodbye.

'Thank you for being so understanding and letting me crash for a couple of nights.'

Tabitha stuffed her hands into the deep pockets of her cargo trousers and met his blue eyes. 'No problem. It's been, um, really good to meet you.'

'Yeah, you too.'

They looked at each other for a moment, uncertainty sweeping through Tabitha as she weighed up whether she should sever their link completely or stay connected – because there was a connection.

'Hey,' she said softly, reaching out and touching his arm. 'Do you want to swap numbers?'

'Yeah, of course.' He rattled off his number and she plumbed it into her phone before calling him.

'There you go, now you have mine too.' She pressed end call and tucked the phone into her pocket. 'You're meeting a friend?'

'Yeah, he doesn't live too far away – I've not seen him for a while. One of my few friends on the island. I'm going to meet him after he finishes work.' He took a deep breath. 'I'd best let you get on.'

He went in for a hug and Tabitha reciprocated. They held each other for a moment, their arms wrapped tight, her body pressed against his, thoughts drifting to the night before and kissing him in the hallway... not really wanting to let him go.

Raff pulled away first and dipped his head in a goodbye. 'I'll see you around.' He swung his rucksack on his back and walked away, disappearing around the side of the house.

Tabitha stood on the sun-filled terrace, with the pool glistening and only the birds and dogs for company; Misty too, wherever she was. The front gate click closed and she sighed. Raff was gone and she was finally on her own. Wasn't that what she wanted more than anything? They'd swapped numbers, but the chances were, she wouldn't see him again. He'd stolen into her life, shaken it up and was off just as quick. Perhaps there was some material within that for a song.

Fudge and Bailey were the best companions. She took them for a short walk and then they kept her company wherever she chose to work, which ended up being a mix of the pool terrace and the dining table looking out over the garden. It was easy and stress-free and she definitely needed to catch up with work after too many days enjoying the Madeira lifestyle, yet her thoughts kept drifting to Raff, wondering where he was and what he was doing. She considered messaging him, then thought better of it. What would she even say? And for what reason did she want to contact him? Beyond his good looks, he was still a bit of a mystery, yet that was at the heart of why she found him so intriguing.

After a long afternoon on a Zoom call bouncing around ideas with her producer, then trying to focus her mind on polishing and recording the lyrics that she would send in the morning, she called it a day when the dogs started badgering her for food. On autopilot, she fed them and Misty.

The pool had been enticing her all day and with the early evening still blissfully warm and sunny, Tabitha changed into a bikini and dived straight in. The cool hit of water was refreshing and took her right back to the night before when she and Raff had ended up in the pool together.

Thinking about Raff focused her mind onto one of the reasons she'd taken the Madeira house sit. Ollie. Being here was her chance to contact him and put the past behind them; to rid herself of the upset he'd caused that had eaten away at her for years. She floated on her back, gently paddling while gazing up at the sky streaked with wispy clouds like they'd been brushed onto the blue. She couldn't avoid him forever. She didn't want to, despite feeling it was too hard to see him again. She had been conflicted for a long time; she hoped Madeira would be the instigating factor in coming to terms with it.

Refreshed from her swim, Tabitha emerged from the pool, showered and pulled on skinny joggers and a vest top, made a salad for dinner and sat on the sofa.

While eating, she clicked on Ollie's Instagram page. Ollie Pereira, with an official blue tick next to his name, had 28.7 million followers. Tabitha's own Instagram account had a modest 26K followers and many of those had been gained over the last twelve months when she'd posted about her travels as much as the music side of her life.

There was no intro needed to Ollie's page beyond his name and website. The photos spoke for themselves: the poster image for his upcoming US tour, Ollie singing at gigs, on photo shoots, in the studio, interspersed with a good dose of him shirtless. His looks, his abs and his voice had managed to get him noticed worldwide and a legion of fans. He was the complete package and Tabitha had known it since they'd first met in Cardiff at the age of eighteen.

She remembered the day they'd set up their Instagram accounts together and posted their first pictures: Ollie singing at a gig in Brighton and her sitting cross-legged on a sofa with her guitar. She couldn't remember if Ollie had taken that photo or if had been one of their housemates. Either way, they'd been following each other for years, although since their fallout, Tabitha only occasionally looked at his Instagram feed and never liked any of his pictures. Not because she didn't like them, she just didn't want to risk her name popping up. Not that she'd noticed him liking anything she'd posted either, but she did wonder if he ever looked.

She clicked into the private messages and faltered. She was reaching out, that was all. No expectation. All she wanted was to confront him and move on. Patching up their friendship would be a bonus. As Elspeth had said, they were friends. They'd once been best friends. There had been many a time over the last few years when she could have done with his friendship, yet she'd stopped herself from contacting him because she was too angry to do so.

As she thumbed a message, deleting and rewriting it several times before finding the nerve to press send, she acknowledged that it was long overdue to make peace with the past.

There, it was done and sent. If she was expecting a weight to be lifted, she was disappointed. Instead, a knot formed in her stomach, twisting with a mix of anticipation and nerves as she waited for a reply. If he replied at all. She'd blocked him from her life for so long, there was every chance that he would treat her the same way.

Tabitha focused her attention on something else, deciding that relistening to the lyrics she'd recorded earlier would take her mind off things. And it did for a short while. She hadn't expected his reply to be so swift, but less than fifteen minutes later, her phone pinged with a new Instagram message. She didn't open it straight away. Instead, she picked up her guitar and played the finished song. But it was no good. With the knot in her stomach tightening, she couldn't put it off any longer. She set down her guitar, took a deep breath and clicked on the message.

OMG Tabitha! Totally shocked to hear from you, but bloody hell, mate, it's so good to see your name pop up. YES to meeting up. It's been way too long. Fancy a drink this Friday evening in Funchal?

Tabitha realised her hands were shaking as she wrote a reply.

Yes, I'd love to. Friday's great, just let me know what time and where.

She didn't want to say anything else; there would be plenty of opportunity to talk to him in person. Years had gone by without them seeing each other and, if he felt any remorse or discomfort, it certainly wasn't coming across.

She messaged Elspeth.

I did it. Finally contacted Ollie. Going to meet up with him this Friday. Xx

Tabitha wasn't surprised when seconds later her phone rang.

'Oh Tabs, I'm so proud of you,' Elspeth gushed as soon as Tabitha picked up.

'I finally plucked up the courage.'

'I know you want to fix things, but you've got to make him understand the hurt he caused.'

Tabitha ran her fingers lightly over the guitar strings. 'I will, but I really want to move on. I'm fed up of all the negative feelings I have when I see him and I don't know if it's because of what he did or simply that I'm looking at his life from afar. We both know what social media is like and how record companies portray their artists in a way that only ever shows the glamorous side of their life—'

'Mind you, the paparazzi do a good job of showing the darker and real side of things, don't they?'

'True, but with Ollie I feel like I've been bombarded with all the amazing things that have happened to him... Oh, I don't know. This might be a huge mistake, but I need to do something. He's been playing on my mind for so long.'

'I think it's good you're doing this. It's a chance to move forward.'

'It's a start.' Tabitha sighed. 'Enough about me. How are you doing?'

'Oh, you know, just juggling too many things as usual. We've only got another week to finish decorating the barn ready for our first wedding a week on Saturday. Nothing like the pressure of a deadline to get things done.'

'I wish I was there to help out.'

'I keep on saying for you to come visit us – I'm going to bang on about it until you do. Mum and Dad miss you too. We all do.'

'Yeah, I know. And thanks for ringing when I know you're so busy. It's good to talk to you.'

'Are you sure you're okay, Tabs?'

'Yeah, I'm fine. It's been a strange day, that's all.' Although she usually told Elspeth everything, she found it hard to put into words the last couple of days spent with Raff. He was a secret – certainly a secret she needed to keep from Cordelia and Rufus, not one she had to keep from her sister – but for some reason she didn't want to go into it right now.

After saying goodbye, Tabitha gave up on work and poured a glass of wine instead. She messaged Cordelia and Rufus with an update, omitting any mention of their son, caught up with the Callahan family chat on WhatsApp, then curled up on the sofa with a book. She was extra pleased when Fudge jumped up and rested his head on her bare feet, keeping them toasty.

The sun was well on its way to the horizon when her phone pinged. She assumed it would be Ollie about Friday. Her heart leapt when Raff's name popped up.

Are you at the house? Got some pastéis de maracuja you have got to try.

Tabitha frowned and read the message again. Did that mean he was coming over? And what were *pastéis de* whatever anyway?

She thumbed a reply.

Yes, I'm here. Where are you?

She googled the *pastéis* name and discovered they were little sweet tarts similar to the Portuguese custard tarts *pastéis de nata* but with passion fruit. They sounded utterly delicious, but when there was no further reply, it crossed her mind that perhaps he'd messaged her by mistake.

Tabitha went back to reading her book, yet her mind kept drifting and she had to reread the paragraph she was on several times. For the umpteenth time that day, her head had been hijacked by Raff. He'd only left that morning, and yet, the excitement in the pit of her stomach was testament to how much she wanted to see him again.

The bifold doors were wide open, the only sounds a soothing combination of the breeze sighing through the trees and an occasional distant rumble of a car passing by. It wasn't hard to miss the sound of a car on the lane thirty minutes later. It stopped and two doors slammed shut. Bailey remained asleep on the rug, but Fudge's head shot up.

Voices drifted towards the villa – deep and male and filled with laughter.

Fudge jumped down and pattered across the tiles to the terrace, Tabitha right behind him.

Tabitha's insides swirled as she laid eyes on Raff, a grin etched across his handsome face, his rucksack slung on his back as he appeared around the side of the villa. This time, he wasn't unexpected... and he wasn't alone. A second man appeared, not quite as tall but dressed similarly in jeans and a short-sleeved shirt, clutching bottles of lager. Tabitha switched her attention from the friend back to Raff.

'What are you doing here?' Tabitha wasn't sure if she should be happy to see him or not, her physical reaction betraying her head as her insides tingled.

Still grinning, Raff shrugged. 'I didn't think you'd mind.'

Hmm, that was quite an assumption, particularly when he hadn't turned up alone. Raff was one thing, but his friend too...

'And we come with an offering of these.' He held up a small white box, which she assumed contained the tarts, and in the other hand he waggled a bottle. 'And this – the nicest wine on Madeira – in my humble opinion.'

Which he'd obviously already been drinking copious amounts of, considering he seemed to be rather tipsy.

'This is my friend Emilio.' Raff gestured to the dark-haired guy next to him, then back to her. 'This is Tabitha. She's looking after the place while my parents are away.'

'*Olá*, Tabitha,' Emilio said with a thick, most probably drunken accent.

'Hey there,' she said, smiling at him before turning her attention to Raff. 'You didn't drive here, did you?'

'Nah, course not. We got a taxi, from the next village. Figured you might want the company. It gets pretty lonely out here...' He held her gaze for a moment, then walked past her into the villa, a waft of spiced ginger in his wake. With her stomach jangling with nerves, she gestured for Emilio to follow. Part of her was glad to see Raff, but once again he'd taken her by surprise, his friend an unexpected and not entirely welcome addition.

Somehow, after only twelve hours since saying goodbye, Raff was back in her life.

12

On her way back from the bathroom an hour later, Tabitha paused in the doorway of the living room and watched Raff and his mate. Part of her craved this, being around people, letting her hair down and embracing life. It was what she was used to. Actually, no, it was what she used to do before she'd met Lewis. Their relationship had become serious pretty quickly. Encouraged by him, she'd made choices which had impacted her lifestyle but had meant they could spend more time together.

It was obvious that Raff dominated his friendship with Emilio and had done since they'd met during their teens after Raff's family had moved to the island. Tabitha had noticed Emilio mutter, more than once, 'Inez is going to kill me' before downing his drink. Tabitha had discovered that his wife Inez was at home with their seven-month-old son, which accounted for why he and Raff had shown up here after a few drinks out rather than returning to Emilio's house. Raff was rather presumptuous about her being okay with him and a friend gate-crashing, and yet, once again, she'd done nothing to stop him. Hadn't there been as much anticipation at the thought of seeing him again as there was worry? She also had the distinct impression that Raff was a bad influence on Emilio.

They'd had a head start drinking and this time Tabitha was aware of not overdoing things and repeating the night before. Ending up in bed again with Raff, regardless of them not having had sex, would not be a smart move. At least they'd had the decency to bring their own booze with them. But even so, she was allowing Raff to take advantage of her good nature. Deep down, she knew it was because she was attracted to him, even if he was intruding on her personal and creative space.

'What are you doing hiding over there?' Raff's voice cut across the beat of Tom Grennan's *Lighting Matches* album that was playing.

With a resigned sigh, Tabitha left the shadows and joined them.

'Raff say you write songs?' Emilio said. 'You written any I have heard of?'

Tabitha rattled off a list of song titles and the artists she'd co-written with and got a kick out of watching Emilio's eyes widen.

'*É bué fixe*! There are some big names there,' he exclaimed.

Even Raff looked suitably impressed, Tabitha noted.

'Yeah, I write freelance for a record label now. I used to write with artists a lot, but since travelling, I've been working as a topliner, so mostly working remotely on lyrics and melody. Although in between house sits earlier this year, I spent a few weeks in LA writing with an up-and-coming young pop star who's been likened to a cross between Pink and Billie Eilish.'

'But you like working on your own more?' Raff asked. He was sitting on the sofa, resting his elbows on his knees, a lager in his hand.

'It's not really a case of liking it more, I've just felt a need to recently.' She met his eyes, hoping he understood that she didn't want to explain further. 'I'm comfortable working by myself, but I also enjoy that collaboration and sparking ideas off someone else. It's a different process. They're both good in their own way.'

They talked a little more about Tabitha's job before the conversation turned back to Raff and Emilio and the music they were into in their teens and the parties Emilio had at his parents' house when Raff was back from boarding school. After last night, Tabitha went steady on the Madeira wine as she listened. She had a second *pastel de maracuja*, which, with its crumbly buttery pastry, smooth sweet custard and the delicious sharpness of the passion fruit, was just too moreish to only have one of.

As the evening wore on, the romantic notion that Raff had come back to spend time with her and explore the feelings that had been evident the night before began to disappear. While she refrained from drinking more than two glasses of wine, Raff and Emilio quickly worked their way through most of the booze they'd brought with them. The conversation was mainly two friends catching up and she felt very much an outsider. It dawned on Tabitha that it wasn't her Raff was interested in at all, but having a place he could crash and bring friends to. This had been his plan all along, which she'd scuppered by being here.

Tiredness had crept up on her. It was nearly midnight and her peaceful evening had been snatched away. She didn't want to put up with it any longer.

'Hey,' she said, standing up. 'It's getting late. I think it's about time you two left.' She looked firmly at Raff, hoping she was coming across with enough authority for him to actually listen to her this time.

'Good luck trying to shift him.' He nodded at Emilio, lounging on the sofa looking worse for wear.

Tabitha huffed. 'I'm going to make coffee; see if you two can sober up enough to leave.'

She paced to the kitchen, filled the kettle and switched it on. She leaned on the worktop and breathed deeply. She was mad at herself for being taken in by Raff and for letting his attractiveness overshadow his behaviour.

Footsteps sounded on the tiled floor behind her.

'Hey, Tabitha,' Raff said soothingly. 'I didn't mean to upset you. I thought you'd be glad of the company.'

'Not like this, I'm not.' She swung round to face him, only to realise he was standing closer than she'd expected. He'd better not try to kiss her. And yet he didn't have to even touch her for her to sense the pull between them as if a magnetic force was drawing them together. Just as well she'd laid off the spirits tonight...

She tried to focus on what he was saying rather than on *him*.

'I was hoping to stay at Emilio's, but the situation's kinda changed since the last time I saw him.'

'Because he's got a wife and baby?'

He shrugged. 'She wasn't best pleased when I showed up – we er, have a history...'

Tabitha frowned.

Raff looked at her sheepishly. 'She thinks I'm a bad influence.'

Tabitha snorted. 'No shit.'

'I'm just asking to stay here one more night, that's all.'

'No,' Tabitha said firmly. 'Why do you have to be my problem? You're Emilio's problem now. I get that his wife is unhappy, and with good reason, but I'm not doing this.' She turned her back on him, heaped instant coffee into a mug, poured on the boiling water and splashed in milk. 'Call a taxi, Emilio can drink this, then you go back to his place.'

Picking up the mug, and determined to not allow Raff to argue with her, she carried it into the living room. She couldn't work out where Emilio had gone until she heard snoring. Her heart sank.

She walked over to the sofa. He was sprawled out, mouth open, dead to the world.

Raff joined her. 'Looks like we might be staying.'

'You're a dick.' Tabitha slammed the mug on the coffee table, slopping liquid onto the glass. She intended to walk away but turned back. 'How can you be so at ease ingratiating yourself with someone you don't know, somewhere you shouldn't be?'

'I'm used to having to fit into new places and fend for myself. I assume it's the same for you, new places and new people all the time?'

'*I am* supposed to be here though.'

'Touché.'

Trying her best to ignore Raff, and the guttural snores emanating from his friend, Tabitha pulled the bifold doors closed on the night, double-checking that both Fudge and Bailey were inside, still asleep on the rug.

She rushed past Raff to the kitchen and rummaged through the cupboards for a plastic bowl. She went back into the living room and placed it on the floor next to Emilio.

'Just in case,' she said at Raff's bemused expression. 'I'm going to bed. You're doing just fine making yourself at home, so knock yourself out.'

She was fuming now and didn't care about hurting his feelings when he was taking the piss and his friend was lying passed out on the sofa.

As if understanding that it was bedtime, Fudge scrambled to his feet, with Bailey pattering after them seconds later. Tabitha left Raff standing in the living room and escaped into the bedroom, the only place that felt like hers.

* * *

Fudge woke Tabitha as usual by inching his way up her legs until his head and paws rested on her stomach, his big brown eyes filled with love. Or was it hunger? With sunshine streaming through the glass doors and without a hangover or the awkwardness of Raff in bed with her, a feeling of contentedness slowly spread through her. Until she remembered that Raff and his unconscious friend were still here.

The annoyance from last night seeded itself once again. Not only was she awake early, but she was incensed that she now had two blokes to get rid of before she could settle down and work. It wasn't Raff taking advantage that she was most annoyed about, but the truth that if he hadn't been so attractive, she would never have let him stay.

It was Wednesday and a working day; she had responsibilities and a career to focus on as soon as she'd rid herself of Raff for a second time.

With two men in the house, she showered first and dressed in black dungarees and a mustard yellow T-shirt, going make-up-free apart from mascara and a slick of red lipstick.

'Come on then, Fudge.' She smiled at him sitting in the middle of the floor waiting patiently. She ruffled his long silky ears, then headed for the door. Fudge immediately clattered after her, waking Bailey in the process.

It was the smell that hit her first, the staleness of BO, which, on closer inspection, was something far worse. She grabbed hold of Fudge before he got any closer to investigating the bowl of vomit. Emilio was as she'd left him last night, snoring, mouth open and dribble down his chin, except his shirt was now stained with the contents of his stomach. Tabitha tried not to heave. It was just as well she'd left a bowl next to him, although as much was out of the bowl as was in it. The table was littered with lager bottles, an empty bottle of wine was lying on the rug and the mug of coffee was where she'd left it, the spilt coffee now a cold puddle.

With fury raging through her, Tabitha pulled Fudge away and manoeuvred him and Bailey to the kitchen to feed them. She left them eating, stormed back into the living room and pulled open the doors to let in some much-needed fresh air. She breathed deeply, relishing the warmth of the sun and the far sweeter scent of the frangipani flowers as she contemplated what to do.

Sod it, she thought. She'd had enough. She had work to do. Raff and Emilio needed to go.

Touching Emilio's arm, the only bit of him that seemed free of anything stomach-churning, she gently shook him. He groaned and shuffled onto his stomach. Tabitha swore, realising his vomit-stained shirt was now in direct contact with the sofa.

On the table, Emilio's mobile flashed with a call, the phone on silent, the name Inez on the screen. His wife. *Boy, is she going to be pissed*, Tabitha thought as it stopped ringing. The screen showed he had four missed calls and countless unread messages.

As Fudge and Bailey headed into the garden, Tabitha stormed upstairs. She knocked on the guest bedroom door and, without waiting for an answer, barged in.

The blinds were closed and it took a moment for her eyes to adjust and see the shape of Raff sprawled on the bed.

'Ugh, what time is it?' he mumbled, reaching across to switch on the bedside lamp.

Tabitha took in his frown and eyes squinting in the sudden brightness, before her gaze travelled to his bare chest and flicked back to focus on his face. She grimaced at the way her heart fluttered. A knowing smile crept on to Raff's face.

'Emilio's been sick and is still fast asleep. You need to sort him out and leave. I have work to do.'

'Morning to you too.'

Tabitha folded her arms, fed up of his cockiness. 'I'm serious, Raff.'

'Okay, I'll come down in a bit.' He yawned.

'No. You're coming now.' Tabitha stood her ground, glaring at him, wondering if he would defy her.

Raff snorted. 'You might want to leave before I get out of bed.' He gestured downwards to the sheet that wasn't doing a very good job of hiding his lower half. 'Kinda sleeping naked.'

Tabitha flushed, annoyed that he'd somehow got the upper hand and left her flustered. Snapping her eyes back to his face and meeting his amused gaze, she retreated from the room.

He was enjoying making her squirm, she knew. It could have been worse, he could have been lying on top of the sheet... Her cheeks flushed redder at the thought.

Downstairs, Emilio was beginning to stir and his snores had turned into groans. The fresh air and sunshine filtering through the open doors had gone a long way to ridding the room of the smell, but Tabitha knew there was the bowl of sick to deal with and the sofa and rug to clean, which needed to be done before Cordelia's cleaner turned up tomorrow. Not really wanting to have an awkward conversation with Emilio, she scooted behind the sofa and escaped into the kitchen to put on a pot of coffee. She needed some and Emilio sure as hell did too.

Tabitha only returned to the living room when she heard Raff and Emilio talking. Raff was a little less distracting now he was dressed, but Tabitha tried her hardest to avoid looking at him as she placed the tray with the coffee pot, milk, sugar and mugs on the only clear bit of the coffee table.

'I'm so sorry, Tabitha.' Emilio looked up at her, his voice sounding as rough as hers had yesterday morning. His shirt was stained, his hair stuck up in all directions, and the aftereffects of the night before showed in his tired eyes and washed-out face.

'I'm not the only one you're going to need to apologise to.' She gestured to his phone.

He scooped it up and groaned again. He glanced at Raff. 'I have to work today. Told you going out was a bad idea.'

Work is the least of your problems, Tabitha thought.

Raff shrugged. 'It's not like I see you often.'

Tabitha just didn't understand him. Was he really so self-centred he didn't understand how his behaviour impacted others? It was obvious that Emilio's wife had an issue with Raff – he'd said so himself – and yet Tabitha had no doubt that he'd been the ring-leader, encouraging Emilio to ignore his wife and go out drinking. Tabitha would be pissed off too, if she was in the wife's shoes; she was cross being the one to have to deal with them infiltrating her space. And she really did feel like that, desperate to be by herself again, enjoying her quiet life, working and exploring on her own terms without the inevitable disruption and confusion of another person. She'd been caught up in a misguided moment of drunken lust, but that was most definitely over.

Emilio took his phone and stood on the threshold between the living room and the terrace to call his wife.

With his face wrinkled in disgust, Raff picked up the bowl of sick and headed towards the bathroom. *Good, he deserves to clear that up*, Tabitha thought as she started gathering together the empty bottles.

Emilio spoke to his wife in Portuguese, but his voice was strained. There were large gaps of silence where Tabitha assumed he was getting an earful from an irate wife at home with a baby.

Bailey trotted in and jumped onto the armchair he liked to sleep on in the morning, kicking off the cushion and turning round and round until he settled down.

'You're finally comfortable, eh?' Tabitha scratched the top of his head. She looked towards the garden, expecting to see Fudge somewhere close by. She frowned. 'Where's your buddy?'

Aware of Emilio's voice getting louder, Tabitha walked past him out onto the terrace and shaded her eyes as she peered down the garden. Misty usually disappeared all day, only returning in the evening, but Fudge was either stuck to Bailey's side or following her.

She wandered round the side of the pool and onto the lawn. The tense sound of Portuguese drifted out, fading the further she walked as she peered between the bushes and the clusters of palms and banana plants for any sign of Fudge. At the bottom of the garden, she turned back and squinted, trying to see if he'd somehow slipped past.

With her heart thudding, she made her way back up the garden, double-checking as she went, walking along the length of the pool closest to the villa. It was unlike Fudge to disappear. Panicked, she rounded the side of the villa, wondering if he'd wandered around to the front. It was shady on this side with a patch of grass and palm trees straining towards the sun. Tabitha walked between the bushes that screened the garden from the driveway and her heart sank.

Fudge was nowhere to be seen and the gate was wide open.

13

Tabitha rushed back into the villa, hoping beyond all hope that she'd been mistaken and Fudge was somewhere inside. She heard the desperation in her voice as she called his name. Emilio was still on the phone and Bailey was still curled up on the armchair. Fudge wasn't anywhere.

Her heart faltered at the sound of footsteps coming along the hallway. Tabitha turned on Raff the second he entered the living room.

'You left the gate open.'

'What?' He frowned at her.

'Last night, when the two of you turned up pissed, you didn't close the gate behind you. I can't find Fudge.'

'I'm sure he's here somewhere.'

'And what if he's not?' Her nostrils flared as she challenged him with a glare, anger and worry coursing through her, along with annoyance at his lack of concern or urgency.

Emilio ended the call and muttered something in Portuguese.

'Everything okay?' Raff asked in a tone that Tabitha assumed meant he knew that everything was far from okay but he felt he should ask anyway.

'*Não*. Inez is coming to get me.' He looked even more washed out than when he'd woken up. He looked from Raff to Tabitha. 'Can I use the bathroom?'

'Do what you like.'

Tabitha didn't care that she was snappy. She was incensed, although her anger needed to be directed at Raff and not his mate, who was going to get a big enough bollocking from his wife.

As soon as Emilio disappeared into the bathroom, Tabitha turned on Raff. 'You're an idiot. I don't know what you were thinking coming back here last night. And to leave the gate open...'

'I honestly thought we'd closed it.'

'*I'm* responsible for the dogs while your parents are away.' Tabitha's voice rose with each word. 'I don't know what issue you have with them and I don't care if you don't care about them, but the dogs at least—'

'Hey, Tabitha, calm down.'

'No, I won't calm down! You're full of yourself. You turned up here in the middle of the night, treating the place like you live here, despite the fact I'm the one looking after it.' Feeling slightly better for releasing some of her pent-up emotion, she took a deep breath. 'We spent a lovely day together and I fell for your charm, but I understand now that it was all a ruse just for you to stay—'

'That's not true.'

Tabitha held up her hand. 'You bugger off to a friend's and I think I have the place to myself again, but no, you waltz back with booze and treats because you two need a place to party. At least his wife had the sense to kick you out, which is exactly what I should have done in the first place. You're the one in the wrong. You need to leave. I should have made you go the night you got here. You've been bullshitting me all along. No wonder your parents don't want anything to do with you.'

'Oh, that's low.'

'Well, what do you expect me to say? Oh, it's fine? Yes, they may be your parents but you've crashed their place without them knowing, and invaded my privacy.'

'You really didn't mind me invading your privacy the other night,' he said with a hint of a smirk.

'That's what you took from all of that! You really are an idiot. Go get your stuff and leave.' She shook her head and paced across the tiled floor to the open doors. She put her hands on her hips and breathed in the ocean air. She stayed like that until Raff's footsteps retreated across the living room and up the stairs.

He was an arse, but a mighty fine-looking one. She was mad at herself for her heart trumping all rational thought. Nope, it wasn't her heart, it was the part of her that had lusted after him the other night, that had gone all funny when her fingers had traced the Smurf tattoo on his abs, that had kissed him and wanted to do a whole lot more.

Her feelings for Raff were the least of her worries as, with increasing anxiety, Tabitha searched the villa for Fudge. She checked every room, looking in cupboards and under beds in case he'd managed to get trapped somewhere, but she couldn't find him. As sheer panic set in, she felt even sicker than she had the morning before, her fear that he must have escaped out of the gate confirmed.

With her heart racing, she returned to the living room and made sure Bailey was still curled up on the chair before closing the bifold doors. The second Emilio emerged from the bathroom and Raff came downstairs with his rucksack, Tabitha pocketed the house keys and grabbed Fudge's lead.

'I am very sorry, Tabitha,' Emilio said, holding out his hands. 'Inez is waiting, but I can help clean up?' He gestured to the sofa.

'No. You need to go. I have to find Fudge.'

Emilio nodded and clutched Raff's hand. They thumped each other's backs in a manly hug.

Clenching her jaw, Tabitha stalked to the front door and held it open for them. A car was waiting on the lane with the engine running. Emilio grimaced as he slipped past Tabitha and walked towards it.

Raff turned to Tabitha. 'I can finish cleaning up.'

'No,' she said firmly. 'You're leaving now too.'

Raff swung his rucksack on his back and followed her outside. After locking the door, Tabitha stalked across the drive and waited until Raff had come through the gate before closing it. She rushed away along the lane, too angry to even say goodbye. The smorgasbord of emotions he'd evoked in her over the last couple of days was insane, from shock to annoyance, happiness and passion, back to annoyance and now anger.

'Hey, Tabitha.' Raff had to jog to catch up with her. 'Let me come with you. Help you find him.'

She shook her head and kept walking. 'I don't need your help.'

'Come on, please, Tabitha. It's the least I can do. I know the area and where he gets taken for a walk.'

Tabitha didn't have the energy to argue. He was infuriating. He was probably used to getting his own way. The only reason she wasn't going to flat out refuse his help was because finding Fudge was more important than anything. If it meant putting up with Raff for a little longer, then so be it. At least he seemed to care.

She took the same route that she'd walked the dogs on the weekend, the awful churning in her stomach worsening the further she went with no sign of him.

'Sometimes my parents walk the dogs down to Jardim do Mar –

at least they used to,' Raff said, keeping pace with her. 'It's probably the best place to look.'

'Fine.' Upset caught in Tabitha's throat as she motioned for him to go ahead.

He took a lane that led down steps to a viewpoint with tables, the wooded hillside jutting all the way to the ocean. They started down the steep path with stone steps cut into the grass- and bush-covered hillside, lined by prickly pears. Tabitha kept imagining she could see a flash of tan and white, but her hope of seeing Fudge was dashed with every turn of the zigzag path.

Apart from Tabitha calling Fudge's name every minute or so, they searched in silence. In her rush, she kept slipping on the loose stones and uneven steps but managed to keep her footing. Raff kept up with her, although more than once she heard him skid on the path and swear under his breath.

They reached a sharp turn with an uninterrupted view over the village below with its cream and white walled houses topped with rust-red roofs nestled between the patchwork greens of the hillside, and the foaming white of the waves breaking on the narrow pebbled shore.

'Tabitha.' Raff caught up with her and touched her shoulder. 'He wouldn't have come down this far, not on his own.'

Tabitha turned her back on the view and looked up at him. Her face was flushed and sweat dribbled into the small of her back from walking so fast, but mostly she was trying not to burst into tears.

'How can you be so sure?' she demanded.

'I just am. You know what he's like; he sticks with Bailey. If it was the two of them missing, then who knows how far they'd go, but Fudge on his own... I think he would have turned back.'

'Then how have we managed to miss him?' As she said the words, the sick-inducing feeling that she'd been trying so hard to bury hit her. 'What if he went the other way, up onto the main road?'

'I'm sure he didn't do that.'

'Stop saying you're sure about stuff when you don't know.' She brushed past him and started back up the path, the going even tougher slogging up the hill. She should have checked up on the road first. Absolutely anything could have happened with fast cars shooting by and a dog with absolutely no road sense. Cordelia had warned her to not take the dogs off the lead anywhere near a road, but if Fudge was out on his own...

It was an anxious twenty-minute hike back up the hill and Tabitha's heart was in her mouth as they reached the main road. She hardly dared look.

Raff strode past her, his voice breaking through her worry. 'He's not here, Tabitha.'

She glanced up and down the road. A car flashed by and then a van in the other direction, but no sign of Fudge, just the grey tarmac edged by grasses. The desperate worry turned into tears that she'd been bottling up all morning. The situation with Fudge had well and truly tipped her over the edge.

Raff took her elbow and led her away from the road and back onto the lane.

'It'll be okay.'

'You don't know that,' she said through sobs.

Raff put his arms around her and hugged her tightly. She didn't immediately pull away. The feel of being encircled by him was soothing as her chest heaved against his, her tears dampening his T-shirt. It felt safe in his arms and comforting, even if he was the cause of her upset. Perhaps it was physical contact she longed for, rather than an emotional connection with someone. If anything, coupled with the situation leading to her break-up with Lewis, the last couple of days had proven that emotions were a pain in the backside.

Although the hug was needed, she knew that Raff was everything she should avoid. The events of the past couple of years had shown her she was better off on her own; it was easier and simpler to only rely on herself. And if she was craving human contact, then Elspeth's offer to stay with them was there. The company of her sister and brother-in-law, along with big squishy hugs from her cute-as-a-button nieces, would do her a world of good – not the attention of the strapping six-foot, tattooed, easy-on-the-eye but unpredictable and mysterious man who held her in his arms.

Tabitha wriggled free from his embrace and wiped away her tears. She looked up at Raff and tried to keep her voice steady. 'I don't know what's happened between you and your parents and I don't really care, because, whatever it is, it's not my problem. I'm going to have to tell them the truth, though. They need to know that Fudge is missing and they need to know how and why it happened, which means I'm telling them about you.'

Raff looked far from happy, but he didn't argue.

'Let me at least come back with you and we can call them together,' he suggested.

'No, you're not coming back.' Another tear slid down Tabitha's face. 'You've done enough. I have an incredibly difficult call to make to your parents and you won't be any help. You need to leave for good this time.'

'Honestly, Tabitha, I'm so sorry.' Raff reached out and touched her arm. 'I was drunk and wasn't thinking...'

'No, you didn't think. Everything you've done since breaking in that night has been for yourself. You're utterly selfish.'

She'd been drawn in by him and the barriers she'd put up around her heart had come down a little with his company, yet he'd completely betrayed her trust. And now, with poor Fudge missing, he'd put her in an impossible position with the whole house sit, not to mention the parents he was estranged from.

Without another word, Tabitha walked away, leaving Raff at the top of the lane. She didn't look back and only unclenched her fists once she rounded the corner and knew she was out of sight. It was done, whatever thing they'd briefly had going on was over.

The villa came into view. Part of her had hoped to see Fudge sitting outside the gate waiting for her, but, of course, he wasn't. Another sob caught in her throat, while the feeling of dread that at best he was lost, at worst... She couldn't begin to contemplate that. Her chest hurt at the thought of having to break the news to Cordelia about her 'baby'.

'Tabitha!' The voice was faint but recognisable.

Tabitha swung round and backtracked to where the lane that led to Julie and Anton's house converged with Rufus and Cordelia's. Julie was jogging up the lane, waving her arms wildly.

14

'Are you looking for Fudge?' Julie called as she slowed down. 'He's at mine!'

Sheer relief flooded through Tabitha at Julie's words. Her heart still pounded, but the feeling of horror at having lost Cordelia's beloved dog dissipated. She glanced back to where she'd left Raff at the top of the lane to tell him the good news, but he'd already gone. She bit her lip. It was his fault that Fudge had escaped to begin with; it was good that he was out of her life.

Without wasting any more time thinking about him, Tabitha jogged down the lane to meet Julie.

'I'm so glad I saw you,' Julie said breathlessly as she stopped in front of Tabitha. 'Fudge was in our garden. I have no idea how he got there.'

'Is he okay?'

'He seems to have hurt his paw, but other than that he's fine, just looking rather sorry for himself.' Julie frowned as she caught her breath and looked at Tabitha properly. 'More importantly, are you okay?'

'I am now.' Tabitha could imagine what a hot mess she must

look. A feeling of wanting to laugh and cry at the same time overwhelmed her. 'I've been so worried, looking for him everywhere.'

Julie placed a cool hand on her arm. 'Well, it's all okay now,' she said soothingly. 'Come on, he'll be pleased to see you.'

With her heart still fluttering, Tabitha followed Julie down the lane to her house. It was smaller than Rufus and Cordelia's but built with a similar stone. Julie opened the front door and ushered her inside, through to the modest open-plan living area.

At the sight of Fudge lying on Julie's wooden floor licking his paw, Tabitha slumped to her knees and snuggled against his warm, soft fur. She kissed the top of his head and gently hugged him to her. 'You gave me such a fright.' She pulled away slightly and tickled beneath his chin. The way he looked up at her made her heart melt. She never wanted to feel that awful worried-sick feeling ever again.

'He's been constantly licking his front right paw and hobbled his way in,' Julie said, 'so I think he's hurt it on something. Might be worth getting a vet to check him over.'

'Yes, I will.' Tabitha wiped her eyes on the back of her hand and turned to Julie. 'Thank you so much.'

'I didn't do anything. I just heard him whimpering and found him in the bushes. I think he must have somehow scrambled through a gap in the hedge from the lane.'

'We... I've been looking for him for the last hour, thinking he would have headed away from the house and not gone in this direction. I didn't even think to check here first.'

'He got out through the gate?'

'Um, yeah. It was left open.' Tabitha flushed, realising to tell the full truth would be to admit that Raff had been there when he shouldn't have been. Now that Fudge was found and she didn't have to make that dreaded phone call, she decided not to say anything more, even if it made her look bad.

'I'm going to put the kettle on,' Julie said. 'I think you could do with a cup of tea.'

'That would be lovely, thank you.'

Tabitha was insanely grateful for Julie's understanding and the way she didn't comment further about the gate situation. She must know Cordelia's rules about the dogs as she'd looked after them in the past, but she wasn't going to make Tabitha feel bad. She seemed to have a heart of gold.

* * *

They sat on Julie's sofa with cups of tea clasped in their hands and Fudge lying on the floor between them. Tabitha had been watching him closely and with the constant licking there was obviously something bothering him. At least he could walk, albeit with a slight limp.

'It's just as well it was today when I wasn't working that Fudge decided to escape,' Julie said, 'otherwise goodness knows how long he would have been stuck in our garden for. You'd have been worried to death.'

Tabitha couldn't even contemplate feeling more worried than she had been. Julie being home had saved her from having to call Cordelia with terrible news.

'I tell you what, when we've finished our tea, I'll drive you to the vets. The one Cordelia and Rufus are with isn't far away. It's where we used to take our dog.'

'You had a dog?'

'A German pointer called Jasper. We lost him eight months ago.' Julie reached down to stroke Fudge. He paused licking his paw to lick her hand. 'Absolutely broke my heart.'

'I'm so sorry.' Tabitha sipped her tea. 'Have you thought about getting another one?'

'We've talked about it, but neither of us are ready. Jasper was such a part of the family, you know, it's still raw. It would feel as if we were replacing him somehow. But I miss his company, his quiet presence. I still catch myself turning round to talk to him or I get to the door and reach for his lead, then remember it's not on the hook because he's not here...'

'Oh Julie, that's so sad.'

Julie nodded and smoothed out the creases in her cream cropped trousers. 'I comfort myself with the knowledge that he had a good life and we were better off for having him in ours. We grieve because we loved; it's as simple and as painful as that.'

* * *

After checking that Bailey was okay at the villa, Julie drove Tabitha and Fudge to the vets. A bruised paw was diagnosed, but it didn't seem to be fractured. They came away with pain relief tablets for Fudge and a bill which Tabitha happily paid. She knew she had to let Cordelia know what had happened, but she decided she'd leave out the bit about Raff.

With an invite from Julie to come over on Saturday for coffee and cake, which Tabitha willingly accepted after all her kindness, Tabitha carried Fudge from the car into the villa. Bailey greeted them with a waggy tail, spinning round in circles as she made her way to the living room.

A huge chunk of her day had gone, so after finishing clearing up the mess and shampooing the stains out of the rug and sofa as best she could, Tabitha spent the rest of the afternoon working, trying to catch up with everything she should have been doing over the last couple of days while she'd been distracted by Raff. At seven, she fed the dogs and Misty but didn't fancy spending time cooking. She rooted through the fridge for salad and cooked a cheese omelette to go with it.

With Fudge, Bailey and Misty curled up for the evening in their usual spots, Tabitha composed a message to Cordelia and Rufus in their WhatsApp group.

Everything's fine, I promise, but Fudge managed to hurt his paw. He was limping a bit, so as a precaution I took him to the vet. He's perfectly fine in himself, no need to worry. He's got some pain relief tablets and the vet said with a bit of rest he should be back to normal in a couple of days.

Tabitha attached a photo of him curled up asleep on the sofa and, with worry developing in the pit of her stomach again, she sent the message. She felt bad for bending the truth and mad, once again at Raff, for the situation arising in the first place. Yet, an hour later, when Raff messaged her, and after a phone call from a worried Cordelia during which Tabitha managed to allay her fears and ensure her that Fudge really was okay, she felt it would be mean to ignore him.

What's happening with Fudge? Have you found him?

Yes, he's okay. Was in Julie's garden all along. She thinks he scrambled through the hedge. Your parents know he's safe.

She left it at that though, not asking how he was or if he'd found somewhere to stay. He was a grown man and perfectly capable of fending for himself. She wasn't going to spend any more time thinking about him.

After an emotionally exhausting day, Tabitha went to bed early with an equally exhausted Bailey and Fudge her only company, as it should have been from the beginning.

* * *

It was a week since Tabitha had arrived on Madeira and she was behind with work after so many distractions. The cleaner, Dolores, was arriving this morning for two hours, so Tabitha set herself up in a shady spot on the terrace and kicked off her day with a Zoom call to her producer at the record label. They confirmed three weeks in Nashville in November for her to write with a new up-and-coming country singer with a pop vibe. The dogs kept her company; Fudge in particular stuck by her, and although he was still limping, he seemed better, following her everywhere.

In the evening, she searched through house sits and started to figure out her plans for the rest of the year. Elspeth had said about staying with them and there was no reason why Tabitha couldn't. She could work from there and have her own place to stay while getting to spend time with them all. A hug from her sister was long overdue. Despite having been incredibly upset with him, Raff's hug when Fudge had been missing had felt so good. Her thoughts were taken over by her hazy memory of kissing Raff in the hallway – hot and passionate, his hands tingling against her bare skin. And that's where the memory ended. But that was messy and complicated. A hug with her nieces and big sister was what she wanted.

After all the commotion with Raff and Emilio, then Fudge, Tabitha's mind had at least been taken away from worrying about seeing Ollie again, but when a message pinged onto her phone with the time and place to meet in Funchal the following evening, thoughts about him resurfaced.

Elspeth phoning after she'd got the kids to bed would have

been a good distraction except all she wanted to talk about was Ollie.

'What are you going to say to him, Tabs?'

'I don't know,' Tabitha said with a sigh. 'A lot probably. We have years' worth of stuff to catch up on.'

'And even if you haven't seen him, you know pretty much everything about him. His life is plastered over the internet.' There was a brief pause. 'Do you think you'll meet his girlfriend?'

'I hope not.' Tabitha wrinkled her nose at the idea of being joined by his model girlfriend. 'I'm hoping it's just me and him, but I guess he might invite other people to make the situation less awkward. Although he does sound happy about it in his messages.'

'Well, it's a good thing.' Elspeth paused again. Tabitha knew her sister was building up to saying something that she thought she perhaps shouldn't say. 'Are you going to tell him everything that's happened to you over the past year or two? You know, about Lewis, about the baby...'

Tabitha's jaw clenched as she fought with her emotions. She didn't want to think about having lost a baby. It had been an early miscarriage, something that happened to countless women, and yet Elspeth bringing it up now hit her hard. A gut-wrenching upset that had followed her for the last twelve months. 'Why would I say anything about that to him?' She could hear her voice, strained and tearful.

'I'm sorry, Tabs. That was thoughtless of me. It's just I know you used to tell each other everything—'

'Back when I trusted him, I did. I haven't talked to anyone about what happened apart from you and Mum and Dad.' Tabitha curled her feet beneath her and gazed out through the open doors at the darkening sky. Her brothers and other sister knew what had happened too, but she hadn't discussed it with them. No, what she'd done was run away. Talking to Ollie about their fallout would be a massive step, going beyond that into the events that had happened since felt way too personal and painful. It was as Julie had said, to grieve was to have known love. The strength of her feelings about something that she had barely been able to wrap her head around had shocked her to her core. How could she love something that hadn't even seemed real?

'You've gone quiet, Tabs.'

'Yeah, sorry, I'm overthinking tomorrow. I just need to meet him and see how I feel spending time with him again. See how he reacts to me, then take it from there.'

'That sounds rather wise. And you know where I am if you need to talk. Any time, Tabs. Just call me.'

15

Travelling on her own didn't faze Tabitha; she could cope with delayed flights and the nail-biting rush to catch the last train, navigate her way around an unfamiliar city or make small talk with a stranger, yet the thought of seeing Ollie after all these years made her hands sweat and gave her butterflies. The last time she'd felt this nervous had been before she'd told Lewis about the miscarriage – the pregnancy he hadn't even known about. Even the memory of trying to put into words her feelings and her thought process for having not told him left her in a cold sweat. If she'd been able to do all of that, she could certainly have a drink with Ollie.

Despite saying to Elspeth the evening before that she didn't want to overthink things, she couldn't help but feel as if she needed to get tonight right, from what she was wearing to how to approach the situation with Ollie. Allowing their friendship to disintegrate had been the easiest way for her to get past the hurt he'd caused, but the trouble with that was she'd never got round to dealing with those feelings. She'd avoided him and ignored his messages and calls to the point where, swept up in his own success, he'd given up trying to contact her.

It was fine to be nervous, Tabitha reasoned as she stared at herself in the bedroom mirror, debating if the sleeveless black playsuit paired with bronze sandals and chunky bangles hit the right going-out-yet-casual vibe. She had reached out and that was a good thing. She couldn't continue to keep running away from situations or push her emotions deep inside to deal with later. Sometimes the best time was right now. This house sit on Madeira was the perfect opportunity to face up to past disappointment and find a way to move forward, perhaps even regain some semblance of a friendship with Ollie.

After a faltering start where she'd holed herself away from everyone, her motto over the past six months at least had been to embrace new opportunities and see where they would lead, all while figuring out where she wanted to be. That was the key thing: where. She knew what she wanted to do – at least for the next four or five years – build the songwriting career she'd worked hard for, maybe even get back into touring as a musician. The more difficult question was how to figure out where she belonged when she felt so adrift. Perhaps tonight was the first step on that journey.

* * *

It felt extravagant getting a taxi to Funchal rather than driving, but Tabitha needed Dutch courage and couldn't face seeing Ollie for the first time in years without having a glass of wine or two. Unless he'd dramatically changed, which from his social media was unlikely, a night out with him would be alcohol-fuelled and he wouldn't take no for an answer. With a sinking feeling, she realised that Raff reminded her a little of Ollie. They had a similar confidence, were at ease with themselves and around other people, had the gift of the gab and knew they were good-looking. Even before Ollie had become famous, he was like that, with a cheekiness you couldn't help but like, dimples when he smiled and boyish good looks that made people assume he was in a boyband even before he was a pop star.

The taxi driver dropped her off in front of a posh hotel on the edge of Funchal's old town and she made her way up to the 360° rooftop bar. She was early, but with nerves jangling her stomach, she'd rather be first and settle down with a drink to calm herself.

Ollie had booked a table. She noticed the waiter appraising her when she gave the name Ollie Pereira. He was well known worldwide, but on Madeira he was thought of as a local boy done good, even if he had grown up in the UK. The waiter led her past the bar and beyond the long curved pool that edged the rooftop to a corner table with a view over the city. He returned with a glass of *poncha*, a local drink made of sugar cane rum, honey, sugar and lemon juice, along with small bowls of lupin seeds and unshelled peanuts.

As Tabitha sipped the exceedingly good and refreshing liquid and gazed over Funchal glittering gold in the darkness, the nerves began to ease. She could do this. It was an opportunity to fix at least one part of her life and technically it was the easiest compared to wading through the confusing and muddled feelings left from the break-up with Lewis.

She didn't have long to wait and mull over the past. It was Ollie's familiarity that hit her first. Along with her family, Elspeth in particular, Ollie had been her closest friend. Between the ages of eighteen and twenty-five, they'd been best friends, never allowing partners to get in the way of their friendship, even when their relationship was questioned by one or two of those partners. As he strode across the rooftop bar towards her, she realised he had changed a little; his look was edgier and there was more of a swagger, a confidence he'd grown into, perhaps having got used to his fame. She noticed the glances in his direction as he rounded the pool with green and purple lights reflecting in its surface – he certainly wasn't trying to hide who he was.

Ollie neared her and Tabitha stood. When he went in for a hug, she didn't resist. And it was a proper bear hug, his arms wrapped tight around her as if he was making up for years' worth of missed ones.

He released her and held her at arm's-length. 'You look bloody amazing, Tabitha!'

'So do you.' A jumble of emotions fought to the surface and she didn't know what she felt: happiness, anger, relief, confusion or a mix of everything.

Ollie did all the talking as they sat down. He was loud and all-encompassing, making Tabitha realise how much she'd mellowed over the last few years, slowly swapping touring the world and perpetual late-night drinking for a quieter life. He was upbeat and obviously pleased to see her and as they got all the niceties out of the way about how Ollie's parents were and Tabitha's family, it felt as if no time had passed and they'd slipped back into the comfortable friendship they'd once had. Yet there was much that needed to be said.

Ollie ordered a bottle of white wine and once the waiter had uncorked it and poured them each a glass, Tabitha knew it was time to turn the conversation to the real reason why she wanted to meet.

Ollie knocked his glass of wine against hers. 'Cheers, Tabitha.' He took a sip and shook his head. 'It really is so good to see you.'

Tabitha took a deep breath. 'You understand why we haven't seen each other, right?'

Ollie leaned back and looked away.

Here we go, Tabitha thought, noticing how he crossed his arms, as if he was protecting himself. She assumed the people around him were all yes people, at his beck and call, praising him, sucking up to him, enjoying his fame and all its trappings. Tabitha didn't care one jot about how famous he was because she still didn't see him that way, even after all this time.

'You're talking about the song, right?' he eventually said.

'Of course I'm talking about the song!' She hadn't meant to raise her voice. Ollie flashed her a worried look. She lowered her tone. 'Do you have any idea how much you hurt me?'

'You wouldn't talk to me, Tabitha.' Ollie leaned forward and placed his glass on the table. 'After the final, I tried calling you, messaging – I even turned up at your place later that week, remember, but you refused to see me.'

'Because I was so angry with you, that's why. *You* didn't talk to me. You kept me in the dark about what you were going to do, led me to believe that you were going to sing our song, that my name would be mentioned live on TV as the co-writer. You must remember that you didn't talk to me or reply to my messages during the two days leading up to the final show. I put it down to you being crazy busy with everything that was going on. But that wasn't the case at all, was it? You were just avoiding me. It worked out rather well for you that I was too nervous to watch the final live at the studio so watched it at my parents' house instead. The whole family was there, friends too, all squeezed into my parents' living room, and then what happened, Ollie?'

His jaw clenched and he avoided meeting her eyes. 'I sang our song,' he mumbled.

'And...'

'Said I'd written it.'

Anger flashed through her. 'Exactly. *Claimed* that you'd written it. No mention of me whatsoever.'

She waited for him to say something, but he took a long swig of his wine instead.

She sighed. 'Why didn't you talk to me? Why weren't you upfront about what you were planning on doing?'

'And what, you'd have been okay with that?' He kept his voice low, but tension ebbed through it.

'Probably not, but you never gave me the chance. You were cowardly, hiding what you were going to do, allowing me to believe that you were going to tell the world about the song *I* wrote, and instead, you made a fool of me in front of everyone. That was what was unforgivable.'

'I had my reasons.'

'I'm sure you did; I just wished you'd shared them with me, like a friend would have done.' She picked up her glass and took a gulp, the smooth, dry wine now bitter on her tongue. Animated chatter from the surrounding poolside tables mixed with the catchy beat of Dua Lipa's 'Levitating' distracted her for a moment. She frowned and turned back to Ollie. 'What were your reasons?'

Ollie's nostrils flared. 'Bad judgement and a misguided decision.'

'It was your decision to claim the song as yours, was it? Or were you influenced?'

'Of course I was influenced,' Ollie said sharply. He glanced around and lowered his voice. 'Do you have any idea of the pressure I was under? Once I was a part of the show, it was a total rollercoaster, pulled in all directions, and the further I got, the more pressure there was. It was a money-making exercise and I was deemed to be someone who could make the record label a lot of money.'

'Even before you won?' she said in disbelief.

'Yeah, the whole way through the competition – it was all leading to me winning.'

'Are you saying it was fixed?'

'No, of course not. But the producers, hell, everyone on the show, the judges included,' he stressed, 'felt it would be an even bigger final and sound even better if it was announced that I'd written the song.'

'Well, you got all the attention you wanted, totally focused on you, didn't you?' She was trying so hard to control her churning anger, that her hands ached from gripping the edges of her chair. 'By leaving my name out of it, you didn't have to share the limelight. You understand that sort of platform would have made my career – at the very least it would have got me noticed by the people who mattered.'

'You got there, though; look how well you're doing.' He leaned close, nudging his shoulder against hers as if trying to make light of the situation.

'You have no idea.' Tabitha shook her head. 'I stopped writing for months – my confidence was knocked by your betrayal. I felt like I'd missed my big break, while I watched your career skyrocket. Not to mention you cheated me out of royalties. But I picked myself up, started gigging again, played guitar, met the right people and wound up getting bigger and bigger gigs until I was touring the world with One Love.'

'That's how you ended up doing all that? Because you stopped writing?'

'You broke my heart that night and I *believed* you'd purposely destroyed our friendship. Why else would you have done something like that and kept me in the dark over it? The fact that you didn't understand the hurt you caused has made me so sad. But you know what, regardless of all that, you're right. I should have talked to you and told you how upset I was, because I've behaved the same by not being open and honest about my feelings. It's eaten away at me for years.' She unclenched her fists and sat back in her chair. 'It was our dream, Ollie. The dream team, remember? You the singer, me the songwriter.'

'I know, we were a great team... And I know it was your song. I gave you ideas, but you wrote it.' There was a sense of nostalgia in his voice as his eyes traced her face.

'You know what saddens me the most? It's not that I should have had a share of those royalties or that my name should have been mentioned on one of the biggest TV shows in the world, but that I lost your friendship.'

'You never lost it, Tabs. I'll always be your friend.' He reached for her hand and took it, smooth and warm in hers. 'I'm so sorry I didn't talk to you first and that I gave in to the pressure. And I'm so sorry about what I did. I know it was wrong. I can never apologise enough or repay you.'

'You can. You can make things right.' She wasn't going to spell it out and she certainly wasn't going to ask anything of him. He needed to work that out for himself, prove to her how good a friend he really was. Everything she'd been doing over the last seven years was in an attempt to move on. She wasn't going to look back with regret or waste any more time feeling bitter.

Sharing a drink and chatting, it almost felt as if the last few years had been erased and they were back to simpler times when they'd shared similar hopes and dreams about their future, about breaking into the music industry with a bang: Ollie singing, Tabitha writing. But they couldn't claw back that lost time. Their lives had diverged and she was a different person to the one who had cheered him on that night from her parents' living room. She was certain he was different too – fame, money, the experiences he'd had, the new friendships, relationships and life he'd led would undoubtedly change someone.

'This can be a new start for us, eh?' He squeezed her hand and leaned closer, trying to catch her eye beneath her curls.

Tabitha realised she'd been totally lost in her own thoughts, staring at his fingers entwined in hers. A tattoo of a dragon edged beneath his watch strap. One she didn't recognise. All the ones decorating his arm were new. She looked up and met his piercing blue eyes and suddenly felt self-conscious sitting and talking so intimately with him, no longer the best friend she'd known so well but a relative stranger, and a famous one at that.

She slipped her hand from his, picked up her wine and took a large swig, the chatter from the surrounding tables screaming back into earshot.

'Did your girlfriend mind you meeting me?' she asked, aware of how packed the rooftop bar was.

Ollie sank back into his chair. 'We're not really together any more.'

Tabitha raised an eyebrow. 'Oh?'

'It's a bit complicated.' Ollie glanced away, obviously uncomfortable talking about it. 'And it's not public knowledge, which I kinda want to keep that way. We need the right time to, er, you know, go public.'

Tabitha didn't know because she didn't live her life in the public eye with everyone knowing her business like Ollie did. It was only what she chose to put on Instagram or TikTok that gave anyone a clue into her private life. And her private life was exactly that. Social media was focused on her songwriting, her collaborations and, more recently, her travels.

A clatter of heels and animated chatter caught their attention. Three women, with their arms hooked in each other's, were making a beeline for them. *No, not for them*, Tabitha thought, *for Ollie*. With their eyes fixed on him, they were all lip-glossed smiles, sparkly tops and short skirts.

'Oh my God! You're Ollie Pereira!' the woman in the middle with a northern accent said as they reached what had been their quiet corner of the bar.

Ollie flashed them a dimpled smile. 'The very one.'

Tabitha sat back in her seat as the three girls crowded around him. It wasn't that she envied him the attention, it was just she couldn't help thinking that a portion of his stratospheric success should have been hers. Could have been. She knew fame and fortune or Ollie's world-renowned success could never be guaranteed, but he had effectively stolen her song and taken a real shot at fame away from her, without having the guts to face up to her and be truthful. That was what she minded. She'd said as much, but she wasn't certain he truly understood. How could he? He'd had no time to, swept up in a shiny new life filled with new people. His ex-girlfriends had been students or barmaids, worked in River Island or in human resources; now they were models or actresses, in the public eye as much as he was.

The women encircled their table, all of them not much older than their late teens, their attention firmly fixed on Ollie. He stood and hugged each of them. Their excited squeals flew into the air, as they said how much they loved him, asked him when he was going on tour again in the UK and mentioned how cool it would be to get a selfie of them all together.

'Hey, this is my friend Tabitha,' Ollie said. He gestured towards her, forcing the girls to part enough to include her. 'She's an epic songwriter who's written for people like One Love and Deedee.'

'OMG! I love Deedee!' the girl standing with her arm wrapped round Ollie's waist exclaimed. 'But not as much as I love you!'

'I should think not!' Ollie laughed. 'Tabitha, do you mind taking a picture of us.'

It wasn't a question and she shouldn't mind, yet she did. It was just something about the way Ollie said it and his expectation of her that grated on her nerves.

One of the girls handed Tabitha their phone and she stepped behind her chair to get them all in. They filled the frame; Ollie beaming in the middle, all tanned skin, dimples and tousled hair, with three equally tanned young women hanging off him, all pouty lips, beach hair and plunging necklines.

'Sorry about that,' Ollie said as the girls eventually left, clutching their phones, no doubt ready to post the photo on Instagram.

'I guess you're used to it, all this attention.' There was no bitterness; that was the last thing she envied any longer. What she was sad about was how different he seemed. Despite his familiarity, the memories they shared and how easily they'd chatted together, there was a distance that she wasn't certain they could ever bridge.

Tabitha sipped her wine and listened to Ollie talk about the madness of his jet-set life and how he and his newly ex-girlfriend were trying to work things out but wanted to keep the difficulties of their relationship private. Tabitha wasn't sure that Ollie meeting her in a public place for a drink was the wisest idea, not that it bothered her, but she did wonder how it would look to other people. He asked if she was seeing anyone and she said a truthful no, but decided she didn't want to talk about Lewis, despite the many times during their break-up when she'd thought it would have been good to have Ollie's shoulder to cry on.

Tabitha was oddly relieved when the evening naturally came to a close. Ollie had an early phone call on the Radio 1 breakfast show and Tabitha had a good forty-five-minute journey back to the villa.

'Hey, I'm having a party next Wednesday for my birthday,' Ollie said as they walked across the bar together. 'I'd love you to come if you'll still be on Madeira?'

'Yeah, I'll be here.'

'Great,' he said, kissing her on each cheek. 'Let me know the address of where you're staying and I'll send an invite. And no present needed, I mean it, Tabs. Just your company.'

Huh. No presents. That sounded about right; after all, hadn't she already given him the biggest gift of all?

* * *

It was late by the time Tabitha got back to the villa. Bailey and Fudge greeted her with wagging tails and once she'd locked up, eagerly followed her to the bedroom.

Tiredness washed over her as she brushed her teeth, changed into her night clothes and clambered into bed. The emotions she'd gone through this evening had left her wrung out; they'd talked and they'd both apologised. They'd reconnected and he'd invited her to his party and she'd been happy to accept, a part of her wanting to have him back in her life. Yet somehow, lying there, she felt more disconnected from him than she ever had done. They'd both moved on; they'd been independent of each other for years. So much had happened, not least for her. He'd never even met Lewis. That relationship would have been one she would have shared with Ollie. She wondered if Ollie would have liked him. He always used to have something to say about her boyfriends, although not always bad things. Perhaps she'd been foolish to expect to feel miraculously different and happier now that they'd seen each other. It would have been naïve to think a broken friendship could be fixed so easily.

She yawned and rolled over, accidentally shifting Fudge as she did. The other side of the bed was empty and yet Fudge was intent on sleeping as close to her as possible. She shuffled until she was facing the sliding doors, the curtains keeping out the dark night. In her sleepy state, an image of Raff sprawled next to her filled her thoughts. As she drifted off to sleep, Tabitha wondered where he was and how he was doing.

16

Tabitha's sleep had been filled with dreams, fleeting images that faded within seconds of waking. She'd gone to sleep thinking about Raff, yet woke up thinking about Ollie. She was relieved to have coffee with Julie to look forward to that afternoon, while a morning to catch up on work would occupy her mind. And it did. She laser-focused her attention to get started on a new song, so she had little time for anything else besides brushing the dogs and letting them out in the garden – Fudge was limping less, but she didn't want to overdo it by taking him for a walk – before having a sandwich for lunch and heading along the lane.

Julie greeted Tabitha with a hug. Tabitha felt as if she towered over her, bold and bright with wild curly hair, red lipstick and saffron yellow dungarees against Julie's dark-blonde locks, pale skin and the muted colours of a simple jeans and T-shirt combo.

'Anton is out walking with a friend,' Julie said as she led her into the open-plan living area at the heart of the house, with patio doors that opened on to the garden. 'And he's not often here during the week either as he works in Funchal. I work two days a week at the International School, which I love, but it's lovely to have days during the week to myself to potter in the garden or sometimes have coffee with friends.' She gave Tabitha a shy smile, which left her unconvinced about how often Julie actually entertained friends.

Tabitha peered through the open doors at the long expanse of garden, the grass neat and well-cared for, broken up by curved borders packed with colour and the feathery plumes of pampas grass.

Tabitha turned back to Julie. 'You don't have a pool?'

'We've thought about it but never got round to doing it.' Julie shrugged. 'The garden keeps me busy – it's my passion. I wish you'd been here earlier in the summer when the Pride of Madeira were flowering, and the jacaranda trees in spring covered in purple flowers are just stunning. We did invest in a hot tub a couple of years ago, which we love.' She smiled at Tabitha. 'Would you like tea or coffee? Or could I entice you with some Madeira wine?'

'A coffee would be lovely, thanks.' With the amount of alcohol she'd drunk over the last few days, the thought of wine turned her stomach.

While Julie made the coffee, Tabitha settled herself on the patio, taking in the extensive garden which made the most of the ocean view. Right at the far end, Tabitha spied the gap in the bushes where Rufus and Cordelia's garden was just visible, although their villa was completely hidden by trees.

Julie joined her and placed a tray with a pot of coffee and a plate of biscuits on the table. She set about pouring the coffee, added milk and handed Tabitha the mug.

Tabitha leant back in her chair and relished the heat. The patio was a suntrap, and despite the clouds clustering further out over the ocean, the sky above them was clear. An occasional bird call mixed with the rustle of leaves, which could easily be mistaken for distant waves crashing on rocks.

Misty was stalking up the garden towards them, stopping to make detours around the flower beds which were filled with late-summer colour.

Tabitha cupped her mug of coffee and turned to Julie. 'Misty spends a lot of time over here?'

'Quite a bit. I try not to encourage her too much and I never feed her,' Julie said seriously, her eyebrows furrowing. Tabitha could imagine Cordelia tutting over Misty disappearing into Julie's domain. 'I like having her around, though.'

Misty reached the patio, wrapped herself around Tabitha's legs and then sat next to Julie's chair.

'She's good company, huh? After losing your dog?'

'Yes, Misty's been a blessing.'

'And she obviously enjoys being here too.'

Julie's smile spoke volumes as she stroked Misty, who purred contentedly.

'I'm sorry not to be looking after the animals this time, but I'm glad you're staying. Bailey and Fudge in particular need the company. Cordelia and Rufus made the right decision getting a house sitter. It's certainly much better for the dogs.' Despite what had happened to Fudge, her words were sincere.

They chatted more about Julie's teaching job and the practicalities of Tabitha's remote working, while enjoying the sunshine and coffee. Despite Julie's timidness – at least on the surface – she was easy to talk to and eager to listen.

Tabitha drained her coffee and placed the mug on the table.

'Is Raff back by any chance?' Julie's gentle voice cut through the stillness.

Tabitha looked sharply at her and frowned, taken aback by the sudden and surprising question.

'Who?' She feigned innocence, although she was unsure why she felt the need to cover for him after he'd upset her so much.

Julie studied her for a moment. 'Rufus and Cordelia's son, Raff. I thought I saw him in the garden.' She shook her head. 'I'm sorry, I'm forgetting that they probably didn't say a word about him. Believe it or not, they have a son.' Her usually dulcet tone had an edge to it. 'But they don't talk about him and they've pretty much kept him out of their life for the last few years.'

'Why? What happened?' Tabitha felt uncomfortable hiding the truth, but she was intrigued to have the chance to hear Julie's side of things.

Julie sighed. 'I don't know the full story, but from what I did manage to gather, they accused him of stealing – there was already plenty of tension, which made the whole situation blow up. We're not exactly close to Rufus and Cordelia, despite making the effort. They, um, like to keep themselves to themselves. Socialise with their own friends.'

Julie said 'friends' in a way that Tabitha understood meant she and Anton weren't included. It wasn't hard to believe that Cordelia didn't have friends like Julie – they were obviously very different – yet it made Tabitha wonder if there was a bigger reason for the divide between them. Cordelia had a troubled son who she'd erased from her life – things might not be quite as perfect as they seemed on the surface.

Julie sipped her coffee and cast a glance at Tabitha. 'We bought this house a few months after Rufus and Cordelia had moved to Madeira. We thought they were a childless couple, didn't even twig that they had a son until he came home for the Christmas holidays.'

'Came home?' Tabitha frowned, still feigning innocence.

'From boarding school.' Julie shook her head. 'Raff was ten and they took him out of his last year of primary school in Surrey to move here before promptly shipping him back to England a few months later to start his secondary education. Most of the time, it was just Rufus and Cordelia here, working and socialising, the only inconvenience being when Raff came home for the holidays.'

'That must have been difficult for him,' Tabitha said, acknowledging the criticism in Julie's words even though her tone was neutral. She remembered the upset Raff had been trying to control whenever he'd talked about his parents.

'Oh, it certainly was. He'd come home most holidays, but sometimes he'd stay in England with his grandparents, particularly if it was Christmas or half-term. Sometimes his parents would fly over and join them.' Julie folded her arms. 'He was one troubled child. It wasn't fair on him; he was given no choice about leaving their life in England and then was torn from his family. That was the hardest thing for him to deal with.'

'How do you know so much?' Tabitha was intrigued to find out more about Raff's past and the stony look on Julie's face. She didn't seem to be the type of woman who would get het up about things.

'I often used to look after Raff when his parents were out or went away. In the early years at least.' Julie sighed. 'He was a lost soul.'

Tabitha frowned. 'So his parents left him despite him being home for such a short time?'

'Surely they were entitled to continue their social life and not let a mere inconvenience of a son get in the way?' Julie's sarcastic tone matched the look on her face. She sighed again. 'When he was older, they'd go away on business – or sometimes on holiday – and if he didn't want to go with them, which he usually didn't, then he'd stay here on his own. He was old enough and sensible enough, but I felt so sorry for him. I'd invite him over for dinner and he ate with us most days. I think he was glad of the company, the security too of having someone there for him when his parents weren't.'

It was hard to ignore the bitterness in her voice.

'You know him well then?' Tabitha said softly.

'I *knew* him well.' Julie smoothed a hand down an invisible crease in her jeans. 'He used to talk to me a lot, until he hit his mid-teens and closed up like so many teenagers do. And as he got older, he came back less and less. After paying for boarding school, his parents supported him through university, but by that time he didn't need them, apart from their money. I strongly believe by that point the damage to their relationship had been done.'

Tabitha considered how different Raff's upbringing was to hers. Although she'd never felt as if she had a sense of belonging anywhere, she had always been surrounded by the love of her parents and her siblings. Home had been wherever her family was. Raff had missed out on that entirely.

'I honestly think his parents believed that by giving him the best education money could buy, they were setting him up for life,' Julie continued, 'and he would be grateful for the opportunity, but they failed to listen to his pleas.' She pressed a hand to her chest. 'What I've seen is a man who has been hugely let down by his parents. They uprooted him from his life, his school and friends at a time that's so challenging for children, that tricky transition from primary to secondary school. Instead of him moving up with some of his friends to a local comprehensive or even starting afresh at a nearby private school, they moved countries, tore him away from his beloved dog – don't get me started on that – and sent him back to England to boarding school while they made a new life for themselves here.' She cupped her hands around her mug of coffee and looked quietly at Tabitha. 'Of course, that's just my take on it as an outsider.'

Tabitha bit her lip. Considering she was the one responsible for the house and animals while Rufus and Cordelia were away, Raff's behaviour, putting that all in jeopardy, had been inexcusable, yet she was beginning to get an understanding of where his behaviour stemmed from and why he had little respect for his parents or their house. He doted on the dogs and cat, that much had been clear, and he'd seemed genuinely upset at being the cause of Fudge going missing.

Tabitha's eyes travelled down the lawn to the gap in the bushes by Rufus and Cordelia's garden. Her mind wound back to the earlier part of the conversation when Julie had mentioned seeing Raff. Raff had left three days ago.

Tabitha frowned and turned back to Julie. 'You said you thought you saw Raff? When was that?'

His name felt familiar on her tongue and Tabitha wondered if it would sound that way to Julie. She had no idea why she felt the need to cover for him, but she wasn't quite ready to confide in Julie yet.

'Yesterday,' Julie said, her quiet tone returning.

Tabitha nodded in what she hoped was a nonchalant way, despite her heart pounding. As she changed the subject to Misty and the dogs, she hoped Julie hadn't spotted her surprise and confusion.

They talked a little more. The garden and its perfumed air was soothing, the sun deliciously warm, the distant ocean shimmering, the endless blue making Tabitha imagine sailing to faraway places. After a pleasant and eye-opening couple of hours, along with an invite to have dinner one evening, Tabitha said goodbye to Julie and headed back to Rufus and Cordelia's villa. The walk back gave her time to ponder how Julie had thought she'd seen Raff only the day before when he'd actually left earlier in the week.

The house was quiet with Bailey and Fudge both fast asleep on the rug. When they barely raised their heads at her return, she immediately dismissed the idea that the dogs would know if Raff was still around. But how could he be?

The dogs woke up as Tabitha wandered past and opened the

bifold doors to the pool terrace. The garden was large with hidden areas, the neat grass yellowed in places after the summer heat, broken up by pockets of verdant bushes and splashes of white trumpet-shaped flowers and large blue ones swaying on tall stems.

Her eyes travelled to the office tucked away in the bottom right corner. Barely visible from the house, with muted silvery-grey wood walls screened by tropical trees, she hadn't paid it much attention. It was Rufus and Cordelia's office and she had no reason to go there, which, when she thought about it, would make it the perfect place for Raff to hide out.

Tabitha paced down the garden path, the dogs fully awake now and trotting after her. She only stopped when she reached the wooden deck in front of the office. Tabitha seethed at Raff's audacity – *if* Julie had been correct. Perhaps she'd got the days muddled and she'd actually seen Raff when he'd been here. Tabitha hoped that Julie had been mistaken because she wasn't relishing the thought of another confrontation.

The door was closed and locked. She rattled the handle in frustration before holding her hands to the glass, blocking out the sunlight to peer inside. There were two desks set up in an L-shape, plus a sofa against the back wall. Raff's rucksack was leaning against it.

Tabitha pulled away from the window with a grimace. So, Julie was right. Yet after everything she'd told her about Raff and his relationship with his parents, Tabitha was conflicted, wanting to be angry with him, yet feeling for him deeply. He must have the keys for the office and had been sneaking around without her even realising.

Not only that, but Bailey and Fudge were truly rubbish guard dogs. And Raff knew it.

17

Tabitha sat out on the office deck with her guitar and the iPhone Voice Memo app open, strumming chords, the beginning of something taking shape in her head. Words scattered the page of a notebook, discordant at the moment, just snatches of an idea. It was an idyllic spot, tucked right at the end of the garden and hidden by shady palms and banana plants with their massive, almost crepe-like leaves. The hedge was low, allowing an unspoilt view across the ocean, which was iridescent in the fading light. As well as it being a beautifully clear evening to watch the sunset, she was so conflicted about Raff that she'd decided to stay on the deck to catch him when he returned. His rucksack was inside so he'd have to come back at some point and she was determined to talk to him.

The sun slid towards the horizon, turning a shimmering gold as it met the pearly-grey ocean. If Tabitha hadn't been so annoyed and if, after nearly three hours of waiting, she didn't need a wee so badly, it would have been a magical experience. Yet the words flowed and a melody was beginning to take shape, upbeat but with an edge of melancholy, much like most of the music she'd written over the past year.

With dusk, the temperature dropped a little and darkness took over. Tabitha shivered. The dogs paced the decking, impatient for their late tea, and she fed them the treats she found in her pockets. Moonlight pooled onto the ocean, rippling silver-white where the waves formed. The magic of sunset was rapidly fading now Tabitha was uncomfortable, hungry and thirsty, not to mention thoroughly pissed off.

She was tempted to give up and head back to the villa when a shadowy figure appeared around the side of the office.

The figure faltered, but before he could back away, Tabitha shot out of the chair and grabbed him, her hand clasping his muscled arm.

Raff's eyes were wide. His look of shock made her stakeout worthwhile.

'Bloody hell, Tabitha! What on earth are you doing?'

She increased her grip. 'What am I doing?' Her voice was overly shrill, while her heart thumped.

Raff gazed down at her, the shock on his face morphing into tenderness. She let go of him and he held his hands up in mock protestation. 'You found me.'

'You're finding this funny, huh?' She shook her head. 'What are you playing at?'

'Nothing.' He reached out as if to touch her shoulder but thought better of it. 'I didn't mean to upset you – I figured you wouldn't even realise.' His voice was firm and steady as he looked pleadingly at her.

Tabitha folded her arms. 'You've been down here all this time?'

'Yeah... sorry.' He shrugged. 'How did you find out?'

'Julie said she thought she saw you yesterday.'

He glanced in the direction of Julie's shadowed garden. 'Huh. She did, did she?'

'I asked you to leave.' Whether it was the anger coursing

through her or being back in Raff's presence, she was feeling flustered. 'You shouldn't be here, you have no right to, not after the way you behaved.'

He stepped closer, the waft of his citrusy cologne hitting her, the intensity of his gaze making her briefly drop hers. 'Let me be honest with you.'

'It's about time you were.'

He annoyed and intrigued her in equal measure, and she knew the flustered feeling stemmed from the wayward thoughts that had continued long after she'd kicked him out.

Raff looked at her steadily. The moonlight only reached the edge of the office deck, making his face shadowed. 'I've got nowhere else to go, that's why I stayed.'

'There are no other friends you can crash with?'

Raff wrinkled his nose. 'Not really.'

'You've pissed off all their wives?'

'That's about right.'

'Because you're a bad influence.'

He cocked two fingers at her. 'You got it in one.'

Tabitha shook her head, but at least he was being honest. 'What's wrong with a hotel?'

'Financial situation,' he mumbled. His jaw clenched. 'It's a perfect storm of being between things and selling the house with my ex. Money's tight.'

She could see the difficulty he was having in admitting that. 'How did you even get in here?'

Raff pulled a set of keys from his jeans pocket. 'I had keys cut the last time I was here.'

'Which presumably your parents don't know about?'

'No, they don't. And I want to keep it that way. Please.'

Once again he was asking a huge amount of her.

Tabitha folded her arms. 'You do realise I'm supposed to be

sending your parents an update. You're expecting me to lie yet again?'

Raff reached out, his hand tentatively connecting with her shoulder, making her glad of the material of the T-shirt between her and his fingers.

'I'm not asking you to lie; I'm just asking you to not mention me. Unless you have already?' His fingers trailed down a little further, connecting with her skin for the briefest of moments.

She held his gaze and shook her head. 'I didn't tell them anything apart from Fudge hurting his paw and needing some pain relief.'

Raff nodded slowly. 'And the dogs are both okay, aren't they? Misty too? There's no need to say anything, apart from the truth; their beloved pets and house are all fine.'

'They are now,' Tabitha said.

Raff tucked his hands beneath his armpits. 'I'm figuring things out week by week at the moment.' He gave her a sly grin. 'I guess I could always take up pet sitting and travel the world like you.'

'You'd be rubbish at it.' Tabitha tried her best to ignore the softening in her heart and the way she had begun to feel sorry for him having no place to go. It was not her problem, even if he kept making it so.

Tabitha didn't quite know what to do, which gave Raff the opportunity to unlock the door to the garden office. 'Come on in; it's chilly this evening.'

Her fiery rage at confronting him was slowly dissipating, and she realised she had goosebumps. She'd got tired and cold sitting outside. She also realised that they needed to sort out the situation they were in. What on earth was she supposed to do now?

Tabitha stepped inside, brushing past him. She was overtly aware of him. He filled the space in a way that was noticeable. He oozed sex appeal and she knew he knew it. She wondered if he sensed her internal battle of wanting to hate him rather than... What? Fancy him?

He was good-looking and fit as anything, but he'd behaved in a way that was deeply unattractive. That was what she should be focusing on, not the way his toned and tanned muscles made her go squidgy inside.

'Is that a bathroom?' She pointed at the door of a space not much bigger than a cupboard in an attempt to move her thoughts away from Raff half naked.

'There's a sink and toilet.'

'No shower?'

'No, um... I was considering sneaking into the house to get a shower when you were out but thought that might be overstepping...'

'You think?'

'Which is why I didn't,' he quickly said.

Tabitha huffed. 'If money's an issue, how did you pay for the flight over?'

Raff's eyes grazed the floor. 'I got a cheap one. It's not that I don't have any money, it's just I'm living from month to month and don't have enough to rent somewhere on Madeira, at least until the house sale goes through.' He looked back up at her. She couldn't help but notice the sorrow in his eyes. 'I've got myself into a bit of a financial situation, which I will get myself out of, it's just going to take time. Until now, I've been sofa surfing with friends in London.' He watched her intently, his full lips pursed, his eyes roving her face waiting for her response.

Tabitha felt she had every right to question him further – and she would – but not right now. Apart from him starting to open up to her – if only because she'd caught him out – it wasn't hard to see the vulnerability etched in his frown and the worry in his eyes. She was still desperate for a wee and wanted to have time to think away from him and his distracting presence.

She walked the couple of paces to the door. 'I need to feed the dogs.'

'What do you want me to do?' he called after her.

Tabitha turned and fixed him with what she hoped was a cool glare. 'I don't know yet, but you've not exactly given me much choice, have you?'

'No, I'm sorry.'

His earlier smirk had vanished and for the first time he looked genuinely serious. She didn't have the heart to kick him out, not now she knew he was in financial difficulty – if he was telling the truth. She wanted to believe him, to trust that everything he was telling her was the way things really were, but he'd already taken advantage of her generosity and she didn't want to be played for a fool.

18

With their stomachs full, Bailey and Fudge settled on the rug in front of the glass doors. Outside, only pinprick stars, the silver-white of the moon and the gentle glow from the garden office broke up the inky blackness. Now that Tabitha knew Raff was staying there, there was no point in him hiding, so he'd turned the outside lights on. How desperate must he have been to stay somewhere without a shower or any cooking facilities? Yet she still wondered if he was really struggling or simply playing on her good nature. She was having difficulty telling the truth from fiction.

Tabitha had been itching to phone Elspeth ever since she'd got back from Julie's, but she knew she wouldn't have the time to talk until she'd got the kids to bed. It was nearly nine now; the day had run away with her, waiting for Raff to show up. After sending a message to Cordelia with an update about the dogs and Misty – and leaving out any mention of Raff – Tabitha plonked herself on the sofa and called her sister. Fudge, eager to have a lap to sleep on, jumped up, settled next to her and rested his head on her thigh.

The phone rang and rang and Tabitha was about to give up when Elspeth answered with a tired but happy, 'Hello, Tabs.'

'Hey there, it's good to hear your voice. Are the girls in bed?'

'Sort of. Nancy's being a pain in the you-know-what... Gethin can deal with her.'

'If it's easier, I can phone back later.'

'Nope, I need the break. You're not going anywhere.' Elspeth sighed and Tabitha imagined her sinking into the depths of the sofa out of earshot of her screaming youngest, which was ear-piercingly loud even on the other end of the phone. 'I want to know all about your evening with Ollie.'

Without meaning to, Tabitha sighed.

'That bad, was it?'

'No, it was fine.' Tabitha picked a dog hair off her dungarees. 'It was just strange seeing him again. In a way, it felt as if no time had passed and there were moments when we slotted back to how things once were, but in another way, there was a massive gulf between us. So much has happened. He's changed; *I've* definitely changed. We've lost seven years of friendship that we can never get back – at least not to the way things were.'

'You sound confused,' Elspeth said gently. 'But that was to be expected. He hurt you and massively damaged your friendship and your trust in him.'

With everything that had gone on today, Tabitha hadn't had much time to dwell on it but she knew she was conflicted about things. 'Did I overreact though?'

'No, of course not! He stole your song, Tabs. We were all encouraging you to sue him, remember. You took the high ground and walked away for your own sanity. Didn't want the drama or the stress. You put your mental health first and were the bigger person.'

'But he tried reaching out – he said to say sorry and make amends. It was me who ignored him and effectively made things worse.'

'I think it's completely understandable that you didn't want to see or speak to him. I know how angry and disappointed you were.'

'Him not being open with me is what upset me the most, more than him claiming the song to be his own. Instead of being truthful, he took the coward's route and just didn't tell me. He led me on too, letting me believe it would be my big break as well. Ah, I don't know.' She stroked Fudge's soft ears and tried to quash the pent-up emotion that was threatening to spill. 'Everything feels a bit of a mess at the moment. Ollie's not the only thing I'm muddled about.'

'Oh?' Elspeth said.

'I'm in a bit of a situation.'

'You are?' Elspeth sounded worried. 'What's happened?'

Tabitha thought back over the past week, which was tarnished by the unexpected arrival of Raff and the subsequent confusion and frustration he'd caused. She took a deep breath and ploughed right into the events since he'd turned up in the night, skipping over the bit about them kissing and ending up in bed together. Elspeth listened intently, offering an occasional 'huh-uh' and 'oh really', while in the background Nancy's screams intensified. Tabitha filled her sister in right up to the events of this evening.

'And he's about your age, right?' Elspeth asked once Tabitha had recounted her story.

'Yes, thirty-one.'

'And good-looking?'

'That's what you've taken from everything I've just said?'

'No, that's not *all* I've taken from it,' Elspeth said calmly, 'it's just that's the bit I've taken an interest in. So, is he, good-looking?'

'He's not bad.' Tabitha decided to underplay his hotness.

Elspeth squealed. 'You like him!'

Tabitha could tell from Elspeth's tone that she was grinning.

'No! It's nothing like that.' Tabitha bit her lip and gazed down the dark garden to the faint glow of the office. The memory of their drunken kiss was still fresh despite the haziness of what had apparently not happened afterwards. The memory of waking with a banging headache to the sight of Raff lying next to her in just his jeans, his ripped chest on show, was pretty much etched onto her brain as well. She focused her attention back to Elspeth. Nancy's crying had turned into a full-blown tantrum to the extent it sounded like something out of a horror movie. 'Don't you need to go and sort out Nancy?'

'Nope,' Elspeth said swiftly. 'Gethin's coping fine. Once she gets into this state, there's nothing anyone can do until she allows herself to calm down. Sometimes you just have to let the tantrum run its course. Plus, I want to hear more about this bloke.'

'You're impossible. I want your advice about a weird situation, not encouragement over a man I barely know.' Tabitha sighed.

'Sorry, Tabs. I'm only teasing.'

'It's all so weird and unprofessional.'

'Back up. When you say it's unprofessional, is it because you've done something with him to make you feel that way?'

Tabitha knew exactly where Elspeth was going with this. Her sister could always see right through her; even hundreds of miles away and over the phone. 'Not exactly… but kinda, yeah.'

'Ooh! You've slept with him, haven't you?'

'No, nothing quite like that.'

'Because that would make it a pretty tricky situation.'

'Yeah, I'm well aware of that. We had a bit of a drunken snog, though, and wound up in bed together, but apparently nothing happened.'

'Apparently?' Elspeth's voice went up an octave.

'According to him, we didn't have sex. I don't remember much.'

'Oh lordy. And after he was a drunken nightmare, you kicked

him out and he's been staying in the garden office sneaking around, unbeknown to you.'

'That's about right.'

'Wowsers.'

'How do things like this happen to me?'

'You mean, why are you lucky enough to have a hot bloke crash your idyllic house sit on Madeira?'

Tabitha hmphed with frustration. Elspeth meant well, she knew, desperately wanting to see her happy and in love again, but that wasn't something that Tabitha had been looking for. 'But I don't want anyone in my life. I don't want a relationship, and you know why that is? Because although I was the one who broke up with Lewis, I did love him.'

'I know you did, Tabs,' Elspeth said softly.

'I loved him and he tried to make me into someone I'm not.'

'I understand that. I know you weren't happy with him even if you were in love. Sometimes that's not enough. He was the wrong guy for you.'

'I keep thinking maybe I'm better off on my own. To find anyone who will understand me and be okay with me living my life the way I want to will take a miracle. And before you say it, I understand that you need to compromise in a relationship, but not to the extent of someone trying to completely change who you are when they knew what you did for a living in the first place.' Tabitha huffed, relieved to get that off her chest. 'I guess what I'm trying to say is, Raff being here might sound like a good thing to you, but, trust me, it's the last thing I want. *He's* the last thing I want.' She bit her lip and gazed at the twinkling office lights. 'Rufus and Cordelia have entrusted me with their home and pets and then he's strolled right in and behaved like a... Like he owns the place.'

'But he's their son, right?' Elspeth interjected. 'Surely that's not too much of a problem?'

'You'd think. There's bad blood between them. Exactly what all the ins and outs are, I'm not quite sure.'

'Don't you think it's about time you asked him then?' Elspeth was the voice of reason she needed. 'You're perfectly in your right to. You're the one who's supposed to be there. Like you said, you're there in a professional capacity, looking after the house and animals while, I should add, you're supposed to be working. It's not as if you're on a constant jolly, travelling around the world living it up, even if I believe that's what you're doing most of the time.' Elspeth laughed. 'If he's there when he shouldn't be and you're letting him stay, even out in the garden office—'

'I haven't said he can stay yet.'

'Okay then, *if* you let him stay out of the goodness of your heart, then you absolutely deserve answers. And whether you like it or not, you've already got yourself involved with him – getting drunk and snogging him probably wasn't the smartest move if you wanted him out of your life.'

'Aarrghh!' Tabitha exclaimed. Fudge's head shot up from her knee. She stroked him and mouthed, 'Sorry, buddy.'

Elspeth chuckled. 'I'm only stating the truth, Tabs.'

'I know you are; that's why I'm annoyed with myself.'

'At least he's a distraction from Ollie. Why don't you take him a peace offering – cook him a meal and have a chat over dinner. Perhaps that way he'll open up to you.'

Without knowing much about him, beyond him being a similar age to Tabitha and assuming he was good-looking, Elspeth was encouraging her to get to know him better. The trouble was, despite a small part of her wanting to kick him out completely, take the keys off him and demand he leave for good for a second time, a bigger part of her had been drawn in by him, by the things he was hiding, the things Julie had told her about him, by his gumption and confidence, not to mention the feeling he evoked in her. On some level, Elspeth's idea was the right one, to take the middle ground and find out more before making a rash decision. Even if her sister was desperate for her to hook up with someone she didn't even know. Elspeth wanted to see her happy again and settled, rather than a nomad of a sister, the only member of the family still with itchy feet and nowhere to call home.

19

When Nancy's screams reached full volume, Tabitha and Elspeth said goodbye, with Elspeth making Tabitha promise to keep her updated on the Raff and Ollie situation.

Tabitha took her sister's advice and cooked dinner. Enough for two. It was a simple dish of spaghetti with sun-dried tomatoes, but it felt like a peace offering of sorts. She dished the pasta into two bowls, grated over some São Jorge cheese and, with a bowl in each hand, headed down the garden with Bailey and Fudge.

'Knock, knock,' she called from outside the closed office door.

The door swung open and Raff looked at the bowls and then at her in surprise.

'I thought you might be hungry.'

'I am, thank you, but you didn't have to do this.'

'I know.'

They sat outside on the office deck, Tabitha cross-legged in a chair, the bowl cupped in her lap. Raff had turned on the fairy lights that edged the overhang of the roof. They cast a warm light over them, banishing the darkness to the grey shadows of the surrounding palms and banana plants. It was an idyllic spot, looking out over the ocean, the endless black shimmering silver when the moonlight caught the ripple of incoming waves.

Tabitha lifted up a forkful of wound spaghetti. 'This was my sister Elspeth's idea.'

'It's a good one and much appreciated.' He finished chewing his mouthful. 'Are you close to your sister?'

'Yeah, she's my big sister but the one closest in age to me, although she's still four years older.'

'You're the baby of the family?'

'Uh-huh.' Tabitha nodded as she chewed and swallowed the spaghetti. 'Elspeth is married with two young children – my nieces are utterly gorgeous but a handful. I love them to bits. They used to live in Camberwell, so not too far from me in Wimbledon, but at the beginning of last year they moved to Wales and started The Wildflower Hideaway, this incredible glamping place in the Brecon Beacons, so I didn't get to see them as much.'

'You must really miss them, travelling around like you do?'

The sudden lump in her throat took her by surprise. 'I do, but the desire to get away from everything and everyone was stronger than me wanting to stay with them for a while – which they offered.'

'You needed to get away?'

Tabitha nodded. 'Completely. Even from the people I love. Mostly from them. It was too hard being around everyone.' And it was too hard talking about it now. Elspeth had urged a peace offering in making dinner for Raff, not a heart-to-heart, unless of course he opened up about himself first. She deserved that much after the events of the last few days. 'Julie talked about you, when I was over there this afternoon.'

'Oh?' Raff stopped chewing and cast a worried look in her direction.

'Don't worry, I didn't tell her you'd been here, although I feel like I should have because she's so lovely. She really cares about you.' Tabitha focused on winding spaghetti onto her fork, aware that she was talking about emotional stuff. 'She said how much you struggled moving here only to be sent to boarding school, forced away from your dog...'

'Jeez...' Raff put his nearly empty bowl on the decking. 'This is stuff I've not talked about with anyone for a long time. I kinda try not to give it any thought.'

'Because it's too upsetting?'

'Because it still hurts like hell,' he said, his voice cracking.

'Oh Raff, I'm sorry to have brought it up.' She reached out and briefly touched his knee, feeling the need to comfort him.

'It's fine. I don't come back here often and usually it's from necessity rather than wanting to, but perhaps it's a good thing to confront the past. Julie in particular was my one constant through my teens. I was only here during the holidays and the older I got, the less I came back. And, honestly, I spent more time with Julie and Anton than I did my own parents. They're good people and I know how my parents talk about them.' His jaw clenched and his face darkened. 'They have very different personalities, which says it all really.'

'Instead of sneaking around here, why didn't you just go to Julie's? I'm pretty sure she'd welcome you with open arms.'

'Oh, I know she would, it's just I don't want to ever put her in a difficult position with my parents, plus they've done enough trying to help me "fix" my life in the past; I don't want to be a burden to them.'

'I'm sure they wouldn't think of it like that.'

'You know them that well, do you?' he said sharply.

Tabitha was taken aback.

'I'm sorry.' Raff ran a hand through his hair. 'That was uncalled for; I know you were only trying to be helpful. Everything back here is complicated; everything back in London is too. Perhaps what I really need to do is escape somewhere, bounce about from one place to another where no one knows me. Run away. That's what you've been doing, right?'

Tabitha nodded, accepting it was only fair to open up to him since he'd begun to share a little with her. 'The short version is I was in love, but we weren't right for each other. We both went into the relationship knowing that we were very different, except instead of accepting our differences, he slowly started to chip away at the things that made me, well, me.'

'Like what?'

'My job for one. I was a musician as much as a songwriter – I've never craved the limelight, but the buzz of performing, that's on a whole other level. Touring with bands, playing the guitar, singing backing vocals, being a part of a massive show, whether in a stadium or an arena...' Tabitha imagined it now; instead of looking out on the moon-dappled ocean, it was a sea of faces, screaming fans waving their arms in the air, singing along to a song she'd co-written. It was the thrill of performing that she missed, yet hearing a song she'd written on the radio or watching it performed on TV equalled it, just in a different way.

'He stopped you doing that?' Raff asked.

'He didn't give me an ultimatum as such, just wore me down, you know that kind of shit. A lot of conversations focused on how difficult it was for our relationship with me being far away for long periods of time.' Tabitha heard the bitterness in her voice. 'I was living in central London but moved in with him in Wimbledon because he had a nicer place, then when things got serious and he started talking about buying somewhere together, he suggested I quit touring – he didn't want us to make that kind of commitment unless I was going to be home more.'

'That sounds like an ultimatum to me...'

'I should have seen the signs then, but what did I know, I was in love – or at least I believed I was – and for once it felt like a proper relationship.' Tabitha shrugged in a way that suggested love trumped everything, and so she'd thought at the time. 'It *was* a proper relationship rather than a casual thing, hooking up with one of the backstage crew on tour.'

'That's what you used to do?' He raised an eyebrow.

'Don't look at me like that. That was my life back then. Shoot me for having fun.'

'Nah, I get it. Sounds pretty sweet.'

'It was, but not something I would have carried on with forever. It's just I wanted to decide that in my own time. And the whole settling down in one place thing. Ugh.' She pretended to shiver.

'You like being free. I understand that completely.' He leaned back in his chair and looked wistful, pursing his lips as if considering whether he should say anything else. 'The one thing going to boarding school gave me was confidence – being away from home, meeting new people, making new friends, travelling on my own during school holidays to family in the UK or back here. I'd led a pretty sheltered life up till then. Uni was the same and I only came back here because I didn't have the money at the time to fend for myself, but as soon as I finished and started earning, I was gone. I've done lots of things and been successful in my own way, but nothing that has ever made my parents proud.'

Raff echoed what Julie had said earlier about Cordelia and Rufus and their opinion of their son. It was a heart-breaking admission, particularly when she came from a big family with parents who supported her and her siblings no matter what. She wanted to say that she was sure his parents were proud of him, but it would be empty words. She didn't know that. And there must have been a reason why Cordelia and Rufus, when welcoming her into their home to look after their beloved dogs and cat, had failed to mention they had a son. Julie had said something about Raff stealing... Not that she was going to bring that up now. The fact that there were no family photos on display spoke volumes. It would be heartless to try to make Raff feel better when she didn't fully understand where the breakdown of his and his parents' relationship stemmed from.

It was dark and quiet at the bottom of the garden. The fairy lights only cast a little light and the shadowy palms gave the impression of the darkness looming closer. A couple of moths fluttered, but apart from that and an occasional rumbling snore from one of the dogs, the night was still, the sound of the ocean distant.

'As we're being honest with each other,' Raff suddenly said, breaking the stillness, 'there's actually another reason why I'm here. It's not just about money – or lack of it.' He gazed thoughtfully out into the night. 'A friend's getting married and I didn't want to turn down the invite. It seemed perfect, coinciding with the house being empty. Or so I thought.' He gently nudged his fist against her shoulder.

'I scuppered your plans.'

'Far from it,' he said, glancing at her. 'I've enjoyed your unexpected company, although I'm not sure you'll say the same about me...'

Tabitha was uncertain how to answer that, so she left him hanging. Although, when she really thought about it, there were moments over the past few days when she'd enjoyed his company too. What she hadn't been prepared for was him taking advantage of the situation and abusing her trust.

And then there was Elspeth, encouraging her to get to know Raff, rather than berating her for having allowed a strange bloke to crash at the villa. But was being lonely a good enough reason to throw caution to the wind and let someone into her heart? Because that was what she feared was beginning to happen with Raff. They kept on being drawn back together – mainly because of Raff's situation – but there was an undeniable connection. Were they destined to be nothing more than a fleeting moment in each other's lives, friends or something more? Either way, she liked this more thoughtful, quieter side to him. His looks had initially attracted her, while his easy-going nature and flirtation had won her over. Now it felt as if she was finally getting to know him a little.

She contemplated what she should do. Her head was telling her to walk away, to not allow him to elbow his way into her life for a third time, yet her heart was screaming louder to give him another chance, to have more time to get to know and understand him, to peel away the layers. Her life wasn't straightforward, her emotions were all over the place, so why would it be any different for him? And weren't they both doing the same thing, escaping everything while trying to figure out the direction their lives should take? Not that she should open her arms and invite him in to the house she was responsible for without conditions; she needed to be able to trust him first.

Her phone pinged, dragging her attention away from her decision. She clicked on the message from Ollie.

I can't even begin to explain how good it was to see you again. Seriously, I've missed you like crazy. I know I've made huge mistakes and hope I can make it up to you. Can't wait to see you again next week. X

Acknowledging the fluttering in her chest his words evoked, Tabitha switched off the screen and looked across the fairy-light-lit deck at Raff. 'I tell you what, if you don't mind bunking in here, you can stay.'

'Tabitha, I don't know what to say.' He grinned at her. 'Thank you.'

'You do realise you've already being doing what I'm now saying you can do.' She laughed, a sense of ease seeping through her now that she'd made up her mind. 'And come in and have a shower whenever you want.'

She scooped up the empty bowls and stood up.

'I really appreciate this,' Raff said, standing up as well.

Tabitha was about to go when a thought about Ollie's party hit her. She'd envisioned rocking up on her own, not knowing anyone besides Ollie, something that never used to faze her, but things had changed since then. 'And, um, I'm going to a party on Wednesday evening – I've been invited by an old friend. He's partly the reason why I wanted to come to Madeira, to try to salvage our friendship. If you fancy coming along, it would be good to have the company, but don't feel you have to.'

'I'd love that.' Raff grabbed her free hand, leaned in and kissed her cheek. 'Thank you for everything.'

'Night, Raff.'

20

Elspeth phoned Tabitha first thing the next morning. Tabitha groaned as she grabbed her mobile. She'd already been up to feed the dogs and let them out but had crashed straight back into bed. She looked at the time: 9.04 a.m. Early on a Sunday for her, not for her sister with a three- and four-year-old.

'Hey, E.'

'Sorry, didn't mean to wake you.'

'You didn't.'

'Liar.' Elspeth laughed, adding to the background giggles of Olivia and Nancy.

Tabitha stifled a yawn. 'They sound happy.'

'That's because they're just finishing off blueberry pancakes with lashings of maple syrup, although more has gone on them than on their breakfast. I just couldn't wait any longer to find out how it went with Raff. I was expecting you to message me, but then figured you might have been a bit busy last night...' Her words were loaded.

'Sorry to disappoint you, but no, I wasn't "busy" in the way you mean. It just ended up being too late to message, that's all.'

'Did you take my advice?'

'Yes.'

'And…'

'You were right, he opened up.' Tabitha shuffled into a sitting position. Sunlight squeezed through the gap in the curtains, casting a narrow block of warm light across the wooden floor. 'The only trouble with that was the more I found out about him, the harder it became to ask him to leave.'

'Was that what you actually wanted to do?'

'Well, no.' Tabitha rubbed her forehead. 'Oh, I don't know. Either way, I said he could stay in the garden office. It seemed the best compromise. I like talking to him. There's also something appealing about him, even though I know it's probably a bad idea to get involved – as a *friend*, because that's all it is before you say anything.'

'I wasn't going to say…' Her voice trailed off as Olivia's cut in.

'Mummy, Mummy, Mummy.'

Tabitha imagined Olivia's sticky maple syrup fingers tugging on Elspeth.

'I'm talking to Auntie Tabitha.'

There was muffled noise and a thump as if the phone had been dropped, then scrabbling.

'Hold on,' Elspeth said. 'Olivia wants to say hello.'

There was more fumbling while the phone was passed over.

'Hello, Auntie Tabitha.'

Overwhelming love flooded Tabitha's heart at her niece's angelic voice.

'Hello, Olivia. I hear you're having pancakes for breakfast. Lucky you.'

'I like blueberry pancakes. Daddy made them.'

'They'll set you up nicely for a busy day of playing.'

'Mummy said we're going to get a dog.'

'That's not what I said, Olivia,' Elspeth's voice swiftly cut in. 'I said Auntie Tabitha was looking after two dogs again and that *maybe* one day we'd get a dog.'

'I like dogs.'

'I know you do,' Tabitha said, imagining Olivia's squashable cheeks and the serious look she probably had on her face.

'She's wandered off.' Elspeth was back on the phone. 'She has the attention span of a gnat.'

'Hard work, eh?'

'Yep. Just as well they're both so adorable.'

'How are you managing with the wedding prep?'

'Mum and Dad are arriving tomorrow to look after the girls for a few days while we get the barn finished ready for Saturday, which is a relief. Olivia's still only in school during the morning until the week after next, so it's been quite a juggle.'

'I wish I was there to help.'

'No you don't, Tabs,' Elspeth said kindly. 'Although you've got to come home sometime.'

'Do I really, though? It's what Mum and Dad did, spent their lives travelling around.'

'Yes, but—'

'I know what you're going to say, that they had each other.'

'Well yes, they did. And us lot. They were never on their own.'

'Perhaps I like being by myself.'

'Do you?'

'I'm comfortable travelling around on my own.'

'That's why you sent this Raff guy packing, eh?' Elspeth said sarcastically.

'I see something of myself in him – he's at a place in his life he's not certain about, his insides in turmoil, for different reasons than me, but we have that in common.'

'I knew you liked him.' Elspeth sounded smug.

'I do like him,' Tabitha said more sharply than she meant. 'Doesn't mean anything more than us being friends is going to happen though, so don't even go there.'

'Talking about Raff, he diverted my attention away from us talking about Ollie yesterday. Have you heard from him since you went out?'

Tabitha sighed, still uncertain how she felt about rekindling their friendship, although it felt like smouldering embers rather than it being ablaze. 'He did message me last night and he invited me to his birthday party on Wednesday.'

'Ooh, that sounds promising.' Elspeth paused. 'You should invite Raff to go with you.'

'I already have.'

Elspeth snorted. 'You're just friends... Yeah, right.'

With Elspeth making Tabitha promise to send regular updates to take her mind off getting the barn finished in time for the looming wedding with eighty guests, they said goodbye.

Tabitha missed her terribly. She missed all of her family, but Elspeth and her mum and dad in particular made the time away hard. And her nieces. Tabitha adored being an aunt, not just to Olivia and Nancy, but to all of her other nieces and nephews. Being the fun aunt was the best, but the maternal feelings that had crept up on her over the last couple of years had taken her by surprise. Initially, she'd put it down to being head over heels in love with being an auntie, but then, after being terrified when she discovered she was pregnant, an early miscarriage, which she assumed she would feel relief at, had in reality torn her apart.

A sob caught in her throat. She grabbed a pillow and hugged it, the wave of grief hitting her so unexpectedly that all she could do for a minute was cry into it as she allowed the upset to echo through her. Fudge moved up the bed until his paws were on her legs, his head cocked, wide eyes looking at her. Tears streamed down her face as she proper ugly cried. Getting pregnant had been the last thing she'd wanted, yet the moment it was taken away she'd realised it had meant everything.

Tabitha grabbed a tissue and dabbed angrily at her face. She'd run away to try to escape feeling like this. She didn't understand how to deal with losing something she never knew she'd wanted in the first place.

Fudge was still watching her intently; she couldn't help but smile. She was glad of the dogs' constant, lovable companionship. And, she realised, she was glad that Raff was here too, albeit at the bottom of the garden.

Reconnecting with an old friend and letting a new one into her life felt like a step forward. After Madeira, perhaps she would head to Wales and take Elspeth up on her offer of staying for a few weeks. It had been too long and the tug of home... No, not home, because she wasn't sure where that was. The pull of family was what had become so strong.

Tabitha forced herself out of bed and banished her thoughts with a swim in the pool. *What better way to start a Sunday*, she thought as she swam a couple of lengths. With the sun warming her shoulders, the water was the perfect temperature. She rested her arms on the side of the pool and gazed down the garden, the gentle slope allowing a glimpse of the deep blue of the ocean between the palms and tropical bushes. Apart from the birds of paradise flowers and the hammock slung between the palms, there was nothing but fresh green and soothing blue.

The garden office was well-concealed by the trees; it was easy to see how Raff had managed to stay hidden. She wondered what he'd been up to for the last few days.

Tabitha pushed away from the edge and glided across the pool on her back, the tepid water and sun caressing her skin.

A door banging at the bottom of the garden disturbed the

peace. Tabitha flipped onto her front and swam back to the edge of the pool. Fudge, lying on the patio, lifted his head as Raff strolled towards the villa.

'Morning,' Raff said, shooting her a smile before dropping to his knees to ruffle Fudge's ears.

Fudge manoeuvred as close as possible to Raff, climbed up his legs and pushed his nose into his face. Raff was so good with the dogs and they seemed to adore him. The thought that she was rather jealous of Fudge being in such close proximity to Raff crossed her mind. She felt relieved that the rush of heat working its way up from the pit of her stomach was tempered by the cool water.

It was just as well Elspeth couldn't see this scene playing out: Tabitha in the pool in a bikini; Raff half naked, his chiselled chest gleaming in the sunshine.

'You slept okay?' Tabitha turned her thoughts to polite conversation.

'Yeah, not bad.' He switched his attention from Fudge to her. 'I really do appreciate you being okay with me staying.'

'What have you been doing for food?'

'Bought stuff in the village market.'

'And what have you been doing down in the office each day?'

'Working.' He shrugged. 'I used to work as a video game designer a while back so have taken on some freelance work to tide me over.'

'How do I not know this?' She rested her arms on the terrace paving. 'For some reason I didn't think you were working.'

'It's a fill-in job. I've kinda bounced from one thing to another most of my life. I'm pretty good at turning my hand to anything. Keeps life interesting. As well as waiting for the house sale to go through, I'm waiting on my first royalty payment too.'

'For what?'

'My debut novel.' He looked sheepish, his voice tentative as if it wasn't something he usually revealed. 'The first of three thrillers written under a pseudonym.'

'So you're a writer too.' Tabitha smiled; just something else they had in common.

Raff smoothed his hand along Fudge's back, then stood up. 'I was, um, going to have a shower if that's okay?'

'Of course.'

'Although a dip in the pool first looks rather appealing.'

The way he was looking at her made her wonder if it was the pool or her in it that he meant.

'Come and join me then.' She meant to come across as friendly, yet she was aware her excitement made it sound flirty.

Raff kicked off his trainers and dived in, neatly breaking the surface of the water and sending ripples towards her. He swam to the middle of the pool before emerging not far from her.

'I do get why my parents moved from Surrey to here. The life-style's frigging ace.' He slicked a hand through his wet hair before front crawling his way to the other end of the pool and back again.

Tabitha leaned on the side, her elbows resting on the warm paving stones, enjoying the feeling of weightlessness and the sun on her damp shoulders as she watched the muscles in Raff's arms tense with each stroke.

After doing ten laps, he swam over and joined her. 'You're not swimming?'

'Nah, just enjoying the view,' she said, smiling slyly.

Raff grinned. 'You do realise the view's that way.' He pointed behind her.

'I know,' she said as innocently as she could. She didn't want to continue being grumpy with him, not when they could be friends and she could enjoy her time with him. It wasn't as if that thought didn't appeal to her... She reached for her phone which was next to her towel and motioned for Raff to join her. He slid his arm around her waist, his fingers tickling her skin beneath the water, while she put her arm around his broad shoulders. 'Say cheese.'

She snapped the selfie, the two of them with big smiles, their tanned skin beaded with water against the hazy green of the garden. She released her arm and returned her phone to the safety of the terrace, while Raff backstroked away, the sun making his chest gleam.

Tabitha swam past him. 'Time to work.'

'On a Sunday?'

'Need to catch up somehow.' She climbed up the steps and out of the pool, sensing Raff's eyes on her as she dripped water on the paving.

* * *

They spent the rest of the day doing their own thing – Tabitha working in the living room with the doors wide open and the dogs lying at her feet, while Raff largely stayed in the garden office. In the evening, they shared another meal, this time prepared by Raff, a seafood salad that was so much nicer than the pasta dish she'd cooked the night before, as they chatted about Raff's work designing video games and writing a series of pacy thrillers.

The next couple of days passed by uneventfully and in harmony, much to Tabitha's relief. She had the time and headspace to work, even with Raff at the bottom of the garden. He was working too and kept to himself during the day, disappearing on the Monday evening for a couple of hours, which made her wonder if he was trying hard to stay out of her way. The trouble was, her heart kept betraying her head whenever he was around, and when he wasn't, she was conscious of how much she missed him. A silly infatuation, connecting with someone after craving time on her own.

On Tuesday morning, a bottle of Madeira wine arrived from Ollie, along with the invitation to his party at a club in Funchal, which once again left Tabitha conflicted over how she felt. That evening, she rang her mum and had a long catch-up before being passed over to her dad and then Elspeth. If her sister was disappointed that Tabitha didn't have any juicy news, she didn't let it show. Elspeth sent photos of her and Gethin wearing paint-splattered T-shirts and standing next to a newly painted sunny yellow wall at the end of the spacious barn. It was beginning to look as if they'd be able to host a wedding there on the weekend. Tabitha considered sending the selfie she and Raff had taken together in the pool, but then thought better of it – she'd never hear the end of it if Elspeth actually got to see what he looked like.

Wednesday evening, the night of Ollie's party, came round quickly. Tabitha had booked a taxi for nine, so they'd get to the club by ten. The day had been filled with remote meetings and little time to concentrate on writing and her head spun with a million things, especially the thought of seeing Ollie again. She'd retreated to her room to get changed and had tried on three or four outfits before finally feeling happy.

Tabitha had never considered herself to be a nervous person. She was fine meeting new people and had the confidence to walk into a room full of strangers. But with Ollie it felt different. The damage to their friendship had left her uncertain about where she stood with him. There might be people she would know from way back at his party, although them being on Madeira rather than in London made that less likely. What she did realise as she got ready was she was grateful that Raff was going with her.

She felt cool and confident in tight black leather trousers, a plunging V-neck top, strappy gold heels and chunky bracelets. She was ready to party and realised that she missed this, getting dressed up and going out, something she'd rarely done over the past year. There had been opportunities during her month in LA, but she'd shied away from being sociable, focusing solely on work. The last time she'd properly gone out was New Year's Eve in Devon with her two sisters and their husbands to the local pub. This was different. This was a night out for her friend's birthday, plus she was going with a new friend. Bring it on.

21

It was dark by the time the taxi arrived. The dogs and cat had been fed and would be okay on their own for a few hours. Tabitha locked up and met Raff on the drive. He looked good even in jeans and a T-shirt, but wearing fitted grey trousers and a black, short-sleeved linen shirt, he was even more handsome than usual. Her eyes trailed over him before she realised he was doing the same to her. When his eyes eventually met hers, he flashed a knowing grin.

The taxi driver raced along, in and out of the tunnels of the coast road, snatches of the city coming into view every so often. Funchal twinkled in the night, lights scattering the hillside all the way to the ocean. From the relative darkness that surrounded the villa, Funchal blazed with the promise of nightlife and dancing till late, leaving Tabitha tingling with excitement.

They'd mostly been quiet on the journey, with Raff on his phone and Tabitha replying to messages and updating her social media, while a local radio station played pop music in the background. As they drove further into the city, Raff spoke to the driver in Portuguese, getting him to drop them off a short walk away from the club.

However much she'd craved peace and time to herself, as she walked through the club doors, there was no getting away from the longing she felt for recapturing that time in her life when going clubbing or playing at a gig was the norm. The bass pulsed, increasing as they walked beyond security into the heart of the club. Tabitha paused momentarily, enveloped in the heat and the all-encompassing thump thump thump as she watched the crush of people on the dance floor, a mass of tanned writhing limbs. Mirror balls glittered, while strobe lighting cut across the dance floor, showing a snapshot of smiling faces, flushed cheeks, hands in the air, a plethora of strangers in slow motion, all as one, lost in the moment.

If she closed her eyes, Tabitha knew she'd be transported back to being on stage and hearing the roar of a frenzied crowd. Performing had been addictive, and now her senses were overwhelmed by the heat, the noise, the beat, the smell: hot skin, sweat, spilt drinks, the mingle of perfume and aftershave. It was everything she thought she no longer wanted, yet right now she couldn't think of anything better.

Tabitha took Raff's hand and led him through the club, bypassing the crush on the dance floor, towards the VIP area. Ollie spotted them and waved them through security.

'Ollie Pereira's your friend?' Raff shouted in her ear.

'I didn't think you were into pop?'

'I'm not; I know who he is though.'

Ollie's fame left her a little starstruck too, the idea that her friend was a big enough star to warrant security and this amount of attention blew her mind and it wasn't as if she wasn't used to being around rock stars. It was different, though, seeing the change in someone she'd known since they were both skint students.

'Hey, Tabitha!' Ollie greeted her with open arms and enveloped her into a hug that was familiar and greatly missed. 'Once again, you look bloody gorgeous.'

'Thank you.' Her cheeks flushed with so many people watching. 'I hope you don't mind, but I brought along a friend. Ollie, this is Raff. Raff, Ollie.'

'Hey, good to meet you.' Ollie clasped Raff's hand before frowning a little. 'How do you two know each other?'

'Long story,' she laughed.

'Just as well we have all night then.' He draped an arm across her shoulder and, beckoning to Raff, led them further into the plush and glittery VIP area.

Ollie sat down, patting the leather seat next to him so Tabitha was on one side, Raff on his other. More people joined them and glasses of *poncha* were handed out.

'So,' Ollie said, 'tell me the long story.'

'I'll give you the potted version.' Tabitha sipped the punchy liquid. 'It was a complete accident that we even met. The place I'm house sitting belongs to Raff's parents, but Raff had intended to stay there while they were away—'

'In my defence,' Raff cut in, 'I didn't realise that Tabitha would be there—'

'When he turned up unexpectedly in the middle of the night...' Tabitha continued.

'And you let him stay?' Ollie's look was one of disbelief mixed with a hint of mischief.

Tabitha realised that it really was mad that she'd not only let a complete stranger stay, but she'd now invited him on a night out.

The woman sitting on the other side of Raff started talking to him, while Tabitha continued the story of how she and Raff had wound up at the party together. The more she explained, the more Ollie's expression and comments changed from confusion to full-on amusement, despite her omitting the drunken snog and them ending up in bed together.

Tabitha tried to focus on Ollie, but the woman deep in conversation with Raff was ridiculously attractive, with long blonde hair and slender tanned legs emerging from a little black dress. She kept touching Raff's arm.

'You like him, huh?'

Tabitha's eyes flicked back to Ollie grinning at her.

'I, um...'

'Don't be coy with me,' he said. 'I know you, remember.'

'I do like him, as a friend.'

'Yeah, right.' Ollie smirked.

Tabitha took in the familiarity of Ollie's dimpled cheeks, baby-blue eyes and his sandy-coloured hair, still styled the same, although perhaps it had receded a little. The crinkles around his eyes when he smiled were deeper, but he was as handsome as he'd always been. No doubt she'd changed too, but they were still the same people inside, even with life taking them on very different journeys. She didn't want to be cross with him, but he had no idea about her, her life, her feelings, what she'd been through – none of it.

'I'm not sure you're in any position to make assumptions about me and Raff.' Her words were sharper than she'd intended. 'I'm not ready to move on from my last relationship – something you know nothing about.'

'Don't get cross, Tabs. I'm teasing you, like I've always done.'

Tabitha breathed deeply, took his hand and held it in her lap. 'I know you are,' she said, softly this time. 'I've missed that. The truth is, despite everything, I've missed you.'

'I've missed you too.' His smile had changed to a look of genuine concern. 'But are you okay?'

'Yeah, I'm getting there. A lot's happened in the last couple of years – things that I wanted to talk to you about, like I would have done before, you know...'

'You can talk to me now.' He squeezed her hand tightly.

Tabitha shook her head. 'Now's not the time or the place.' How would she even start to unravel the events and feelings that had consumed her over the last few months. Back when their friendship had been rock solid, she would have told him everything and done anything for him. Her expectation that he'd do the same for her had been misjudged. She'd tried hard to deal with that and the breakdown of their friendship and although this was the start of fixing it, she wasn't prepared to fully open up to him. She released her hand from his and raised her glass of *poncha*. 'Let's concentrate on you instead, after all it's your birthday.'

He knocked his glass of beer against hers. 'Cheers, Tabitha. I'm really glad you're here.'

'Me too.' She enjoyed the refreshing kick of lemon as she took a sip. Although it might not be the time to delve into her heartache, it was the perfect opportunity to put an end to the upset that had interrupted their friendship. 'I really am sorry I never reached out before, but I think it's taken me until now to be in a good place with my career and how I feel about, well, everything.'

The blonde woman was leading Raff towards the bar. Tabitha forced her attention away from them and back to Ollie.

'It's ancient history,' he said. 'I'm the one who has a hell of a lot of making up to do. You have nothing to be sorry for.'

Tabitha nodded, knowing she didn't. 'I'm trying to move forward and not look back on things with regret. I don't want us to not talk or see each other.'

Although he'd been the one to break her trust and disappoint her, her anger at being let down in front of her family and cheated out of a life-changing moment had diminished over the years. Even if an apology wasn't necessary from her, it was a weight off her shoulders to say sorry as much as it was appreciated to hear it from him.

22

A radio station producer arrived, someone Tabitha didn't know, someone who took Ollie's attention away. Of course she'd been right in thinking he wouldn't spend the whole party with her, even if she'd come on her own. Long gone were the days when they'd be clamped to each other's sides, when he'd look out for her. It was expected and inevitable, but her heart ached for their lost friendship and that they'd never again share the closeness they once had. Reconnecting with him was always going to be emotional.

She tore her eyes away from Ollie chatting animatedly to the radio producer and searched the sea of faces. Most were strangers, a handful she recognised, like Ollie's bubbly and efficient PA, but mainly because she'd seen them on Ollie's social media rather than in real life. The one person who was conspicuously absent was Ollie's model girlfriend, which made Tabitha wonder if they weren't intending to keep up the pretence of being together. She no longer knew all the ins and outs of his life. Tonight was a stark reminder about how much their lives had diverged.

Tabitha looked for Raff, eventually finding him by the bar, still talking to the beautiful blonde. The stab of envy took Tabitha by surprise and she had to remind herself that although they'd come together, they weren't together in the other sense, exactly as she'd pressed upon Ollie.

Picking up her drink, she decided to be brave and mingle. She could hold her own in a room full of Ollie's friends. As she introduced herself as a songwriter and witnessed people's reaction to her songwriting credits, it dawned on her just how far she'd come from that devastating night when Ollie had shunned her for a glittering career of his own.

Ollie did the rounds too, being a good host and chatting to everyone, lapping up the attention as he'd always done. He was a born performer, whereas Tabitha had always been happy to be in the background. She kept a lookout for Raff, although he seemed perfectly comfortable mingling too, no longer talking to the blonde, which Tabitha couldn't help but feel relieved about, but drifting between groups and chatting with Ollie as well.

Three glasses of *poncha* later, Tabitha went to the bar and ordered a gin and tonic. She felt nicely tipsy, with the buzz of being out at a club still there. The barman slid the drink to her. She leaned on the bar, looking past the VIP area to the pulsating mass on the dance floor, wishing she was down there.

An arm around her waist tugged her from her daydream. Raff's breath tickled her cheek. 'Since getting here, I've been offered cocaine and propositioned by a twenty-three-year-old blonde model. How's your night going?'

Tabitha laughed and looked from the dance floor into Raff's amused eyes. 'By the sounds of it, not quite as exciting as yours.'

'Ah, there's still time.'

'What? To snort cocaine and hook up with a model?'

He shrugged. 'If that's your vibe.'

'Is it yours?'

'Used to be. The drug bit at least; would have been hellishly lucky to have pulled a model back then. I was a bloody mess.'

'Being here isn't too much of a temptation then?' Tabitha asked tentatively, hoping he wasn't going to take offence.

He shook his head. 'Nah. Although I don't profess by any stretch of the imagination that I have my shit together as much as I should by now, that kind of temptation is a big no. I'm never going back to those days.' He looked at Tabitha intently and waggled his glass. 'Drinking I can manage – believe it or not, I do know when to stop. With drugs, it was a whole other story.'

'And the model? She didn't tempt you?' Tabitha smiled in a way she hoped wasn't too suggestive, although his gaze and close proximity was making her insides do that fluttery thing again.

Raff smiled broadly and leaned even closer. 'Truthfully, I much prefer redheads…' He left the words hanging and swigged his beer. 'You had a good chat with Ollie boy over there?'

It was Tabitha's turn to shrug.

'Bit like that, eh?'

'I'm not really sure how I feel. One minute, it's like time's rewound and it's exactly like it used to be, the next minute, it feels as if I'm talking to a stranger. I guess it's early days and he's surrounded by new friends. I need to move forward and not dwell on the past. That's what this whole last year has been about.'

'Sounds like good advice – for myself too.' Raff's hand fell from her waist. He pointed across the club. 'There's an outside bar if you fancy getting some air?'

Tabitha nodded and they escaped with their drinks to a terrace where the music wasn't quite as loud and the back wall of the bar was covered in leafy fronds nestled between shelves filled with bottles of spirits. After the heady heat and pulsing lights inside, outside was refreshing, the air warm but sweeter, the night broken up by the city's lights glowing far up the mountainous terrain all the way down to where the Atlantic Ocean lapped the bay.

'Honestly, what's the deal with you and Ollie?' Raff asked as they squeezed onto the end of a cushioned sofa, their thighs touching.

'What do you mean?'

He nudged her arm. 'You know what I mean. I've been chatting to him and he seemed rather keen on knowing what our relationship is.'

'He did?'

'Yeah, trying to find out in a roundabout way if we're *together* together.'

'What did you say?'

'I told him we're just friends.' He kept looking at her as he sipped his drink. 'Because that's what we are, right? Friends?'

'Yeah, totally.' It dawned on her that she very much liked that idea and had been thinking exactly that when she'd been getting ready to go out. Not that she'd rule out anything more happening with him...

'But just the way he was talking about you and asking after the two of us made me wonder what you two are to each other.'

'Friends.' Tabitha shrugged and waved her hand. 'We used to be best friends and then shit happened.'

Raff made an 'uh-huh' sound that suggested he didn't believe a word she was saying.

'I know what you're insinuating, but we're just friends, that's all.'

'You're honestly telling me the two of you never had one drunken night and slept together?' Raff's voice was incredulous.

'That's exactly what I'm saying.'

'And he's not gay?'

Tabitha snorted and shook her head.

'Right...' Raff was still looking at her with obvious disbelief. 'It's just even with whatever it is that happened between you, I can see how well you get on together, see the way he looks at you—'

'He doesn't look at me in any way. You're seeing things that aren't there.'

'Yeah, well, I'll be the judge of that.' He sipped his beer. 'I'm only thinking of the other night, you and me, all the flirting and drinking, which, er, would have led to us doing a lot more than kiss if you'd been compos mentis, if you get my drift.'

'I do, but I don't usually jump into bed with men I've just met.'

'I was the exception, was I?'

Tabitha pursed her lips. 'I was drunk.'

'So what you're telling me is you and Ollie have been drunk many times, yet you two never wound up in bed together?'

'That was different.'

'How?'

'Well, for starters we met when we were freshers, we lived in the same halls, had the same bunch of friends and really got to know each other and became best friends. You must have a best friend; you understand that, right?'

Raff snorted. 'Yeah, I do, because my best friend is a bloke, so getting drunk and sleeping together, never going to happen.'

'But you understand about friendship and not wanting to mess that up.'

'And sleeping together would?'

'Absolutely.'

'But how do you know that it wouldn't be the best thing? You're best friends – or at least you were – perhaps you're soulmates and you're missing out on a relationship with him because you're afraid to give it a go?'

'Why are you encouraging this?'

He shrugged. 'Ah, I don't know. Better to try and fail than not be brave enough and never know…'

Tabitha sat back on the seat, her gin clasped in her hand, and studied him. 'It sounds as if you're talking from experience.'

'That's because I am.' He downed the rest of his beer and for the briefest of moments Tabitha expected him to stop the conversation and make an excuse to go and get another drink, but he didn't. 'You know I said that as well as needing somewhere to stay, I came back to Madeira because I was invited to a friend's wedding?'

'Yes,' Tabitha said slowly, wondering where he was going with this.

'Well, that friend – Mai – was the person who I believed was my soulmate.' He raised an eyebrow and looked as if he was about to get up.

'Woah.' Tabitha grabbed his arm. 'You're not stopping there. You have got to tell me more.'

Raff sighed. 'She's five years older than me and I met her at the restaurant I used to work at during the holidays when I was back here. The age difference shouldn't be an issue, but I was sixteen when we first met and that's a massive difference when she was twenty-one. I totally lusted after her, but we also had a lot in common and I was older than my years,' he looked at her pointedly, 'you know, from being an only child and spending time at boarding school, plus I looked older too.'

'When did you make a move?' Tabitha asked. 'As a teenager?'

'Nah, I was twenty. Back from uni for the summer. We'd had four years of friendship and getting to know each other. There'd been girls on and off when I was at uni in London, but no one I felt the way I did about Mai.'

'So what happened? You didn't try it on at work, did you?'

'Nuh-uh. I wasn't that much of a lovestruck fool. We went out one evening. I understand now that she believed it was two friends having a drink, but I was thinking of it as a date. I walked her home afterwards planning to kiss her and imagining she was going to fall into my arms and invite me in for a coffee which would lead to... well, you get what twenty-year-old me was hoping it would lead to.'

'Yeah, I get it. So what did happen?'

'Oh, well, I did kiss her. I think her words were something along the lines of "What the hell are you doing?" Exactly what a bloke wants to hear,' he said wryly. 'For me, the kiss was electric; but obviously the biggest turn-off in the world for her. But what I'm saying is you don't know until you try. I've never regretted it because I always think if there'd been a chance and she'd actually fancied me too, it would have played out differently. Things would have been a lot different.' His brows knitted and he sounded wistful.

'I promise you it's not the same for me and Ollie.'

Raff shook his head. 'You really don't know if you've only ever been friends.'

Tabitha took a gulp of gin and leaned closer to Raff, lowering her voice despite it being impossible for anyone to hear their conversation over the thump thump beat of the music. 'We did snog each other once, at a house party in our third year at uni. Of course it was a drunken thing at the end of a mad night. One of Ollie's mates had copped off with a girl and they were in his bed, so Ollie crashed in mine.'

'And...?' Raff asked, raising an eyebrow.

'We snogged.'

'And...?' he said again. 'Bloody hell, Tabitha, it's like getting blood out of a stone.'

'It was weird.'

Raff laughed. 'Weird?'

'Yeah, in a really icky way. Honestly, it felt like I was kissing one of my brothers.' Tabitha made an 'ugh' face at the memory.

'And he felt the same?'

'Yep.'

'Are you sure?'

Tabitha crinkled her brow. 'Of course.'

'But it was you who stopped the kiss, right? And said it was weird, not him?'

Her brow furrowed deeper. 'Well, yes, but he agreed.'

'Or so he said.'

'Stop it!' Tabitha playfully whacked his arm. 'I was there, I know what happened and how I felt. There was no spark. Honestly, I had zero desire to do anything beyond that one kiss. We hugged and went to sleep, that was it.'

Raff was still looking at her in disbelief. Her hand was still on his arm. Ollie had never made her feel anything remotely like the way she felt around Raff. She dropped her hand onto the seat between them.

'Trust me,' Raff said with a twinkle in his eye. 'He's a bloke; he wanted to do more.'

'You don't know that.'

'Oh I do, Tabitha, don't kid yourself.'

'I wasn't infatuated with him the way you were with Mai, and anyway, he broke my heart worse than if we'd been in a boyfriend-girlfriend relationship. He made promises he didn't keep and was happy for his career to skyrocket while mine stayed stagnant. It's taken me years to get past the upset and hurt and to begin to want to be anywhere near him again.'

23

After chatting together for a while longer, Tabitha and Raff swapped the fresh night air, star-dusted sky and golden lights of Funchal for the pulsing beat, heat and glittering silver lights inside the club. It had been a long time since Tabitha had partied until the early hours of the morning and she felt so alive.

Ollie certainly wasn't short of attention, swamped by clubbers every time he left the privacy of the VIP area. Tabitha did wonder if he'd headed into the main part of the club because he craved the attention. He was well known worldwide, but he was a household name on Madeira, along with Cristiano Ronaldo, and although he didn't live on the island all the time, he was obviously well-loved.

Tabitha hadn't expected to spend much of the party with Ollie, and apart from their initial conversation, they only had fleeting moments together. She'd spent more time with Raff. He was assured enough to not stick by her side all night, allowing them both to mingle and chat to other people before radiating back together.

Over the last few years she'd been conflicted about what she wanted from life and the expectations of those around her, Lewis in particular. Watching her older siblings all find partners and have kids had somehow put pressure on her to do the same, even if none of her immediate family suggested anything of the sort. The freedom now though...

Tabitha had lost track of time, but it was late or early depending on how you looked at it. She and Raff were on the main dance floor. Ollie was somewhere else in the crush with friends, with fans, with clubbers. The beat pulsed through Tabitha. Her hands were in the air, the heat of other clubbers surrounding her, Raff close in front. The movement of other people pushed them closer, the brief connection of hot skin sticky against hers like a lightning bolt. The music pounded, bodies grinding, the pulsing beat ricocheting through her. Lights flashed blue-green, ice-white on the slow motion of dancers in every direction. Freedom, freedom, freedom, thumped through her head in time to the beat.

Tabitha flung her head back, reached her hands higher towards the glitter ball. Hands on her waist. Raff laughing, Raff dancing, Raff inches from her.

Raff, Raff, Raff...

The tempo changed and the music switched beats. Tabitha took Raff's hand and led him through the throng of dancers. She wanted to end the night on a high, to leave the party before the bitter end, to escape before the music died, the lights went up and the magic dispersed. Tabitha slowed before they reached the VIP area and leaned back against Raff. 'I think we should call it a night.'

'Yeah, that's fine by me.'

She was pressed against him. His free hand rested on her hip, his other still entwined in hers. They remained like that a heartbeat or two longer, between the dance floor and Ollie's party. Tabitha thought about reaching up and running her hand along his stubbled jaw, imagined his hands sliding up her body, turning her around until they were facing each other, eyes locked, lips temptingly close from...

'Tabitha!'

Ollie had clocked them. Their trance was broken.

Tabitha moved, increasing the distance between herself and Raff until they were ensconced back in the VIP area. Ollie, clutching a bottle of wine, was dancing towards them.

'We're going to make a move,' Tabitha said as Ollie reached them, realising how the use of 'we' sounded very much as if she and Raff were a couple, rather than just friends.

'You're leaving already?' Ollie flung an arm around both of their shoulders and attempted to steer them back towards the bar.

'It's gone three in the morning, Ollie.'

'When has that ever stopped us, Tabs?'

'That was a long time ago.'

Her late teens to her mid-twenties had been filled with alcohol-fuelled late nights, all the way through university and beyond when she'd toured with bands. Sell-out stadium shows every few days in a different UK city, then a few months spent bouncing from one show to the next throughout Europe, until she gave that lifestyle up to settle down. That was the truth of it. Yes, she'd fallen in love, but as she'd edged towards her thirties, the expectation of friends and family had played their part too. It was hard to ignore friends who had normal jobs, who were beginning to settle down with partners, buy a house, plan for the future. A part of her had craved some stability, to find out what it was like to live in one place for a while, have a home and somewhere she belonged, yet the truth was all that 'normality', for want of a better word, scared the bejesus out of her.

Ollie planted a smacker on Tabitha's cheek and released his hold on her. 'Keep in touch this time, eh?' He was swaying slightly, his arm still clamped across Raff's shoulder and she wasn't sure if it was Raff who was keeping him upright or not. Ollie jabbed a finger into Raff's side and locked his arm around his neck in a rugby-type hold. 'Look after her, mate.' Raising the wine bottle, Ollie released Raff and walked backwards, fixing his drunken gaze on Tabitha. 'Let's make time to write together.' He took a swig from the bottle. 'But not tonight!'

'Happy birthday, Ollie.' Tabitha gave him a wave and walked away, Raff following, leaving behind the dum dum dum beat echoing into the pre-dawn as they clattered downstairs and out into the relative quiet of the street.

Voices drifted down from the club's open roof terrace. A dog barked, setting another one off. Drunken shouts sounded from other revellers a street or two away. They'd partied through the night and it was nearly the start of a whole new day. Tabitha doubted she'd have stayed out this late if she hadn't been with Raff. Ollie had made time for her, for them both, but he was constantly encircled by other people, his entourage and new friends.

Tabitha yawned and Raff laughed.

'Let's find a taxi.' He hooked his arm in hers and led her along the street, away from the drifting music, Ollie and her past.

* * *

They were both quiet, consumed by thoughts, as the taxi drove through the glinting streets of Funchal into the outskirts and the nearby towns that edged the island like limpets clinging to a rock. Now the adrenaline of the night had subsided, Tabitha attempted to sift through her feelings for both Ollie and Raff in a haze of tiredness. Her long-time friend and her new one. One friend who had betrayed her, the other one who'd ignited something inside her. After months of being on her own and keeping very much to herself, her time on Madeira had been drastically different. Maybe it was a good thing to be confronted with the past and deal with it, as Raff had suggested. Ollie was just one aspect, the other was how to get over Lewis, how to move on from the breakdown of their relationship. Did she want to be on her own? She'd thought so. Lewis had constricted her; the more he pushed for commitment, the more she'd pulled away, and yet, becoming pregnant when it was the last thing she'd ever wanted had opened her eyes and her heart to a whole other life, one she hadn't ever imagined. Instinctively, Tabitha's hand fluttered to her stomach.

Raff glanced at her. 'Are you okay?'

'Yeah,' she said, forcing the melancholic thoughts from her head. 'Been a long time since I stayed out this late.'

'I enjoyed myself more than I thought I would tonight.'

'Good, I'm glad.' She reached for his hand where it rested on the leather seat between them. 'Thank you for coming with me. It really helped having you there.'

Raff curled his fingers in hers. It spoke volumes that she was more comfortable around someone she'd only recently met compared to a friend she'd known for fifteen years, even if the last seven of them had been erased. But then she'd never held Ollie's hand in the way she was doing now with Raff – drunken arms around shoulders exiting a bar in the early hours, yes. She'd never thought about Ollie in the way she thought about Raff either. It wasn't because Ollie wasn't good-looking, because he was, thousands of screaming fans confirmed as much, but he didn't turn her on, not like Raff did...

The taxi pulled up outside the closed gates of Rufus and Cordelia's villa. Tabitha untangled her fingers from Raff's and reached for her purse.

'I've got this.' Raff handed the driver the euros and they scrambled from the warm taxi into the pleasantly cool air.

It was still dark, the night invigoratingly fresh after the club, the inevitability of dawn just a short time away. The idea of having to get up in a few hours was the last thing Tabitha wanted to think about. She yawned, wanting nothing more than to make sure the dogs were okay before crashing into bed.

The taxi drove off, leaving absolute peace with just the distant sound of the ocean. A dog barked a long way off. Tabitha opened the front door quietly in an attempt to not wake Bailey and Fudge.

'You know what.' She turned back to Raff and leaned in the open doorway. 'It's silly you staying at the bottom of the garden, when you've already slept in the spare room.' She stepped back and held the door open for him. 'So come on in.'

'Are you sure?'

'I'm positive.'

He brushed past her, wafting lager and a deep lemony scent, but it was the warm comforting presence of *him* that she sensed the most.

Misty was in her usual spot on the armchair, while Fudge and Bailey were asleep on the rug in the living room, both of them facing the direction of the door as if keeping an eye on where the humans had gone. Their ears pricked at Tabitha's and Raff's footsteps and they trotted over, breaking the tension that Tabitha felt at being back in the house with Raff after a night out together.

Tabitha dropped to her knees and ruffled both of their ears. 'Did you wonder where I'd gone?'

'They probably think it's morning and time for food,' Raff said. 'Do you need help with them?'

'No, it's okay, thanks.' She stood back up. 'I might as well feed them now, then crash. I'm struggling to keep my eyes open.'

'Yeah, me too. I'll get my stuff from the office in the morning.' Raff screwed up his face. 'You know what I mean – when I wake up later this morning. So, if you're sure…' He stepped closer and kissed her cheek, his stubble brushing her skin.

Tabitha considered pulling him in for a proper kiss but faltered and the moment was gone. As she watched him retreat up the stairs to the spare room, she wondered if he'd been thinking the same but had decided he might be pushing his luck...

Tabitha fed the dogs and let them out into the garden for a wee, yawning as she waited for them, tiredness sweeping over her. With them back inside and the doors locked, Tabitha made her way to the bedroom in a daze of sleepiness, hoping that Bailey and Fudge would settle back down. She managed to clean her teeth and get into her pyjama shorts and vest top. The effects of the alcohol had worn off long ago, with the hit of fresh air after leaving the club a tonic before the long taxi drive back. And now, as she slid beneath the covers, her mind whirled as fast as a merry-go-round as she thought back on the night with Ollie and Raff. Mostly her head was consumed by Raff, imagining him lying in the spare bedroom not a million miles away from her...

24

Tabitha's eyes flew open, uncertain what had woken her. Sunshine poured through a gap in the curtains. She groaned and rubbed her eyes, wanting desperately to go back to sleep.

A woman screamed.

With her heart racing, Tabitha threw off the cover, making Fudge jump awake. Her head was spinning as she launched herself out of bed. Growling, Bailey skittered to the open door.

It was Thursday morning. Tabitha frowned. What was special about Thursdays... *Shit, the cleaner*. She shot from the room, with the dogs chasing after her.

Clutching a cloth, the cleaner, Dolores, was pacing across the living room muttering in Portuguese.

Raff, in just his pants, clattered down the stairs. *Shit*.

'*Me desculpa mesmo*,' he pleaded.

Tabitha had no idea what it meant, but it definitely sounded apologetic. She looked between Raff and Dolores. 'What's going on?'

Dolores let out a stream of Portuguese aimed at Raff. Red-faced, he held up his hands.

Shaking her head, Dolores turned to Tabitha. 'I come next week. No more today,' she said firmly as she shoved the cloth into her bag and marched to the front door.

'Shit,' Tabitha repeated out loud as she followed her.

'I say to Cordelia, I not well, I not clean.' Without another word, Dolores slammed the door behind her.

Tabitha retraced her steps back to Raff in the living room. 'I completely forgot she was coming today.'

'Yeah, she got a bit of a shock. I, um, was wearing less than this.' He motioned downwards. Tabitha's eyes trailed over his rather snug-fitting black pants. 'Could have been worse, though.'

'How could your parents' cleaner walking in on you naked be any worse?'

He grinned and motioned between the two of them. 'We could have been in bed together, like the other morning...' He let the words hang.

Tabitha shook her head. 'You're impossible,' she called over her shoulder as she went to the kitchen, not wanting him to see the reaction his words evoked. It was true; it could have been worse. The cleaner wasn't going to say anything to Cordelia and it obviously hadn't bothered Raff to be walked in on like that... Maybe it was time for her to stop worrying quite so much and be a little more carefree. 'Fancy a coffee?'

'Hell yes.'

Instead of going upstairs to put on some clothes, he followed her into the kitchen and leaned against the counter while she switched the coffee machine on.

'Apart from being rudely woken, how are you feeling this morning?' she asked to fill the brief silence.

'Like I haven't had much sleep.'

He was hugely distracting, his muscled arm and the side of his chest just visible out of the corner of her eye as she waited for the coffee to trickle into the pot.

'To be honest, when I heard the door open, I, er, thought it was you. I certainly wish it had been you.'

Tabitha didn't know how to reply to that. Her cheeks flushed uncontrollably at the idea he'd have been okay with it being her. If she was being perfectly honest, it was something that had crossed her mind... But maybe him standing half naked suggesting things like that was to tease her, to make her aware that he could sense the chemistry between them.

The coffee couldn't drip through fast enough. Her thoughts were heading in a direction she really didn't want them to go. Except she did. Why was she hell-bent on nothing happening between her and Raff when her insides were screaming to let it? She'd only known Raff for less than two weeks and in a little more than ten days she'd be leaving the island. So perhaps it was okay to let her thoughts wander to Raff naked in bed and be open to the possibility of something more happening. It may have been a whole drunken thing the other night, but the attraction between them had been obvious and still was.

Tabitha concentrated on the coffee, getting the milk from the fridge and a spoon for the sugar as newfound worry fuelled her thoughts. It had been easy the other night after an unexpected whirlwind of a day getting to know each other, and then again last night at a party, tipsy on a few gin and tonics. The sinking feeling was because the more she got to know him, the harder it would be to have a fling and forget about him. Raff had wheedled his way into her time on Madeira and inched his way into her heart in a way no one ever had, apart from Lewis – and look how that had turned out.

Perhaps he sensed her discomfort. 'I'm going to go change into swim shorts and have a dip in the pool,' Raff said. 'Meet you on the terrace for breakfast?'

'Sure.' Tabitha nodded, relieved when he left the kitchen. She got two mugs from the cupboard and leaned on the counter. He really was distracting, and yet, she enjoyed having someone to share the little things with: eating breakfast together, having someone to chat to and bounce ideas off. Raff was everything she didn't think she wanted and yet, deep down, he seemed to be everything she craved.

Raff was already in the pool when Tabitha emerged with a tray onto the sunlit terrace, the dogs on her heels. His tanned arms sliced effortlessly through the water as he lapped the pool. Tabitha placed the tray with the coffee and bowls of fruit and yogurt on the table and sat down. Fudge settled next to her, his fur soft against her bare leg. She would miss them like crazy when she left. As Raff turned at the end of the pool, his body streamlined in the water, she realised the dogs weren't all she'd miss.

Snatches of lyrics had been forming over the last couple of days – disjointed ideas, but they were slowly shaping into something coherent. She needed to hone them to see if she had something worth continuing with. Tabitha felt inspired by Raff. He was a mystery and he'd intrigued her from the beginning – a worthy subject to focus her songwriting on, at least.

A message from Cordelia in their WhatsApp group brought Tabitha thudding back to reality.

Morning, Tabitha. As we didn't hear from you yesterday, we just wanted to check that everything's okay?

With the anticipation of the party the day before, she'd completely forgotten to check in with Cordelia and Rufus. Not that they'd needed to know that she was going out – they'd said they were fine with her doing that for short periods of time, but with Raff here and after the craziness of this morning with the cleaner...

With her heart in her mouth, she thumbed a reply.

So sorry I didn't message you, it was just a busy day and it slipped my mind. All is fine. Bailey and Fudge are sitting with me on the terrace. Misty is sunning herself in the garden. Hope you're still enjoying your time in Tanzania and can relax now.

Tabitha took a photo of the dogs sitting by her feet and attached it to the message. Not that it eased the guilt as she watched their estranged son emerge from the pool, rivulets of water streaming down his torso and dripping onto the paving stones.

Raff grabbed a towel from the sun lounger and rubbed his hair. Tabitha's phone pinged again as he sat down opposite her.

Thank you, Tabitha, you've put my mind at rest. Sunshine and blue skies here and I'm about to take a dip in the pool. Bliss. Enjoy the rest of your day.

Tabitha sent a thumbs up in reply.

'Is that my parents?' Raff asked, slicking a hand through his damp hair.

'Yeah. I forgot to message them yesterday. Your mum scheduled the days for me to check in with them.' Tabitha picked up her coffee and blew on it.

'Huh, figures. She's always been a control freak – everyone has to revolve around her.'

'I don't really mind. She's not the first owner to request me to check in with them.'

'The cleaner hasn't said anything to them?'

'Dolores said she was going to tell your mum she was ill and didn't come round.' Tabitha looked across the table at Raff, trying her hardest to focus on his face rather than his water-beaded chest. 'It's going to be difficult not telling them the truth when they get back, you know, about you, about what really happened to Fudge. I don't like the thought of lying to them.'

'You won't technically be lying, just omitting a few things.' He looked at her in a way she couldn't quite figure out; was there amusement there or a hint of sadness? 'I'll be gone before they get back – there will be no trace of me.'

Tabitha assumed he was trying to reassure her, but his words left her feeling empty. In a little over a week, Tabitha's time on Madeira would be over, and Raff would be exiting her life as quickly as he'd appeared. She needed to sift through her emotions and work out how she really felt about, well, everything. She'd been putting it off for too long, spending the last twelve months in denial, pushing her feelings to the back of her mind as she bounced from place to place, never staying long enough to connect with anyone other than her four-legged friends. Here her experience had been completely different. Raff would be hard to walk away from, yet she realised it would be him walking away from her. Well, not technically her, he would leave Madeira before she did, to get on with his life, the same way she needed to get on with hers.

Tabitha sipped her hot coffee. 'I wasn't completely truthful when I said last night that it had never crossed my mind that Ollie and I could be more than just friends.'

'Where did that come from?' Raff laughed.

Tabitha shrugged. 'I don't know. I've been thinking about a lot of things. I loved him to bits – I mean as a friend – but, admittedly, there were times when I noticed just how damn attractive he was.'

'Was?'

'Oh, well, he still is, but I don't fancy him. Not any longer. And I didn't really back then. I appreciated his good looks, but it was his friendship I treasured. There were times when I wondered if we could take our relationship from friends to lovers without damaging it. I was being honest with you, though, about my one and only kiss with him turning out to be a big turn-off.'

'For you,' Raff said with a smirk. 'Once again, I'll stress it was mostly definitely not how he felt.'

'Maybe not, but I'm sure he's over it now. I'm pretty certain we'll never be able to return to having as good a friendship as we used to have.' A light breeze swayed the leaves of the banana plant behind Raff. Everything about the garden was soothing, sun drenched and tropical, the perfect combination of various greens with an occasional pop of colour. Tabitha put her coffee mug down. 'What about you and Mai? How are you going to feel seeing her getting married?'

'I'm actually really happy for her.'

'You are?'

'We were friends and it was only my mistaken belief that there could be something more that made me attempt anything. To tell you the truth, it's a relief knowing that she's with someone and happy. We were never best friends like you and Ollie, but we've managed to stay in touch over the years. Knowing she's comfortable enough to invite me to her wedding, that's good enough for me.'

It was suddenly clear to Tabitha that they were both going through a similar experience, confronting people from their past and finding a way to move on without holding a grudge. 'You've made peace with the fact that you're just friends then and that's all it's ever going to be?'

'Yep, 100 per cent. I got over being rejected a long time ago, but her getting married is closure. My life mostly feels topsy-turvy, mainly to do with my relationships, so to know absolutely where I stand with her is a good thing and much needed.'

'Do you mean romantic relationships or the relationship you have with your parents?' Tabitha asked gently.

'Both. My relationship with my parents has been strained since we moved here. Romantically, it's a bit of a shitshow too. Me and my ex wanted such different things, and, to be truthful, it's been a bit like that with every girlfriend, which makes me think either I'm the problem or I go for the wrong type.' He looked sheepishly at her. 'I should be a recluse, live by myself in the middle of nowhere with just a dog or two for company.' He reached down and scratched Bailey behind his ears.

'I've often thought that might be the best thing for me too...' Tabitha gazed across the garden to the smudge of deep blue ocean merging with the paler sky. 'But then I'm not sure if I could cut it living so far from anywhere. I like the grit and pulse of city living, but I've been spoilt over the last year staying in the heart of Paris and Barcelona.'

'It's the same as anything, when you live in the country you crave the things you're missing from city living and vice versa. I wonder if there is such a thing as a perfect place?'

'My parents have found it.'

'They have?'

'A restored cottage in the Devon countryside with a patch of land where they grow veg and have chickens, which also happens to be within driving distance of beaches and a town with lots going on.' Tabitha shrugged. 'The best of everything. Although, to be fair, they did spend four decades moving from country to country for Dad's job, so they lived in enough places to figure out what they wanted. I don't think I've done that yet.'

'You've not travelled enough?'

'I'm not sure I'll ever not want to travel.'

'I feel the same, but I also want to put down roots, you know. Find somewhere that I feel at home.'

'That's not here on Madeira?'

'God, no.' Raff shook his head and drained the remainder of his coffee. 'And it's definitely not in London either, although I'll have to head back there before my parents return. Ah,' he waved his hand, 'one day I'll figure it out.'

Tabitha met his eyes. 'I'm sure I will too.'

'Hey, I was just wondering,' he said, holding her gaze. 'Seeing as I've been your wingman – so to speak – at Ollie's party, how do you fancy being my plus-one at Mia's wedding on Saturday?'

'Really?'

'Yeah. She left it as an open invitation for me to bring someone along, which I never intended to, but I know she'll be relieved if I don't rock up on my own and, uh, I'd really like you to come with me.' He looked bashful, his usual confidence having vanished. His tanned cheeks might even have flushed a little.

Tabitha adored that he'd asked her. 'Yeah, I'd love to come, thank you.'

'Great, it is an overnight thing with a celebratory breakfast on the Sunday too, so you might have to see if Julie can feed and check on the dogs while we're away.' He scraped his chair back, stood and flicked the towel over his shoulder. 'I'm going to shower and head down to the office to work. I'm sure you've got stuff to get on with too. See you later.'

An overnight thing. That was all Tabitha could focus on as Raff retreated inside. Was he embarrassed? Or had he asked quickly and escaped in case she changed her mind? It was obvious that they both wanted to spend more time with each other and going to a wedding and staying over would certainly allow them to do that. The rush of excitement flooding through her suggested exactly how she felt. She'd considered taking their relationship a step further; perhaps a fling would get him out of her system.

25

The day flew by with Raff locked away in the office at the bottom of the garden and Tabitha switching between working at the dining table and on the terrace. She built on the thoughts that had been floating around her head over the last couple of days. Lyrics tumbled and melodies swirled. Snatches of ideas began to form on the page and in the guitar chords. Lyrics about love lost, about the freedom of being true to yourself, of the tentative steps towards the possibility of new love, a new future. Tabitha hadn't wanted to write about Raff, but somehow his presence and influence had seeped into her and were now forming a song. What he had done was open her up to the idea that she could move on, that she could free herself from the worry of repeating the same mistakes that she had with Lewis.

Elspeth messaged her at lunchtime.

How did the party go? Hope you had a good time. I NEED to hear all about it but rushed off our feet with barn/wedding prep. No time to call at the mo but will do tomorrow evening and we can chat properly. If we're not finished by then, we're going to be screwed, so fingers crossed. Much love, E xxxx

Tabitha sent a quick reply with lots of kisses and wished her luck.

Early in the evening, after Tabitha had finished working, she walked the couple of minutes along the lane to Julie and Anton's house. A fog of tiredness had descended over her as the day had worn on. Four hours' sleep plus a hangover may have been doable when she was twenty-two, but a decade later she was most definitely struggling. She'd got out of the habit of late-night partying; she wanted to blame Lewis, but she'd allowed him to mould her into the partner *he* wanted her to be. Even though she thought she'd be better off on her own, she realised now it wasn't what she wanted. What she wanted was to be with someone who was onboard with how she wanted to live her life, someone who wouldn't try to restrict her, someone who would help her to achieve her dreams instead of crush them. Perhaps that was too much to ask.

Tabitha reached the house and rang the bell. There was a car in the drive, so she assumed someone was home, but when there was no answer, she wondered if Julie was out the back. She went through the side gate and into the garden. She spied movement and spotted Julie in a sun hat pruning climbing roses.

'Julie!' Tabitha called. When Julie waved, she headed down the garden.

'What a lovely surprise,' Julie said with a welcoming smile.

'I came to ask you something, but I thought you might want to know how Fudge is doing as well.'

'That was going to be my first question. I've been wondering how you both are.'

'He's much better. Can even jump down off the bed now.'

'Good, I'm glad.' Julie shaded her eyes. 'I don't suppose you've got time for a drink?'

'Yeah, I'd love one, thanks.' It was the least she could do when she was going to ask a favour. Not only that, she liked Julie's quiet and steady company. She had a calming effect, and didn't seem to have any drama in her life. She was surprisingly easy to talk to as well, which made her feel even more guilty not telling her about Raff.

Julie took off her gardening gloves and left them and the secateurs on the grass. Tabitha walked back up the lawn with her.

'Anton's not home yet,' Julie said, leading the way into the open-plan kitchen and living area. 'Would you like tea, coffee or wine?' She glanced at her watch and smiled. 'It is wine o'clock after all. I'm going to pour myself a glass if you'd like one too?'

'Why not,' Tabitha said. 'Hair of the dog and all that. I went to a party in Funchal last night and have been battling a hangover all day, so a glass of wine might just help.'

'It sounds like you had fun. You went by yourself?' Julie reached into a cupboard for two wine glasses and took a bottle of white wine out of the fridge.

Tabitha felt her cheeks go hot. 'An old friend invited me. Ollie Pereira – you might have heard of him? Pop star, ex-*The Star* winner. He's half Portuguese and has a villa in Funchal where he stays when he's not in his apartment in London.'

'You know him?' Julie's eyes widened. 'I don't know much about popular culture, but I know who Ollie Pereira is. Lots of my students will be incredibly jealous that I'm friends with someone who's friends with him!'

'Yeah, we go way back, friends since before he was famous, but we've drifted apart. It was good to see him again, though. At least it was the start of us repairing our friendship.'

'It sounds as if it was a cathartic experience as well as a fun night.' Julie handed her a glass of wine and led her outside to the patio. They sat facing the garden. Cupping her wine glass, Julie looked at Tabitha. 'So, what did you want to ask me?'

'Oh yes, I nearly forgot.' Tabitha laughed nervously. She was about to bend the truth to Julie again. 'I'm, um, going to be out all day Saturday and overnight – back on Sunday afternoon, so I just wondered if you'd be able to pop in to feed Misty and the dogs?'

'Of course, I'd love to. I can take Bailey and Fudge out for a walk as well if you'd like?'

'Only if it's no trouble.'

'Not at all, they're a joy to look after.' Julie sipped her wine. 'Are you going anywhere nice?'

'Oh, um, only to Funchal again...' She hated lying to Julie, but there was no point unravelling the truth now. 'Although I'm a bit worried about leaving the dogs. Cordelia did say to ask you to look after them if I was out, but I hadn't planned on being away overnight.'

'It will be fine,' Julie said firmly. 'I'd be delighted to look after them, so go and have a great time. No one needs to know.' She paused. 'And how about when you're back on Sunday you come over here for dinner – only if you fancy it and aren't too tired. Anton and I would love to have you over. It would be nice for him to meet you. He's a wonderful cook – I got very lucky marrying him.'

'That's really kind of you; I'd love to, thank you.'

'You can bring Raff with you,' Julie said.

Tabitha looked at her sharply. 'Raff... um...' she mumbled.

'I know he's back.' Julie's gentle voice was filled with amusement. She placed a cool hand on Tabitha's arm. 'I told you I thought I saw him in the garden and also hearing what sounded like a party the other week, I assumed you weren't on your own. And then I saw Raff in the garden again this week. Is everything okay, you know, with him being there?' she said with a more serious tone. 'I don't want to interfere, but I can't ignore the fact that he's at the house with you when presumably he's not supposed to be.'

'No, he's not, but it's fine.' Tabitha laughed. 'It's been a strange couple of weeks. I would have told you, but to begin with I didn't really understand the whole situation with Raff and his parents. Although I'm still not sure I fully understand where it went wrong.'

Julie nodded. 'It's certainly a minefield. But don't worry, I won't say anything – I presume he doesn't want them to know. I'm, um, just surprised you're okay with him being there...'

Tabitha noticed Julie's cheeks flush a little as if she didn't want to ask a more pertinent question. Tabitha could certainly see how it must look from Julie's point of view.

Tabitha took a gulp of wine. 'I wasn't to begin with – it was a bit of a shock him turning up in the middle of the night, but we've kinda got to know each other. It's a long story really... He was staying out in the garden office, but I invited him in. To sleep in one of the spare rooms,' she added, not wanting Julie to get the wrong idea. She decided it was about time she was completely truthful; Julie deserved that much as she'd shown her nothing but kindness. 'And this weekend, I'm going to a wedding with Raff. He invited me. And he came with me to Ollie's party last night. I'm sorry I lied to you, I really didn't want to, it's just been an odd situation.'

'Oh please,' Julie said, batting her hand. 'You've not intentionally lied; I know full well it's Raff who's told you not to say anything. I know he sneaked into the house the last time his parents were away. In Cordelia's eyes, I'm a nosy neighbour,' she looked at Tabitha with a gleam in her eye, 'so I might as well live up to it. Not much gets past me. I should have gone over and said something – not to get rid of him or anything like that, no.' She sighed. 'I wished I'd had the courage to speak to him and invited him to stay here. I, um, I try not to interfere with Cordelia and Rufus and their relationship with Raff. It makes me too angry and just so sad. So I didn't get involved.' She paused. 'Anton and I were never blessed with children, so Raff has always been special to us. You should tell him that I'd love to see him. Well, hopefully I will on Sunday, see you both.'

'You will, yes. Raff's said nothing but lovely things about you.'

Julie flushed, quietly accepting the compliment and the situation. She moved the conversation on to the more comfortable topic of Fudge and Bailey and which levada trail she was going to take them on for a walk while Tabitha was away at the wedding with Raff.

26

It was really rather easy and comfortable living and working with Raff. The drama of the last couple of weeks was in the past and they slotted together, both of them working for a good chunk of the day with Raff only returning to the villa in the evening.

Tabitha was incredibly relieved that Julie now knew the truth about Raff being here and she didn't have to continue lying to her. Raff's reaction had been surprisingly calm: 'not much gets past Julie', followed by, 'she's really invited us over for dinner?'

He didn't say no, though. Tabitha sensed he had as soft a spot for Julie as she had for him. She also noticed the way he said 'us'. The last time she'd been referred to as an 'us' was with Lewis. She'd felt stifled by their relationship and trapped by commitment, but here with Raff she was free and she very much liked the idea of them being 'together'. It felt exciting rather than scary, but then she had swapped the fringes of London for the subtropical beauty of Madeira; it was completely different.

Much like the day before, Friday whizzed by, Tabitha getting more done and written than in the whole of the previous week now her attention could be solely focused on work. It crossed her mind again that she'd been inspired by the events that had unfolded. Perhaps Raff was her muse.

They were eating dinner together that evening when a surprise delivery of flowers arrived from Ollie with a note attached.

> *For your kindness and your forgiveness, which I'm not sure I deserve. You're the best, Tabitha. Beautiful inside and out. Love, Ollie x*

'Yeah right, just friends.' Raff smirked.

Despite brushing the comment off, it did leave her with the niggling thought that her relationship with Ollie had changed beyond all recognition. What were they to each other now?

Raff motioned to the note. 'So why doesn't he deserve your forgiveness? What happened to make you two fall out?'

Tabitha sighed, finished the last bite of the soy-poached chicken and chickpea salad that Raff had made, and told him the whole sorry story.

'I didn't like his music anyway,' Raff said firmly once she'd finished, 'but I like him even less for how he treated you. No wonder you've had nothing to do with him for so long. But hey, with your songwriting success, it turned out you didn't need him anyway.'

Raff's words filled her with joy, because he was right. However much it had hurt at the time, she hadn't needed Ollie. She'd carved a career in a difficult and often cut-throat industry through hard work, perseverance and talent, without stomping on anyone else. She could hold her head high and be proud of what she'd achieved.

Raff took the dogs out for a walk later in the cool of the evening, just as the sun was beginning to descend, and Tabitha took the opportunity to call Elspeth.

The phone rang for ages before Elspeth answered with a tired, 'Hey, I was just about to call you.'

'You sound exhausted,' Tabitha said, curling her legs beneath her on the sofa. This was her favourite spot at this time of the day, sitting on the comfy sofa with the doors open, looking out at the garden which was bathed in the golden light of dusk, the ocean sparkling, the sun beginning to pool onto the horizon.

'I am.' Elspeth sighed. 'Even with Mum and Dad here, there's been a ridiculous amount to do, plus Olivia has been so clingy and will only let me put her to bed. It's been hard. I think she's worried about being at school all day next week – it's a long time for a four-year-old. Plus tiredness and excitement with Granny and Grandad being here and her birthday coming up is not the best combination. Anyway, enough about me, for the first time this week Olivia has actually gone to sleep without too much fuss, Mum and Dad are making dinner and Gethin's still out in the barn ensuring everything is 100 per cent ready for tomorrow. I've poured myself a large glass of much-needed wine and want to hear how the party went with Ollie *and* Raff. You're one lucky, lucky lady.'

'Ollie and I, as you well know, are just friends.'

'Did you talk more?'

'Yeah,' Tabitha said, smoothing out a crease in her maxi skirt. 'As much as you can talk to anyone in a club while drunk. But yeah, we cleared the air; we're talking again.' Elspeth made encouraging 'uh-huh' sounds, allowing her to continue. 'So much has changed for both of us. His fame is off the scale – it's nothing like I've ever experienced. We can never recapture the friendship we once had, but I think I'm okay with that.'

'The main thing is you've reconnected – you must feel better not having the weirdness hanging over you any longer? I know you've struggled with it.'

'Yes, that's true. It wasn't healthy to hold on to so much anger for so long.'

'No, it wasn't, although understandable. As Olivia would tell you – or rather Elsa – let it go... Talking about letting go, what do you think about Ollie and his girlfriend splitting up?'

Tabitha frowned. 'What do you mean? He told me they were separated but keeping it quiet.'

'Well, it's all over social media this evening, so definitely not a secret any more.'

Tabitha swallowed the fluttering feeling in her throat as she thought back to the note that had arrived with the flowers from Ollie, along with Raff's comment about Ollie wanting to be more than just friends. That was the last thing she wanted to focus on, so she decided not to comment. The warm embrace of her family, even this far away, was what felt important.

'I tell you what I am thinking about – as long as you're sure it's still okay for me to come and stay with you in October, then I—'

'Yes!' Elspeth practically screamed down the phone. 'I couldn't think of anything better. We'd love to see you. So you're actually saying you're going to come here after Madeira?'

'It'll depend on a few things as I was planning on staying in Lisbon for a bit, but I miss you guys.'

'We miss you too, Tabs, but I expect you're going to miss Madeira as well, or rather a certain someone.' She chuckled. 'So you made up with Ollie at the party, please tell me you made out with Raff?'

Not that time, Tabitha thought, her mind drifting to that first drunken night. 'No, we didn't, but we did have a good evening together. We talked loads. He was good company and confident, totally fine about going off and chatting to other people, relaxed and up for a good time. The perfect person to go to a party with.'

'So, the opposite of Lewis then...'

'That's not exactly fair, E.'

'No, I know. I'm sorry. It's not that he wasn't fun, it's just he held you back. It happened slowly over time so it wasn't obvious. Hindsight helps, doesn't it?'

'It certainly does.' Tabitha stared wistfully out at the garden, the edges tinged with darkness. The remnants of the sun had sunk below the hedge and only a wash of burnt orange and fiery red remained.

'So, you had a good night and the two of you went back to the villa and...'

'And I told him he could stay in the guest room. It was crazy him sleeping out in the office.'

'Huh, in the guest room. And the owners are still unaware of him being there?'

'Yep, and I plan to keep it that way.' Even after yesterday's events with the cleaner. 'Although I feel guilty, because I'm betraying their trust...'

'It's a difficult one, particularly if they discover he's been there and you haven't said anything...' Elspeth trailed off. 'Sorry, I know you're worried. But what's worse? Being upfront and telling them the truth or them finding out that you lied to them?'

'I know you're right. It's just Raff...'

'Like I said, a dilemma. Sorry I can't be more help. But, talking about Raff, what have you two been doing since you invited him to stay in the house?' Her words were loaded. Tabitha imagined her curled up in an armchair with her glass of wine, anticipating Tabitha divulging juicy gossip.

'Not much, apart from working.'

'And Raff...'

'Working too.'

'Uh, that's so disappointing. I want gossip. I *need* gossip!'

'Well,' Tabitha said, wondering if it was a good idea to tell her sister this or not, but feeling the need to tell her something. 'I am going to a wedding with Raff tomorrow.'

'As his date?'

'Well, his plus-one.'

'So a date then.' She could hear the grin in Elspeth's voice. 'Cool. I look forward to finding out how it goes. It's going to be a good weekend for weddings.'

'I really hope everything goes well for you guys tomorrow.'

'You and me both. This will be such a good income strand for us. The setting is, well, just lush. I can't wait for you to see it finished.'

'Pop lots of photos on Instagram.'

'Don't worry, I will. The same goes for you too. Plus a pic of Raff would be nice.'

'Yeah, yeah,' Tabitha said, smiling.

They said goodbye, Elspeth to finish her wine and have an early night before the excitement and stress of the first wedding hosted in their newly renovated barn, and Tabitha to sit quietly and contemplate how easy her life felt right at that moment, far from the stresses of real life, in a bubble on the island of Madeira as she waited for Raff to return with the dogs.

She opened up the photos on her phone and scrolled to the one she'd taken of her and Raff in the pool. Beaming tanned faces, their arms around each other, Raff's chest on display... She opened up her conversation thread with Elspeth on WhatsApp, attached the photo, paused for a moment, then clicked send.

Within ten seconds, Elspeth replied.

OMG, Tabs! How is he just a friend?!

Tabitha smiled as she wrote a reply.

Just because he's good-looking doesn't mean anything has to happen. I'm enjoying his company.

Elspeth replied with seven laughing emojis, swiftly followed by:

But, seriously, you two look gorgeous together and it's SO nice to see you looking happy. Have fun at the wedding! ;-);-);-) Xxxxx

Tabitha sent a message wishing her and Gethin luck again for tomorrow. She clicked back on the photo of her and Raff. She did look happy. A spontaneous selfie with both of them grinning, smiles that reached their eyes. The realisation that she *was* happy took her by surprise. It wasn't that she'd been miserable while travelling around, but she'd been content to be on her own. Being around people felt too much like hard work, making connections, having meaningful conversations that didn't stray into personal territory. Yet here, despite the ups and downs, she'd begun to crave Raff's company and his friendship. His behaviour and the annoyance he'd caused still hadn't put her off wanting to spend time with him, because it felt easy and natural. He had a way of making her feel good about herself and through the upset, disappointment and uncertainty that splitting with Lewis had caused, Raff showing up had had a positive impact.

Raff returning with the dogs interrupted Tabitha's thoughts. He swaggered in through the bifold doors, followed by Bailey and Fudge, who, after lapping their bowls of water, flopped down panting on the cool tiles.

'Did you see the sunset?' Raff said as he hung up the leads.

'Yep, it was lush. Just one of the things I'm going to miss.' Elspeth's words played over in Tabitha's head, making her go hot. She really would miss Raff too. She cleared her throat. 'What time do we need to leave tomorrow?'

'I was going to book a taxi for eleven, unless you're happy to drive?'

'Yeah, I don't mind driving.' At least with them staying overnight, she'd still be able to drink. She looked at Raff as he sank into the armchair. 'What's the dress code? And, oh my goodness, I should take a present, shouldn't I?'

Raff laughed. 'I've got them a present, which we can sign from both of us.' He met her eyes. 'And dress code is a smart summer vibe.'

'So a summery playsuit will be suitable?'

'I think anything you put on would be suitable, but yeah, that sounds perfect.' He held her gaze and her heart beat faster.

Was this the build-up to the inevitable? The flirtation had continued, even if it was a little more restrained than it had been during those first couple of days. Since then, they'd slowly got to know each other, peeling back the layers of their past, the experiences and relationships that had shaped them both, making the anticipation of the inevitable all the more electric.

27

Beautiful and captivating were the words that sprang to mind as Tabitha admired the half Portuguese, half Japanese bride in a lace wedding dress, the bodice sculpted before flowing into a white skirt. Her smile was infectious and she glowed with happiness. It wasn't hard to see why a teenage Raff had fallen head over heels in love with Mai.

The groom was as handsome as his bride was beautiful, his English and Spanish heritage woven into the day, along with Mai's Japanese and Portuguese roots.

As they stood on the sun-drenched hotel terrace overlooking the ocean, a glass of *poncha* flavoured with passion fruit clasped in their hands, Raff hooked his arm in Tabitha's. It was a perfect start to the tropical-themed wedding and Tabitha soaked up the moment. Beyond the beach below, dotted with umbrellas, sun loungers and people, the ocean stretched endlessly, while in the other direction were the terracotta rooftops of Funchal and its mountainous backdrop, a hazy green in the glorious afternoon sunshine, the tallest peaks obscured by drifting white clouds.

Tabitha and Raff had arrived at the hotel an hour earlier,

parked the car and had been shown to their room. *Their* room. Tabitha had put her bag next to the bed on the side she normally slept on while Raff had made a point of putting his on the sofa. She hadn't said anything.

Then, on the hotel's terrace, where the wedding party had met for drinks, Raff had introduced Tabitha as his friend to the bride and groom, Mai and Edward, and to Mai's parents, before they mingled with the other guests.

A warmth filled her heart as much as the sun warmed her bare shoulders. Her sleeveless blue and white patterned playsuit was perfect for the location and occasion. As they stood chatting to people, with Raff's arm casually around her waist, it took all her resolve to focus on the conversation rather than the feel of him through the thin material as he caressed her hip with his thumb. Whether intentional or not, it felt good.

Mai and Edward's wedding ceremony took place in the hotel's grounds, a beautiful private spot away from the terrace that overlooked the vibrant and colourful beach. White chairs lined the lawn, leading to an archway of dark green leaves entwined with white flowers. The bride and groom stood alongside the best man, who wore a bright orange strelitzia buttonhole, and the bridesmaids in sunny yellow dresses clutching small white and dark green bouquets. Tall palms cast shade around the edges of the lawn, while the deep green of Monstera plants, with their large, tattered heart-shaped leaves, were the perfect backdrop.

Raff's arm was warm against Tabitha's as they sat together and watched his first love marrying her true love. Tabitha squeezed his hand as Mai said her vows; she hoped this would be closure for him.

The sit-down meal was in a large and airy room in the hotel, with its own bar and doors opening out on to the beachside terrace. The tropical theme continued in the white tables and chairs which were decorated with Monstera leaves as placemats, and saffron-yellow and zingy-orange flowers. There was shrimp cocktail to start with, followed by roasted grouper with chorizo on a bed of asparagus risotto, finished off with a cooling tropical fruit sorbet served with passion fruit liqueur.

Marriage wasn't anything Tabitha had ever considered, but she had to admit, bar Elspeth and Gethin's wedding, this one on Madeira was pretty special.

The evening reception kicked off with dancing, followed a little later by sushi canapés which Tabitha happily tucked in to while Raff chatted with Mai's family. She got talking to the groom's best friend and his wife, who lived in Cornwall.

Darkness had descended by the time Mai came over, hooked her arm in Tabitha's and stole her away.

'I just wanted to say how happy Raff looks,' Mai said as she led her out onto the terrace. 'You both do. I'm so pleased he's found someone.'

'Oh, we're not actually together.'

A slight frown creased Mai's flawless skin. 'Really? You look so comfortable with each other.'

'I guess we are, as friends.' They stopped beneath a floodlit palm tree glowing a deep zesty orange. 'It's a bit of a strange situation how and why we've ended up here together, but we do get on well.'

'I can see that.'

Tabitha's heart beat faster, knowing that the attraction between her and Raff was obvious to other people, certainly to someone who knew him well.

'It's been a beautiful wedding,' Tabitha said, wanting to deflect the attention away from herself.

'Thank you.' Mai smiled. 'We were a little worried that the mix of cultures would be a bit of a mess, but I don't think it's been too shabby.' Her English was flawless, her accent only slight and not one Tabitha would have been able to place had she not known her heritage. Raff had said she spoke Portuguese, Japanese, Spanish and English perfectly. Tabitha had picked up French, Spanish and German as a child travelling from place to place, but not with the fluency Mai had.

'It's been a wonderful day. I've pretty much spent my whole life travelling, so I appreciate the mix of cultures. I think you've blended them successfully.' Tabitha sipped her wine. 'Raff said you two met when you were working together?'

'Ah, it feels like a lifetime ago.' She looked wistful for a moment, then laughed. 'I presume he's told you the story about me turning him down?'

'He had mentioned it, yes.' Tabitha grinned.

'Honestly, I thought of him like a younger brother. He was sixteen when we first met and by the time he plucked up the courage to kiss me, the last thing I was looking for was a relationship. I'd had my heart broken and the idea of being involved with someone I loved as a friend did not sit comfortably. He had confidence, I'll give him that. I hated letting him down, but at that time in my life and the age we were, it just felt wrong.'

'I've experienced a friendship not feeling right as a romance, so I totally get that.'

'The thing is, if it had been a few years later, and perhaps if he'd simply asked me out rather than kissing me with no warning, I might have said yes.' Mai touched Tabitha's arm. 'But I think it worked out for the best. For all his demons, for all the stuff he's working through, he's a catch.' Mai raised a sculpted eyebrow. 'I eventually found my soulmate.' She glanced towards her new husband chatting to Raff and a couple of other guests on the threshold of the hotel. 'But it took a long time; I hope it doesn't take so long for Raff.' She gave Tabitha a look which she assumed was trying to convey that she meant her.

'You still live on Madeira?' Tabitha asked, eager again to change the subject.

'My parents do, but Ed and I live in Lisbon now, although my heart belongs to the island.'

'It's not hard to see why.'

'How long are you here for?' Mai asked.

'Only another week. I arrived at the beginning of September.'

'That's a shame; although I presume Raff won't be staying either.' She glanced beyond Tabitha's shoulder, waved and nodded at someone. 'I actually only thought he was coming back for our wedding; I didn't realise he was staying at his parents' house while they were away.' She shook her head. 'I hope he works things out with them; for his sake, not theirs.' Her tone was filled with bitterness. 'He deserves to be happy.' She nodded again at whoever was catching her attention and placed a cool hand on Tabitha's arm. 'The only trouble with being the bride is there are too many people to talk to in too short a time.' She kissed Tabitha on each cheek. 'I'll let you get back to Raff; it really is good to meet you and I hope we'll see each other again.' Her smile as she left to be embraced by one of the other guests was filled with warmth. It left Tabitha with the longing to be a part of something, whether as a couple or seeing her family again.

Raff was deep in conversation with the groom, but everyone was welcoming and chatty so Tabitha wasn't left alone for long. Friends of the couple and then Mai's aunt and uncle came over and chatted to her, and once again she was enveloped in the spirit of the evening. Mai was so happy, it made Tabitha wonder if she'd ever feel that way, if she'd ever be able to let someone back into her heart without the fear of them stifling and restricting her. Perhaps someone who could love her for who she was wasn't out there. Yet when her eyes travelled across the terrace to Raff, the feeling he evoked had an intensity that she'd never felt before. It scared and elated her in equal measure.

After the toast at midnight, Mai and Edward thanked everyone and bade them all goodnight, retreating to their honeymoon suite to cheers and whoops. Tabitha escaped back out on to the moon-bathed terrace.

The rhythmic swoosh of the waves rolling onto the shore below before being sucked back into the dark ocean filled the starry night. They'd started the day on the hotel terrace and she was ending the evening there, after an elegantly tropical wedding. Tabitha wondered how the wedding had gone in Elspeth and Gethin's newly renovated barn and if the weather had been as kind to them in Wales as it had been on Madeira. She was tempted to message her, but at gone midnight, she hoped her sister was heading to bed after an exhausting but hugely successful day.

'Hey,' Raff said, joining her by the wall and resting his arm across her shoulder. 'Sorry I've been gone so long.'

'Oh, that's fine; everyone's really friendly. Mai's lovely,' she said, slipping her arm around his waist.

'I'm glad you like her.'

Away from the light spilling on to the terrace, the mid-September air had a delicious subtropical heat, yet Tabitha was grateful for his comforting warmth. She wished she could bottle the feeling, the quiet contentment and the ease of Raff's presence, there with her but not an intrusion. Looking out at the ocean, she felt as free as she'd ever done. That was what she wanted to recapture, the freedom of following her own path wherever that took her. There was no place to return to, not anywhere she thought of as home, not even her parents' cottage – a place she loved but somewhere she'd never lived. Even if she went and stayed with Elspeth, it could only be temporary, and then what? The nature of moving from place to place while growing up meant that she'd never had roots and when she'd tried to settle down, it had felt restrictive, rather than nurturing. But she'd grown over the past year, through the experience of new places and meeting new people, even if they were fleeting moments.

'Do you want another drink before the bar closes?' Raff's deep voice merged with the rush of the waves.

'No, I think I'm okay, thanks. It feels about time to call it a night.' Her heart skittered at her words. After Mai and Edward had been cheered off, the guests had slowly begun to drift away. Tabitha and Raff were two of the few remaining. Part of her wanted to head to their room to see where things would lead, and yet where they were standing was a blissful spot overlooking the moon-streaked ocean and she was curious to know how Raff had found the evening. 'How are you feeling after seeing Mai getting married?'

'Like I've finally had closure. She's in love with someone else who she's going to spend the rest of her life with, so if this isn't closure, then I'm doomed to let my love go unrequited forever. I think it's time I move on from a lot of things – a bit like you and Ollie moving on from your feud.'

'It was my reaction that forced us apart.'

'Because of *his* shitty behaviour.' He squeezed her tight. 'But, either way, you've made up now and the past is behind you. I need to move forward too. Something I've been trying to do for a long time. With the completion of the house sale with my ex next week, that link will be severed and I'll finally be out of a financial mess, which will make it much easier to move on, although to where, I have absolutely no idea...' He stared out over the dark ocean. Tabitha followed his gaze to the rippling waves that glinted silver as they neared the shore, building up into foaming peaks before breaking with a whoosh.

'It's been a good day.' Raff turned to her. 'Thank you for coming with me.'

'Thank you for inviting me.'

In the brief moment as they looked at each other, Tabitha considered how easy it would be to reach up and kiss him. Like that drunken kiss in the hallway. It felt longer than a couple of weeks ago. Except it wouldn't be a drunken mistake now... and the thought sent her heart racing.

Raff took her hand and the moment was broken as he led her across the terrace towards the cluster of remaining guests and the light, laughter and music spilling out into the darkness. Calls of goodnight echoed after them as they retreated inside and went upstairs, her heart skipping with each step.

They were both quiet as Raff closed the door to their room and Tabitha switched on one of the bedside lamps. The room faced the ocean and the sound of the waves lapping the shore overpowered the distant night-time noises of Funchal.

Tabitha was riddled with expectation, nervousness and anticipation and her stomach twisted in a knot. She remembered Mai talking about Raff's confidence when he'd kissed her as a twenty-year-old. Tabitha could do that: quit worrying that sleeping together would mess up what they had and just kiss him; she didn't think he would say no. She turned to him and opened her mouth.

'It's okay; I'll sleep on the sofa,' Raff said. 'You can have the bed.'

Maybe he wasn't feeling quite the same way after all...

'Don't be silly,' she said, busying herself by taking the cushions off the bed and putting them on the chair so she didn't have to meet his eyes. 'You're not going to sleep on the sofa when there's a perfectly good king-sized bed.' She almost said, 'It's not as if we haven't slept in the same bed before,' but stopped herself. There was chemistry and an attraction, but she'd been worried about taking their fledgling friendship to the next level and he might be thinking that too. Or perhaps he'd simply played on the flirtation to get her to say yes to him staying. Perhaps she was a fool for thinking there was actually something between them when all he'd been doing the whole time was getting his own way...

She riffled in her bag for her pyjama shorts and vest top along with her wash things, while Raff used the bathroom. As soon as he came out, Tabitha shot into the en suite, feeling ridiculously self-conscious, clutching her night clothes so she could get changed in private.

Tabitha finished in the bathroom, switched off the light and closed the door. Raff was already in bed wearing a T-shirt; she remembered his comment about usually sleeping naked. Apparently not tonight.

He met her eyes and smiled. 'I'm setting an alarm so we're not late for breakfast.'

'Good idea,' she said, slipping into bed next to him.

He switched off his phone and put it on the bedside table. 'Night, Tabitha.'

'Night,' she replied lamely, rolling away from him onto her side and tucking her hand beneath the pillow.

The bed was huge. The space between them might as well have been filled with barbed wire, the way they were sticking to their own sides. If Tabitha moved over any further, she'd roll right off. Her thoughts turned to the conversation she'd had with Raff about the time she'd shared a bed with Ollie and they'd ended up kissing. She'd already kissed Raff and, even in her drunken state, she remembered it had been mind-blowingly good, the complete opposite of when she'd kissed Ollie all those years ago. Was Raff just being a gentleman because he didn't quite know where he stood with her? Maybe he was refraining from trying anything on because in a week they'd be parting ways anyway. Maybe he was waiting for her to make the first move... She was second-guessing everything. But why complicate the situation? Why indeed...

Tabitha's head was in overdrive. She moved slightly until she was staring up at the shadowed ceiling, every fibre of her aware of Raff next to her. She should have kissed him earlier, broken the tension *before* they'd got into bed. She assumed he was asleep; his quiet breathing had become deeper and steadier as she lay there tense and unbelievably awake. Presumably being in bed with her hadn't played on his mind like this.

After the day she'd had, it would have been difficult to sleep anyway, but it seemed impossible now with her head consumed by Raff while her body longed for him. Her thoughts returned to that night years ago, in the student house in Cardiff when she and Ollie had snogged. They were friends in bed together and she'd gone to sleep knowing that was all they were, but what had Ollie done? Had he wanted more? Had he lain awake watching her sleep, wondering if he should try to wake her, kiss her again, turn something tentative into something passionate? She knew then, and she was certain now, that she'd only ever wanted to be friends with Ollie, but with Raff... With less than a week left, what did she have to lose?

Feeling uncomfortable and irate at not being able to sleep, she rolled over. Encased in a T-shirt, Raff's back was broad and strong. She shuffled to get comfortable and her foot connected with his calf. He murmured and rolled over into the centre of the bed. Tabitha held her breath as his face stopped inches from hers, his eyes still closed.

He yawned and reached out. His fingers touched her collarbone and glided up to her cheek.

'Are you awake?' he mumbled through a second yawn.

'Uh-huh. I can't sleep.'

'Oh.' Raff brought his hand back to his face and rubbed his eyes. 'Why not?'

'I can't stop thinking about things.'

'About what?'

Tabitha considered lying, but where would that get her? Better to be brave and be turned down than to never know. Something Raff himself had told her. 'About you.'

28

Raff's eyes shot open, slowly fixing on her face as if seeing her for the first time. 'What about me?'

'I was thinking whether or not to kiss you again.'

Raff swallowed. 'And, er, have you come to a decision?'

Her gaze dropped from his eyes to his full lips. Her memory of kissing them was hazy. She'd enjoyed herself tonight and had drunk plenty, but it had been a sophisticated wedding with food and no lethal shots. Unlike their first drunken snog, this time Tabitha planned on remembering every single second.

She shuffled closer until Raff's breath was hot on her face. Leaning in, she brushed her lips against his before ducking her hand beneath his T-shirt and smoothing it across his muscular chest. She kissed him deeply, and he responded, kissing her gently, but enough to send a thrill coursing through her body.

She pulled away slightly, wanting to gauge his reaction. In the darkness of the hotel room, she could just make out his grinning face.

'Does that answer your question?'

'I should say.'

It was as if time stood still, the two of them drinking each other in, weighing up the next move and whether it would be a mistake or not. Perhaps this would be the way they'd truly find out how they felt about each other. The last couple of weeks had been a mishmash of emotions, along with the realisation that being on her own wasn't the most important thing but being with the right person was. Whether Raff was the right person or not, she was uncertain, but he could be.

Raff broke the spell, kissing her with a ferocious passion that erased the nonchalance he'd gone to bed with, seemingly unbothered about exploring the possibility of romance. She matched his passion and kissed him back, intending to take things a whole lot further.

Raff smoothed his hands up her bare skin and tugged her top off. His weight on top of her as he rolled her over sent tingles shooting everywhere. Her fingers were just as eager, exploring his firm tattooed chest with enthusiasm. She grasped the edge of his T-shirt and pulled it up and over his head.

With their eyes closed, legs entwined, fingers caressing, lips exploring, they filled the space in the centre of the bed that only a short time before had felt like no man's land. Tabitha was glad nothing more had happened that first drunken night; it would have massively got in the way of the relationship they'd slowly built on, the flirting and attraction meaning this moment was all the more wanted.

Tabitha slid her hands downwards, tracing the firm contours of Raff's stomach. She smiled, knowing she'd reached his Smurf tattoo even though she couldn't see it. She trailed her fingers even lower.

'Arse,' Raff said, catching hold of her hands. 'I so want to do more, but I don't have a condom.'

Tabitha eased her hands out from beneath his, noticing the

disappointment in his eyes. She smiled knowingly, tugged the waistband of his pants down and whispered, 'It's just as well I do, then.'

* * *

Tabitha woke before the alarm to sunlight easing through the gap in the curtains, Raff naked and a feeling of utter contentment sweeping through her. The uncertainty, worry and awkwardness she'd gone to bed with had been erased by a night of passion. As she lay there, relishing the warmth of Raff against her bare skin and the feel of his chest rising and falling, she didn't want the moment to end. A night with Raff had been everything she'd hoped for and more. There was no regret, like there would have been two weeks ago, only a longing to repeat it and keep repeating it. She banished that thought. She was going to try not to think beyond this morning and continue to live in the moment for as long as possible.

The alarm cut through the quiet. Raff groaned, reached out his hand for his mobile and swiped it off.

'Morning,' he said groggily. His frown at being rudely awoken morphed into a smile as he opened his eyes fully and looked at her.

'Morning,' she said, unable to stop grinning as she drank him in.

He yawned and stretched, folding his arms around her and pulling her close, his leg sliding between hers as they kissed.

'So, breakfast with everyone, huh,' Tabitha said, raising an eyebrow.

'We've got a bit of time,' Raff said cheekily, smoothing his hand along the curve of her hip and caressing the inside of her thigh, leaving her barely able to breathe. He kissed her neck as he gently pushed her back. 'Or we could order room service and have breakfast in bed...'

* * *

They did make it to breakfast, although they were the last to arrive. Tabitha was sure from the grin Edward gave them and the look that passed between Mai and Raff that they had a pretty good idea about what had kept them. They joined everyone at the long table and Tabitha basked in being loved up as Raff's hand rested on her thigh. Everything about him had surprised her, from his unexpected arrival to the strength of her feelings, but she relished all of it.

After tucking into a full English breakfast, and once everyone had said goodbye to Mai and Edward who were heading off on their honeymoon, Tabitha and Raff spent a couple of hours sunning themselves on the hotel beach before packing their bags, checking out and retrieving the car. On their way out of Funchal, they stopped off so Tabitha could buy a box of *pastéis de maracuja* for Julie and Anton, then, with the windows wound down, they whizzed along the coast road back towards the quieter southwest side of the island.

Raff connected his phone to the car stereo and was quizzing Tabitha about the songs she'd written as he searched for them.

'Now, this one,' Raff said at a particularly upbeat song Tabitha had co-written with a young and up-and-coming pop star. 'This has got soul. I like it. I like it a lot.'

April's voice was husky, the thumping beat catchy. Tabitha had intended for there to be more grittiness to the song than just fluffy pop and she was impressed he could see that. 'And you're not taking the piss?' She snatched her eyes away from the road to glance at him.

'No, absolutely not. I can appreciate a good song when I hear it, even if it's not my taste in music.'

Tabitha liked the way their easy-going banter had continued. On the beach they'd talked about the night before, both of them grinning like crazy at each other as they'd acknowledged their mutual enjoyment, which had put Tabitha at ease. There may have been the briefest moment at breakfast after Mai had caught her eye and smiled knowingly, when Tabitha had felt self-conscious that her friendship with Raff had moved on, but alone with him now, she'd never felt more comfortable. They slotted together as if somehow he was a missing part she hadn't realised she'd been without. She gulped back a wave of emotion that threatened to spill over into tears.

After a social time in Funchal, the serenity of the villa wasn't lost on Tabitha as they arrived back. It wasn't that she craved peace – many of the places she'd been happiest were in the bustling and pulsing heart of a city, yet there was something about this place that soothed her. Or perhaps it had more to do with the company. She was dying to see her sister, brother-in-law and nieces, but she didn't want to think about leaving Raff.

They dumped their bags in the villa and retrieved an excited Bailey and Fudge. Raff took Tabitha's hand as they walked along the lane with the dogs to Julie and Anton's.

Tabitha glanced at him. 'Are you sure you're okay seeing them again?'

'This is a good thing.' He squeezed her hand. 'I feel bad about not visiting for so long. I miss them.'

Tabitha was conscious of the emotion tugging at his words as they reached the house. Raff briefly hesitated before knocking on the door. Moments later, Julie answered with a smile that lit up her face. She looked between them.

'Raff,' she said quietly, her gaze resting on him. 'It's good to see you.' She faltered for a heartbeat, then pulled him into a hug.

A lump formed in Tabitha's throat as Raff wrapped his arms around Julie. *Bloody hell.* She was going to be a mess by the end of the day, let alone by the time she left the island. All she'd wanted to do over the last year was escape, yet here, Madeira had proved to be a refuge, a place for her to heal, to begin to understand her feelings and what she needed to do next, while Raff… Raff had ignited something within her.

Julie released Raff and held him at arm's-length. 'What on earth have you been doing sneaking around all this time?'

Raff smiled warmly at her. 'Don't blame Tabitha for any of this; it's all my doing.'

'Oh, I believe that!' Julie laughed, her light tone matching her look of mock indignation.

'These are for you,' Tabitha said, handing Julie the box of passion fruit tarts. 'A thank you for looking after the dogs and Misty.'

'It was my pleasure.' Julie hugged Tabitha too and ushered them inside. 'This is my husband, Anton,' she said, motioning to where he was uncorking a bottle of wine at the kitchen island.

Tabitha had spotted photos of Anton when she'd visited before, but he looked different in the flesh, his hair greyer and a little dishevelled as if it needed a good cut, his cheeks rounder, giving him a jolliness she hadn't expected.

'I've heard lots about you, Tabitha,' Anton said, putting down the bottle to shake her hand. 'And, Raff, it's good to see you after so long.' Anton hugged him and said something in Portuguese as he patted him on the back. He released him and looked between them both. 'Wine?'

'Yes please,' they both said, smiling at the way they'd said it in unison. Tabitha met Raff's eyes and her heart beat faster.

Anton handed them a glass of wine each and they followed Julie outside. Cubes of skewered beef were roasting on a barbecue, the fat dripping and hissing on the white-hot coals below. Anton turned the skewers while he and Julie tried to work out when they'd last seen Raff. It had been a long time, they concluded, as Julie led Tabitha over to the patio table.

'What are you up to these days, work-wise, Raff?' Tabitha heard Anton ask as he prepared the salads on the table next to the barbecue.

Even in the late afternoon, the patio was a suntrap. A heat haze shimmered across the garden. Sitting there reminded Tabitha a little of her meal with Cordelia and Rufus the evening she'd arrived. Tabitha had been on edge, steeling herself for the inevitable personal questions that had steamrolled her way. It felt different with Julie and Anton. Although Julie had a quiet demeanour, she was actually rather chatty and easy to talk to, while Anton seemed reserved but affable, nowhere near as outgoing as Rufus.

Tabitha picked up her glass of Madeira wine, wedged her sunglasses in her hair and leaned back, enjoying the blissful warmth of the sun on her face.

'Raff seems happy,' Julie said wistfully. 'Calm too and settled somehow. He's different to how he normally is when he's back here – on edge. Although it has been a while.'

Tabitha dropped her sunglasses back over her eyes and looked at Julie. 'Perhaps it's because his parents aren't here.'

'Perhaps...' Julie said. 'Or maybe it has something to do with you.'

Tabitha deflected the insinuation with a laugh. 'To be fair, though,' she said, watching Raff, broad and strong, towering over Anton as they chatted together in Portuguese, 'he certainly seems more relaxed than he did when he first arrived. We've got to know each other a bit and I think we've been good for each other. He's certainly been good for me…' Her sentence trailed off as her thoughts detoured to the pulse-racing memory of just how good he'd been the night before and again that morning.

'Well, good, I'm glad you're happy with him being at the house,' Julie said without a hint of suggestion, even though Tabitha's cheeks were red hot. 'I know it must be a bit awkward Cordelia and Rufus not knowing.'

Tabitha waved her hand. 'Oh, that's a whole other thing.' She felt bad every time she thought about them, knowing she was withholding the truth.

Julie raised her glass. 'Well, let's say no more about that tonight.'

29

An hour later, the four of them sat round the patio table with only the contented sound of munching filling the air as they tucked into Anton's *espetada*, beef skewers seasoned with garlic, salt and bay leaf and dripping with melted butter. A colourful array of salads filled the rest of their plates, along with Anton's homemade *bolo do caco* bread. It was simple but utterly delicious and Raff, a seriously good cook himself, was particularly impressed, asking Anton a load of questions about how he'd prepared the beef and made the bread.

'One of Raff's many talents,' Julie said to Tabitha, 'is making delicious food. He was always eager to try different recipes when he stayed here during the holidays.'

'Because my mum wouldn't let me cook in her kitchen.' Raff raised an eyebrow. 'Mind you, she didn't cook in it either. Least maternal mother ever.'

'Not everyone enjoys cooking, Raff,' Julie said with a calmness Tabitha had become used to. 'But at least you had the opportunity to hone your skills here. I'm always happy for someone to take over in our kitchen. I'm lucky that Anton loves to cook and is good at it.'

'I can tell.' Tabitha motioned to her nearly empty plate.

'I wasn't surprised Raff ended up working as a chef when he was travelling,' Julie continued, 'but I was surprised he gave it up when he went back to the UK.'

Raff pursed his lips. 'I'm not allergic to working hard, I just didn't want to spend sixteen hours a day, six days a week sweating in a kitchen for someone else.'

Anton leaned closer to Tabitha in a conspiratorial way. 'Raff likes to do things on his own terms.'

'Nothing wrong with that,' Raff said with a grin.

The relaxed banter continued as if Julie, Anton and Raff had picked right up from where they'd left off. It was clear how well they knew each other, Raff and Julie in particular. She'd babysat him when his family first moved to Madeira and then looked after him for longer periods when his parents went away. Even when he was old enough to be left on his own, he'd still chosen to go over to Julie and Anton's for dinner and Julie had been happy to encourage her relationship as a surrogate aunt. Yet Tabitha sensed a distance had grown between them, which had probably been inevitable once Raff had left the island for good. Perhaps Julie wasn't too sure where she stood with him now he was an adult and not having seen him in nearly three years.

Raff and Anton got into a conversation about home brewing beer and they disappeared into the kitchen, with Bailey following. Tabitha and Julie remained on the patio with Fudge asleep between them, sipping wine and chatting about the places Tabitha had lived when she was growing up and where she'd stayed while pet sitting. Tabitha was about to show Julie photos of the Paris apartment and the Shetland pony she'd looked after in the Yorkshire Dales but realised she'd left her phone in her bag at the villa. Not that it mattered, plus Julie seemed riveted just by Tabitha's descriptions. And, of course, the conversation soon returned to

Tabitha's time on Madeira, her reconciliation with Ollie and her newly formed friendship with Raff.

'Can I tell you something, Julie?'

'Of course.' Julie's smile made the corners of her grey eyes crinkle. Her quiet demeanour gave Tabitha the sense that there was underlying sadness there, yet with the surprising enjoyment of each other's company, it made Tabitha want to confide in her. 'Going back to what we were talking about earlier. I don't know if Raff is truly happy, but he's made me very happy after a difficult time and a break-up that was for the best but has left me... I don't know how to put it, hurting, I guess.'

'I did wonder if your reason for travelling had been due to heartache.'

'Heartache is the right word, but it's probably not the reason you're thinking of.'

'Oh?'

'I was the one doing the breaking up – not because I'd met someone else, but because we weren't right for each other. I didn't want to remain trapped in a relationship that was stifling me emotionally and creatively.' Tabitha considered how much she could tell Julie without blurting out the whole story. 'So I finished with him and escaped. I've steered clear of men for the last twelve months and then Raff—'

'Broke into your life.' Julie smiled.

'Literally!'

'You're very much alike, you and Raff. Free spirits. Raff has never followed the norm. He escaped his parents the first opportunity he could, although they pushed him away from a young age. He's confided in me over the years, but his reluctance to come back here put paid to the closeness we once had. They had an epic falling out a few years ago – I think I told you about Cordelia and Rufus accusing him of stealing, but I don't know the whole story and they certainly don't confide in us. I've never broached the subject with Raff because he's rarely returned since his parents drove an even bigger wedge between them.' She shrugged. 'You probably know far more than I do... I, er, assume you and Raff are, um, together?'

'It depends on what you mean by together?'

'Romantically involved.'

'After last night, yeah.' Tabitha couldn't help but grin at Julie over the top of her wine glass. She took a large swig to cover her embarrassment.

'Oh!' Julie said, her cheeks flushing. 'I'm so happy for you. For you both. He's quite a catch.'

'He is indeed, although I'm sure it's nothing that's going to last beyond my time here—'

'Oh you don't know that.' Julie frowned and clasped her hands on the table.

'I wasn't looking for a relationship – I'd escaped from one. A bit of fun I can handle. I've never craved getting married or even being in a happy long-term relationship, what my parents or my sister and her husband have. What you and Anton have.'

Julie dropped her gaze from Tabitha's and glanced away.

'Did I say the wrong thing?' Tabitha touched her arm.

'No, you didn't.' She looked back at her. 'I'm being silly. Anton and I are happy enough.'

'You don't sound that sure...'

'Oh, I don't know.' Julie shook her head. 'I see other couples our age and wonder how they manage to keep the spark alive.'

Tabitha was starting to worry about the direction the conversation was going in. Advice about love was the last thing she'd be able to give.

'Anton and I are friends first and foremost, we always have been, that's how our relationship started and then we fell in love and got married.' She sighed. 'But over the years the passion has faded.'

'Surely that's normal?' Tabitha said while thinking her longest relationship hadn't lasted four years, so what did she know.

'Perhaps. We loved each other – we still do,' Julie stressed, 'but both of us expected our lives to be different. I know I certainly did. I thought children would be a part of our future, yet despite trying everything we possibly could to have a child of our own, it wasn't meant to be.'

Tabitha was at a loss as to what to say. Her heart pounded, the upset of what she'd been through the summer before grinding away at her insides, something she'd been trying hard not to divulge to anyone. The enormity of what Julie had confided left her fearful of saying the wrong thing. She had some understanding about the emotional fallout not being able to conceive had. She remembered Elspeth's heartache when she and Gethin had struggled to conceive Olivia. It was obvious from Julie's demeanour, pursed lips, slight clenching of her fists and the way she avoided eye contact that it was an emotion she still struggled with. Yet when Tabitha thought about it, she did know what to say, not because she understood on any level what Julie must have gone through, but because she'd experienced something of what Julie had – that hope, however brief, when she'd come to terms with her pregnancy that was so cruelly and unexpectedly dashed.

Tabitha found her voice. 'That must have been incredibly difficult, to not have a child when you wanted one so badly.'

'It was. We went through so much, with five rounds of fertility treatment, both in the UK and Portugal – the strain on our marriage, well, on everything, financially, emotionally, physically, was hard to deal with and to keep having a disappointing outcome...'

The way she said 'disappointing' made Tabitha sense it was a whole lot more than that. Her tone suggested it was devastating, and yet she was obviously trying hard to keep it together. Tabitha reached for Julie's hand and held it, wanting in some small way to comfort her, knowing she had no words that would.

'IVF was hard enough,' Julie continued, 'and the absolute disappointment of a fertilised egg not being viable is impossible to explain, but what hit me hardest was the treatment being successful twice.' She pressed her lips together and her knuckles tensed white around the stem of her wine glass. 'I got pregnant twice but miscarried both times.'

The word startled Tabitha. She tensed, her hand involuntarily squeezing Julie's. The statistic of one in four pregnancies ending in miscarriage was a stark reminder that she wasn't alone in her grief, yet she'd clammed up over it, not wanting to talk about it, not wanting to share her heartache, unable to put words to the jumble of confusing and surprising feelings after her own miscarriage, even to those closest to her.

'What did I say?' There was concern in Julie's voice as she clasped Tabitha's hand.

The heartache that had toyed with Tabitha over the last year, hitting her when she'd least expected it, sucker-punched her in the gut. Hot tears spilled down her cheeks.

'I'm so sorry.' Tabitha swiped angrily at her face. 'After everything you've been through and here I am crying like this.'

'You should never apologise for letting out your feelings. And there must be a reason for it?'

Tabitha sniffed, feeling foolish for her upset and thankful for Julie's kindness. 'It was the other reason I escaped – actually, the main reason.' She breathed deeply. 'I had an early miscarriage just over a year ago. I was only about seven weeks along.'

'Oh Tabitha, I'm so sorry.' Julie gripped her hand tighter.

'The thing is, unlike you, I didn't want to have a baby. My first reaction to seeing that positive pregnancy test wasn't joy or even nerves, it was utter devastation because I already knew that Lewis and I weren't right for each other.'

Julie frowned. 'And yet you were pregnant?'

'I know how that seems. I still fancied him, that wasn't the problem.' Sadness wrapped around her words, but accepting it still hurt after bottling everything up was a relief. 'We just weren't compatible on any other level. We wanted different things and he wanted me to change to fit into his life. I had changed for him – my career, my passion for travel. I'd been stuck in one place for far longer than I was comfortable and it had got to the point where I'd had enough. I knew we'd be better off apart and I'd been building up the courage to talk to him when—'

'You discovered you were pregnant,' Julie said quietly.

Raff and Anton emerging from the house cut the conversation short.

Julie leaned close to Tabitha and whispered, 'Thank you for sharing that with me.'

'I now know how to brew my own beer,' Raff announced proudly as he reached them. He glanced between Tabitha and Julie. 'You two all right?'

'Just a heart-to-heart,' Julie said firmly.

Tabitha scraped back her chair and stood up. 'It's probably time we were going.'

She felt flustered, trying to cover her discomfort and conscious of Raff's worried look.

Julie nodded and caught Tabitha's eye. 'Of course. Although you might have trouble waking the dogs.' She glanced down at Fudge sprawled next to her chair.

Fudge actually woke the second everyone left the patio and headed inside. Bailey was having none of it, though, snoring away on the wooden floor as Tabitha tried to stir him.

'You can always leave him here,' Julie said, laughing as Bailey briefly raised his head and slumped back down. 'Although he might wonder where Fudge and you two are if he wakes later.'

'Come on, Bailey,' Tabitha said, gently shaking his shoulder.

He lifted his head again and, at the sight of Fudge, scampered to his feet, shaking himself awake, his clipped nails clacking on the wood.

Tabitha hooked the lead onto his collar and turned to Julie. 'Thank you, both, for a lovely evening.'

'No, thank you,' Julie said as she gripped Tabitha's hands. 'We've enjoyed your company immensely.' She looked at Raff. 'Don't leave it so long next time.'

30

Tabitha and Raff waved goodbye to Julie and Anton and walked up the lane with the dogs, both lost in their own thoughts. Darkness had crept up on them and, after an enjoyable few hours filled with good food, wine and conversation, Tabitha was wrung out and longed to be back in the villa. They went inside, made coffee and settled themselves in the living room, Fudge immediately jumping up and squeezing between them on the sofa, incessantly turning around until he found a comfortable position.

'It's been an odd evening, hasn't it?' Raff said softly, stroking Fudge. 'Odd but nice.'

'Yeah, I get what you mean. It's been quite a day all round.' Her thoughts flipped from the deliciousness of waking up next to Raff, to ending the day having a heart-to-heart with Julie, someone she hadn't even known three weeks ago. Then again, she'd known Raff for even less time, which was hard to believe. Tabitha rested her hand on Fudge too, gently smoothing his soft fur as she reflected on the day.

Raff's fingers brushed against hers. 'It looked like you'd been crying when we left.'

'That's because I had.'

'Why?' His voice was gentle and full of concern.

'Because Julie opened up about some of the things she'd been through, asked some pertinent questions, which, um, kinda made me open up about stuff too. Did you know about Julie and Anton's struggle to have a family?'

'Not explicitly, no, although I guess on some level I sensed there was something wrong.' Raff rubbed his thumb against her finger as he continued stroking Fudge, keeping his eyes fixed on the dog instead of her. 'I've been rather self-absorbed whenever I've been back here.'

'She doesn't blame you for that.'

'I know, it's just she's always been so lovely; I feel bad that I've not seen her recently or really kept in touch at all. She's shown me such kindness over the years.'

'Julie totally understands. I mean, there's a big age gap, it's not like you're friends in the buddy sense. I get the feeling she thinks of you like the son she was never able to have. There's unconditional love there.'

Raff nodded, his attention still on Fudge. He swallowed hard and his jaw clenched. Tabitha realised that he was trying to control his emotions, much like she'd been trying and failing to do during the latter part of the evening. She'd opened up to Julie; she could certainly be honest with Raff.

'I got upset because I told Julie about the miscarriage I suffered a year ago.' Although she said it quietly, somehow her voice filled the room with big words, words she'd been fearful of saying out loud to anyone, finding it easier to run away and pretend it had never happened.

'You had a miscarriage?' He said it as if he was trying to process the words too. It had all got rather serious, rather quickly, but Tabitha couldn't make light of the situation. She felt safe opening up to Raff, comfortable too, his hand resting on hers, his thumb caressing.

'It wasn't planned,' Tabitha continued, 'despite Lewis being eager for us to start a family. That was so far from what I wanted back then. I'd been having serious doubts about us when a positive pregnancy test left me up shit creek without a paddle, so to speak.' She laughed bitterly. 'I was talking to Julie about it because she told me she'd suffered two miscarriages herself.'

'Oh shit, Tabitha, I never realised about Julie and I'm so sorry you went through that too.' His hand remained warm and solid on hers. His eyes narrowed. 'Is this the first time you've talked to anyone about it?'

Tabitha pursed her lips in an attempt to hold back the tears lodged in her throat. Fudge's fur was so soft, it suddenly reminded her of stroking the soft downy hair of a baby, like she'd done when Olivia and Nancy were tiny. The memory of peach-soft skin and that sweet nothing-quite-like-it baby smell consumed her. Since escaping the UK, she'd rarely been triggered in the way she had been today, although sitting outside a cafe in Paris when three mums with their babies had sat at the table next to her had hit her hard. Locking her feelings away had just delayed the inevitable. Escaping but not using the time to process everything was exactly what she'd done with Ollie. She couldn't keep running away because dealing with the emotional fallout was hard.

'If it's too upsetting we don't have to talk about it,' Raff said, in response to her silence. 'I'm sorry I asked.'

'No, it's okay, it's probably a good thing.' Fudge stretched out, kicking his paws into her bare leg. She shifted off the sofa to give him room and sat on the rug. She kept her hand on Fudge as she looked up at Raff. 'My parents know, but it's only Elspeth I've been able to talk to properly. Even then, I've struggled to put into words how I actually feel.' She glanced away, across the luxurious villa with its beautiful garden, glimmering pool and ocean view. No one's life was perfect, however wonderful it looked on the surface. There were always hidden secrets, unspoken heartache and countless lies. Even Rufus and Cordelia's idyllic life hid the heartache of a broken relationship with their only son. Tabitha sighed. 'Perhaps a year of running away from my emotions, from everything, is enough. I need to make peace with what's happened.'

'But at the time it must have felt like the right thing to do?'

Tabitha nodded. 'I wanted to escape from everyone, even the people closest to me who would have helped me get through it, because it felt too hard staying. All my brothers and sisters are in long-term relationships. All of them have kids. I know I'm the youngest, but it was the unspoken expectation that it would be my path too, that because I was with someone and we loved each other we should live together, get married, definitely have kids.'

'So your ex wanted children but you didn't?'

'Not then, no.'

'How did you feel when you found out?'

'Sick, absolutely sick to my stomach and utterly terrified. And you know why? Because I realised I was trapped. I'd been uncertain about my relationship with Lewis for a while, put it down to itchy feet, but it was more than that. We weren't happy together – actually, that's a lie, apparently Lewis was, it was me who wasn't.' Something about the way Raff was looking at her, not shying away from an uncomfortable subject, made Tabitha want to let it all out, to tell him stuff she hadn't even opened up to Elspeth about. She folded Fudge's long silky ear between her fingers. 'I was on my own when I did the pregnancy test and seeing those two positive lines made me feel like everything was closing in on me. I remember leaning on the sink trying to steady my breathing and I had this, like, physical pain in my chest. And it wasn't as if I could pretend it wasn't happening – I had signs, I knew I was pregnant before the test confirmed it – I'd been feeling sick in the morning for a few days. The hormones had left me a sobbing mess.'

'Did you tell him?'

'No, I meant to, but I wanted to get my head round it first and figure out my feelings.' Tabitha breathed deeply, feeling the familiar tension building in her chest. Tears stung her eyes.

Raff shifted off the sofa on to the floor and slid his arm around her.

'I spent so long thinking that I didn't want to have children...' She took a deep, shuddery breath and shook her head. 'Elspeth tried to give me hope, saying it was common to bleed in early pregnancy, but I just knew in my gut, you know, that something wasn't right. And it was at that moment, when the possibility of becoming a mum was taken away, that I realised how much I actually wanted it.' Her voice cracked, the bottled up heartache of the last twelve months unravelling. 'It sounds heartless, but I wanted the baby more than I wanted to be with Lewis.'

'Oh Tabitha.'

He hugged her close and she leaned into him, the tears releasing like a dam had burst. She sobbed into his shoulder, crying harder than she'd ever done, soothed by the comforting weight of his arms wrapped around her.

She pulled away, leaving his T-shirt damp, her face wet with tears. It was a relief to have let it all out, her grief, her regrets, her sadness, the stress, the worry, to finally open up to someone.

'I didn't mean to burden you with all that.'

'I'm glad you did.' His eyes were filled with concern. 'It's not healthy keeping things bottled up.'

He gently pressed his fingers to the centre of her chest, momentarily stilling her breath. It had been hard to open up to Raff, to be truthful about stuff that had plagued her for months and months, but she was glad she had.

'I told Lewis about it after I'd miscarried and he was understandably upset. He didn't get why I hadn't told him, didn't understand my reasons, particularly when he found out that my sister knew.'

'Surely that was your choice?'

'True, but he had every right to be upset. I was honest with him about my feelings, about my concern over how we weren't right for each other. I didn't end it with him then because my emotions were all over the place and I'd just dropped a bombshell on him. But he didn't listen. Instead of backing off and giving me some space to, I don't know, grieve for something I didn't know I'd even wanted, to just get over the awful physical stuff, he chose instead to propose, completely out of the blue just two weeks later.' Tabitha shook her head. 'Even after telling him how I felt about our relationship, he still didn't understand. He even suggested we tried again, despite us not having intended to get pregnant in the first place.'

'So that's when you finished with him?'

'Yeah.'

'And you didn't tell your sister?'

'I told her about breaking up with him and she obviously knew about the miscarriage, but I didn't tell her he'd proposed. I didn't tell anyone, not even my parents, for fear someone would attempt to talk me into trying to make things work. It never felt quite right with Lewis, but I had no idea why. He was a decent bloke, really decent, and I honestly believed I loved him. My whole family did and thought he was the one. But the more he tried to change me into the sort of partner he wanted, and the more serious our relationship became, the more I distanced myself. The more commitment there was, the further I pulled away.'

'It's expectation,' Raff said quietly.

'What do you mean?'

'Your family's expectation for you to settle down – we're

programmed to want that, for our parents to want that for us. It's been similar with my parents, except their expectation for me has been my schooling, then to go to a prestigious university. They wanted me to go to Oxford or Cambridge; I opted for Royal Holloway in London. Nothing wrong with that, and despite dicking around, I managed to get a 2:1, but it wasn't the course or university *they* would have chosen. They wanted me to have a serious career and succeed, to make something of myself in a field they could be proud of. They found wealth through hard work and wanted to set me up, but it feels as if they wanted me to be an extension of themselves. It sounds like your parents and sister and everyone are coming from a good place wanting to see you settled and in love, to start a family... Misguided maybe if it wasn't truly what you wanted, but at least they love you.'

'And you don't think your parents do? Isn't them giving you that sort of education and helping you achieve, their own way of showing you their love?' Tabitha held up her hands. 'Before you say anything, I'm well aware of how that sounds and that it was far from the love and support you needed or deserved. Perhaps they're misguided too.'

Raff shook his head. 'Your family loves you, Tabitha. My parents sent me away as a kid and never had time for me when I was back. I was an inconvenience. They wanted a trophy son and I disappointed them. No, worse. They believe I betrayed them; their trust, their love, their support.'

'Because they accused you of stealing?' Tabitha asked quietly. He went rigid, his back tense, the muscles on his arms clenched. She held him closer.

'Yes, expensive jewellery went missing. It was back when I was having a shitty time in London, when I'd got in with the wrong crowd. One of the few times I escaped back here to try to sort my shit out. They accused me of taking stuff to sell to pay for drugs. I'm not proud of how I behaved and lived my life back then, but I'd *never* have done something like that. I was back here because I was trying to make a positive change, not fuel a drug habit. I've never forgiven them for not believing me over their cleaner. It was a misunderstanding on their part, but it hurt like hell to have the blame thrown at me when I knew I was innocent. I went straight back to the UK. They fired their cleaner not long after. Make of that what you will.' Bitterness threaded through his words.

'Oh Raff,' she said, snuggling closer. 'I don't blame you for not forgiving them, but maybe it's time you confronted them?'

'How did this conversation turn from talking about you to me?' He traced his thumbs across her face, wiping away the rest of her tears. 'You can't do things because it's what your family want. You need to live *your* life, Tabitha, the way you want to.'

'I know, that's what I intended to do. That's what I am doing.' She shifted closer, cupped his stubbled cheeks in her hands and kissed him. She pulled away and smiled. 'Thank you for listening and being you.'

She felt wrung out but also freer somehow after talking to Julie and now Raff. First the miscarriage, then splitting with Lewis had sent her life spiralling. Sitting here with Raff, she felt grounded, as if the merry-go-round of life with all its ups and downs had momentarily stilled.

'Do you fancy going to bed?' He swept a wayward curl off her face.

Tabitha nodded.

'Alone, or er…'

'I don't want to be alone.' She scrambled to her feet and held out her hand. 'But, um, we really shouldn't sleep in your parents' bed.'

Raff's concerned look morphed into a grin. Taking her hand, he stood and led her upstairs.

31

For the second morning in a row, Tabitha woke in bed with Raff. After their emotional conversation the night before, with Raff suggesting she lived her life the way she wanted, it was beginning to become clear what that was, and he was lying next to her. She was getting way ahead of herself, but it felt unbelievably good with his arm heavy across her waist, his bare skin warm against hers. After being on her own for more than a year, she knew she was getting swept up in the deliciousness of the moment. He was hot as hell and the sex was amazing – surely that was why she felt like this?

The dogs weren't in the room. Guilt ebbed through her that she'd upset their routine. Cordelia would not be happy if she knew that Tabitha had put her own needs above those of her beloved dogs.

Tabitha reached for her phone, but it wasn't on the bedside table. She remembered she hadn't had it since yesterday afternoon either. She yawned and tried to slip out from under Raff's arm, but he groaned and pulled her closer, his arms encircling her, his body firm as he spooned her, his hands gliding up to cup her breasts.

'I need to feed Misty and the dogs,' she whispered, laughing as she peeled his hands away and scooted off the bed before her resolve vanished.

She pulled on knickers, threw on her T-shirt from the day before and left Raff sprawled on the bed, naked and enticing.

It was Monday morning and she needed to get up, face the day and get on with work. However much she wanted to, she couldn't stay in bed having sex with Raff.

Fudge was lying on the landing with his head on his paws, probably confused why the sleeping arrangements were different, but he padded downstairs after her. Tabitha found Bailey in his bed in Cordelia and Rufus's room. He woke immediately and followed her and Fudge into the kitchen. Misty slunk in, winding her body around Tabitha's legs.

With the dogs and Misty tucking into their breakfast, Tabitha retrieved her phone from her bag in the living room. It had been there since they'd got back from the wedding. There were missed calls from Cordelia, one made just a few minutes earlier, and a voice message. As she clicked on it, Raff came down the stairs in just his pants.

'Come back to bed,' he said, trailing his hand across her hips. 'Who are you phoning?'

She put her finger to her lips as the answerphone message started.

'Tabitha, it's Cordelia. When you get this, call me back asap.'

That was all there was and she sounded stressed.

'Shit.' Tabitha deleted the message.

'What's up?' Raff asked.

Tabitha jumped as her mobile started ringing and Cordelia's name popped up on the screen.

'It's your mum.' Tabitha waved Raff away as she answered.

'Cordelia, hi,' she said breathlessly. 'I'm so sorry I missed your call before. I didn't have my phone on me.'

'I've been trying our landline too,' Cordelia said curtly, 'multiple times this weekend. There's been no answer.'

'Oh I was next door at Julie's with the dogs...'

'You were?' Her voice was clipped. 'Since Saturday?'

'Oh, I, er...' Tabitha was at a loss. How to explain where she'd been without mentioning Raff?

'We've had an utter nightmare,' Cordelia ploughed on. 'We were on a guided walking safari when Rufus managed to slip down a steep bank and badly twist his ankle. Smashed his phone too. My phone ran out of battery, hence me only being able to try calling you on our home phone until last night as we were in a hospital in Dar es Salaam.'

'Oh my goodness, that sounds horrendous.'

'It is. And it's cut our holiday of a lifetime short.'

'Is Rufus okay?'

Raff was really frowning at her now. Tabitha mouthed, 'I'll tell you in a bit.'

'He's dosed up on pain relief and cross with himself for falling over in the first place, not to mention embarrassed. But other than his pride being dented and being in an awful lot of pain, he's fine.' She sighed. 'What's done is done. We've decided not to go to Zanzibar and come home early instead, which is what I've been trying to contact you about.'

'Oh, okay. When?' Thoughts swirled and a tightness built in her chest.

'We've been travelling for hours already and are in Amsterdam waiting for our flight to Lisbon. If all goes to plan, we should be back on Madeira this evening.'

'This evening?' Tabitha said, her voice suddenly high-pitched.

'Yes, between eight and nine tonight, I think. I know this is disrupting your plans too, which was why I was trying to give you fair warning. Obviously, you can stay for as long as you need, until you sort out where you're going next, but it really hasn't felt as if we have any other option.' Tension coiled round her voice. 'We just want to be home.'

'I'm not surprised.' Panic ripped through Tabitha.

'The dogs and Misty...'

'Are absolutely fine; you don't need to worry about them. They'll be pleased to see you.'

'We'll see you later then.' Cordelia hung up before Tabitha had a chance to say anything else.

'Shit.' She held the phone to her chest.

'What do you mean they'll be pleased to see them?' A frown creased Raff's handsome face. 'What's going on, Tabitha?'

'Your dad's had an accident – he's fine, though,' she stressed as Raff's eyebrows furrowed even more. 'He hurt his ankle and is in a lot of pain so they're on their way home. They'll be back this evening.'

'Ah, shit.' Raff rubbed his hand across his forehead.

Tabitha felt as stressed as he looked. Of all the times to not have had her mobile on her. Of all the times to not have been here. She could only imagine what had been going through Cordelia's head as she'd desperately tried to get hold of her.

'Perhaps this is a good thing,' Tabitha said, attempting to make herself feel more upbeat about the situation.

'How is my parents returning early good?' Raff muttered. He ran his fingers up her arms. 'I thought we'd have longer together.'

That had been Tabitha's initial reaction too, not that her time on Madeira was about to be cut short, but her time with Raff would be. For one weekend, everything had been perfect, and now...

'With them coming back early and you being here, it might be an opportunity to finally talk to them,' she said gently. 'Tell them how you feel about everything.'

Raff dropped his hands from her arms and shook his head. 'That's so not a good idea, particularly with Dad being injured. He's not going to be in a good mood.'

'There never will be a good time, you know.'

'Then maybe that's the way it should stay. I've got on just fine not having anything to do with my parents.'

'Then why are you here now, in their house, if you want nothing to do with them?'

His jaw clenched. 'You know why I'm here. Circumstances. And I was going to leave before they got back. I can't see them. I don't want to see them.'

From all she'd learned about Raff's relationship with his parents, his reaction was understandable, but it would be her facing them. 'I get why you're upset, Raff, but if my time here is anything to go by, sometimes it's good to talk. Perhaps you might even be able to make peace with them.'

Raff tucked his hands beneath his armpits, his chest muscles tensing as he did. Tabitha wished she could rewind the morning and instead be naked beneath the sheets with Raff, enjoying each other and forgetting about everyone and everything else.

'Honestly, however hard you try, however well-meaning you are, you really don't understand my relationship with my parents.' There was a hardness to his voice. 'I've come to terms with being a disappointment to them, but what really hurts is the knowledge that they wished they'd never had me.'

'They don't think like that.'

'Oh, you know them, do you? The brief evening you spent with them trumps my thirty-one years, does it?'

'No, it's just they're your parents—'

'So? I'm way past caring what they think of me and that they didn't believe me when it mattered most. I know I've caused them trouble and disappointed them. I'm sure their life would have been easier without me, and if you don't think they've wished that over the years, then you haven't been paying attention to anything I've said.'

Tabitha held up her hands. 'You've taken it the wrong way. I was only trying to make a *well-meaning* suggestion. You didn't have to bite my head off.'

His demeanour and sudden change of tone had upset her more than she thought possible.

'I can't be here when they get back.' Raff shrugged. 'I'll go to Funchal and get a flight to London. Figure something out then. Another week and the money for the house will come through.'

'No.' Tabitha shook her head. 'You don't get to walk away.' She wasn't prepared for her time on Madeira to come to an end so abruptly and she sure as hell wasn't ready for Raff to walk out of her life. The pain in her chest had returned, making it feel as if her breathing was restricted. 'Do you honestly want to carry on hating your parents while they ignore the fact that they even have a son?'

'Tabitha, it's not that straightforward.'

'Yeah, I get it, it's a messed-up situation, but something keeps on bringing you back here. I don't believe for a second that you would rather carry on the way you have been. I don't imagine it will be easy attempting to regain a semblance of a relationship with them, but surely it's worth a try? What better time than now?'

'Oh, I think any time would be better than now,' he said bitterly.

'You're only saying that because you don't want to talk to them.'

'Of course I don't want to talk to them!'

'You'll have me for support.'

'And how's that going to go down? You've been lying to them while they've been away, letting me stay—'

'Because you asked me to!' Fury rushed through her.

'But still...' Raff unclenched his hands from his armpits and held them up in a 'what can I say' kind of way. 'Do you fancy explaining our situation to them? Explaining everything that's happened over the last couple of weeks and what we've got up to in their house?'

Tabitha folded her arms, her nostrils flaring.

'I thought not.' He started for the stairs, but stopped. His hand rested on the banister as he bowed his head and shook it. He turned and came back over, taking her in his arms. The smell of him was intoxicating, the feel of him making her skin tingle, his bare chest pressed against her sending her heart racing. 'I'm sorry, Tabs. What I said was uncalled for, but I really can't do this.'

Raff kissed her and retreated upstairs.

Tabitha remained in the living room. She breathed deeply, trying to calm her thumping heart as she fought back tears. Utter despair washed over her, still more uncertainty, her feelings for Raff a muddle; she wanted to escape yet hold on to him for dear life too. Instead, she let the dogs out and retreated to her bedroom. *His parents' room*. Despite his obvious anger and reluctance to stay, what hurt the most was his tender use of the pet name that only her family used, coupled with the feeling he evoked when he touched her, when he said sorry, when he held her. Yet, with a sinking heart, she knew that nothing she said was going to change his mind. The gloriousness of the weekend, where they'd been in a loved-up bubble, had burst.

Tabitha showered and dressed in her boy-fit jeans and a vest top, at least attempting to look like she was ready to face the day.

Whether Raff was a coward for not wanting to face up to his parents or right for not letting himself be swayed into forgiving them, it was his decision and she and Raff were nothing more to each other than strangers who had spent a couple of nights together and were now heading their separate ways. They always were going to have to say goodbye; it was just happening sooner than she'd expected, her time on Madeira screeching to a halt with the return of his parents.

Despite wanting to rewind the morning and erase the new tension between them, she didn't have time to with a Zoom meeting scheduled and admin stuff to do that she couldn't put off any longer, particularly now the rest of the week would be disrupted. She managed to change her flight to Lisbon on the weekend to one leaving the next day. Madeira was done and she certainly wasn't intending to spend any longer than necessary with Raff's parents.

Elspeth phoning in the middle of the day took her by surprise. She'd hoped it was Cordelia calling to say they'd be delayed.

'Hi, E.'

'Hey there, I couldn't wait any longer to speak to you.' Her sister's voice was the slice of home that Tabitha was most definitely craving. 'I'm surprised you haven't phoned.'

'There's been a lot going on.'

'Oh really?' she said with interest.

Tabitha gave a hollow laugh. 'You don't know the half of it.'

'Ooh,' Elspeth said, 'then tell me all of it.'

Tabitha sighed and sat down on the sofa. 'First, how did the wedding go?'

'Oh Tabs, the hard work was worth it. Perfect Indian summer weather, a happy bride and groom, incredible photos – the guests loved it and so many commented that it was one of the best weddings they'd ever been to because of the location.'

'Oh Elspeth, I'm made up for you.'

'I could sleep for a week now, though.'

'I bet.'

'Mum and Dad took the kids out yesterday morning so Gethin

and I could have a lie-in. It was just nice to have breakfast sitting outside together, peace and quiet with no kids squabbling. Mum and Dad went home this morning.' She sighed. 'Going to miss them big time.'

'I'm surprised you have time to phone me in the middle of the day.'

'It's Olivia's first full day in school and Gethin's taken Nancy out for a couple of hours. I'm supposed to be catching up on paperwork, but I've stopped for lunch and wanted to talk to you. So, tell me, how was the wedding you went to with Raff?'

Where to start with that? 'It was, er... amazing actually. I don't know if the location would beat your barn in the Brecon Beacons, but it was pretty special.'

'And how did you and Raff get on?'

Snapshots of the last couple of days filled Tabitha's head. 'Are you trying to ask if we slept together?'

'Um, yes.' Elspeth laughed. 'Did you?'

'Yep.'

'Oh my goodness, Tabs! Well...'

'It was everything I'd hoped for and more.' Tabitha sighed inwardly, knowing that nothing further would come of it.

Elspeth squealed. 'I'm so happy you're happy.'

'I was, but things have turned rather pear-shaped.' She filled Elspeth in with that morning's events, emotion weaving through her words. 'So, there you go. Typically, things are not quite so straightforward any longer.'

'Is he still there?' Elspeth asked.

'For the moment.'

'Then talk to him again. Tell him how you feel.'

'I don't know how I feel.'

'Well, you sound upset and I can tell you really like him.'

'I do, but this whole situation with his parents... There's no way

I'm going to be able to get him to change his mind about staying and talking to them.' Tabitha gazed out at the sun-dappled garden, hoping the soothing view would help her tension abate.

'Sometimes it's easier for other people to see the path forward more clearly,' Elspeth said pointedly. 'I knew you needed to escape everything a year ago, that's why I encouraged you. If you think Raff talking to his parents now will help him, then what's to lose?'

'Him,' Tabitha said matter-of-factly.

'Maybe, but he needs to put the past to rest, otherwise he'll never be able to move on. And it's your reputation at stake. If they find out you've been lying to them, how's that going to look? I'm trying to look out for you, Tabs. I can tell you're stressed about seeing them again and having to bottle everything up. By telling his parents the truth, you'll not only straighten the situation out for yourself, but you'll give him an opportunity to open up to them too. You're right, though, he may not thank you for it.'

Tabitha bit her lip, aware that what would be right for her might not be for Raff. 'You're right about me not being able to continue lying to them, not now, not after everything that's happened.'

'Because you and Raff are together?'

Tabitha made an 'uh-huh' sound, her thoughts elsewhere. Were they really together though? They'd spent time together and got to know each other, they'd laughed and argued, not to mention slept together, but none of that meant they were together in the sense Elspeth was suggesting.

Fired up after talking to her sister, Tabitha decided to take the situation into her own hands. So far it had been Raff in control, bending her to his will. It was about time that changed.

Tabitha held her phone in her lap with the screen open to the WhatsApp chat with Cordelia and Rufus. With them returning home early, she couldn't blatantly lie to them. If Dolores came clean, if Julie accidentally mentioned something, if they found out in any other way than through her, she'd feel awful. Elspeth was right about it looking bad. She already did feel bad, having spent the last two and a half weeks not telling them what was really going on.

Her fingers hovered over the WhatsApp message. Raff was being unreasonable. However much she'd grown to love him being here, however much their relationship had developed from strangers to friends then lovers, she wasn't going to continue bending the truth to his parents. She started writing a message.

Hi Cordelia, before you get back, there's something I need to tell you…

32

Cordelia didn't reply until later in the afternoon and when she did, Tabitha realised she didn't know her well enough to work out if she was incensed by the news of Raff being here. Her message was short and to the point.

I see. We'll talk further when we're back. In Lisbon waiting for our flight to Madeira.

If Tabitha had expected to feel better for being truthful, then she was disappointed. Her stomach churned and she was on edge, filled with misery at how her time on Madeira was ending. Unable to concentrate, she stopped working and went to check on the dogs. Her escape and the time to herself that she'd craved so much was closing in around her. Her heart sank at the sight of Raff's rucksack by the door. With her stomach rumbling from skipping lunch, she grabbed a banana and ate it out on the sunny terrace.

Raff took her by surprise a few minutes later, emerging from the garden office, all broad shoulders, tanned skin and ruffled hair.

She couldn't help but think about how she'd been running her fingers through it the night before.

'Hey,' he said when he reached her. 'I've cleared and cleaned the garden office and the guest bedroom so they won't even know I've been here.'

Tabitha discarded the banana skin on the patio table and folded her arms. 'So you're really leaving?'

'It's for the best.'

'For you maybe,' she said, trying to control the hurt in her voice. 'I've already messaged them, though.'

'What do you mean?'

'I told your parents the truth.'

'You did what?' Anger flared in his eyes. 'What the hell did you say?'

'Just that it was a long story and that you were here and I'd invited you to stay for a few days. I didn't go into detail.' She waited for him to say something and when he didn't, she continued. 'Raff, I'm sorry, I can't lie to them about my time here, which means I can't lie about you either. You shouldn't expect me to.'

He rubbed his forehead, a stress reflex, something she'd noticed him do before. 'I know I shouldn't.' There was a tenderness to his words, yet Tabitha felt as if an almighty gulf had opened up between them that she didn't know how to bridge. 'It's my fault expecting you to lie on my behalf and be okay with it.'

Despite their intimacy over the last couple of days, she was uncertain if she should reach out and hug him when he was about to walk out of her life.

'We're involved, Raff. Even if you're estranged from them, I can't lie to your parents about that or my feelings.'

'Your feelings?'

Tabitha swallowed. There was a strained look on his face, not quite horror, but close enough to make her realise that the idea of any sort of feelings creeping into their relationship scared him silly.

With a sinking feeling, Tabitha clenched her jaw. 'Yes, my feelings. I like you. A lot.' She held his gaze, her insides melting, knowing all she wanted to do was sink into his arms and kiss him.

'I like you too, Tabitha, but I can't be here when my parents get back, I'm sorry. Even if they now know the truth. And everything's my fault, okay? Don't let them make you feel guilty for stuff I've done. I'm aware I put you in this position, but, um, I'd no idea when I turned up that night that you, well, would be quite as wonderful as you are.' Their eyes locked momentarily before he brushed past her, the sincerity and meaning of his words snatched by the breeze sighing through the leaves of the palm trees. The stillness, peace and beauty of her surroundings evaporated, leaving a coldness clenching her stomach. She followed him inside, listening to the matter-of-fact words tumbling from him. 'I'm all packed, I've booked a flight to Gatwick for later this evening. I popped round to Julie's earlier to say goodbye and she's going to take me to Funchal; she said to let her know when your flight is and she'll be more than happy to take you too.'

'I'm not going till tomorrow, after your parents are back,' she said pointedly.

If he was feeling at all guilty, he was hiding it well. He glanced at his watch. 'Julie will be waiting; I'd better go.'

Fighting back tears, Tabitha watched him pick up his rucksack and swing it over his shoulder. So this was it. This was how her time on Madeira was going to end, with Raff escaping as abruptly as he'd arrived, leaving her to face his parents alone.

'So, you're choosing to run away, rather than deal with any of this?' Tabitha flung her arms in the air. She wondered if he understood that she included herself in that statement, not just his parents.

'I have your number, you have mine...'

Tabitha laughed bitterly and shook her head. 'Well, that's all right then. See you around, eh?'

He walked to the door, Bailey and Fudge clattering after him. 'Hey, you guys need to stay here.' He squatted and tickled them both under their chins. He stood and met Tabitha's eyes. 'I'm going to miss you.' Before she could reply, he yanked the door open and slipped out, closing it behind him before the dogs could escape.

Tabitha stood in the shadowed hallway, alone again apart from the dogs and cat. It was incredible the impact someone could have in such a short time. Whether he was a coward for not facing up to things or she was expecting too much from someone she was still getting to know, she knew she was a fool for allowing him to inch into her heart, yet here she felt she'd found something in Raff, something that had reignited a passion. But she'd made a mistake. She needed to accept that he'd been using her to get what he wanted – a place to stay and companionship, his actions suggesting their time together meant nothing. A short fling worked out perfectly for him.

* * *

With the afternoon marching on, Tabitha packed and cleared her belongings out of Cordelia and Rufus's bedroom, stripped the bed and put the washing machine on; she'd sleep in the guest room again tonight. The scratch marks on the bottom of Cordelia and Rufus's bedroom door were still there, not that she could do anything about them now beyond apologising and offering to pay for the damage. As she rushed around the villa, cleaning and tidying, the dogs followed her like little shadows, somehow understanding that something was up, neither of them settling down to sleep.

She didn't hear anything further from Cordelia, so assumed their travel plans were on track and they'd get here later in the evening. Tabitha's mind was in overdrive, wondering what they'd make of the whole situation, while she agonised about just how much she should tell them.

Elspeth messaged a couple of times to check how she was doing and Tabitha sent noncommittal replies, not wanting Elspeth to worry and phone her. A conversation with her sister right this minute would reduce her to tears. She just wanted to make it through the next few hours and get to the airport tomorrow before figuring out her next steps.

And then a message from Ollie pinged onto her phone.

I can't get you out of my head, Tabs. So glad we're friends again. Been thinking about you loads, about music, about us and the way things used to be. There's a couple of weeks before the US tour starts. I know you're here for a few more days, but after that, how about staying in Madeira for a bit longer, crash at my place and we can write songs together. Come on tour with me too. It'll be like old times. I miss you like crazy. What do you think? Xx

Tabitha sat down on the guest bed with a thump. It had briefly crossed her mind to contact Ollie and stay on the island, but it had felt easier to change her flight and head to Lisbon for a few days alone as planned. Getting a message like this from Ollie on the day Raff had left, the day his parents were returning early, the day before she was leaving the island; was it fate? Facing up to things had been good for her and perhaps it was time to embrace opportunities and say yes, instead of running away.

She didn't reply straight away, but mulled over Ollie's proposition as she finished hoovering, not wanting Cordelia to find fault with anything apart from the small matter of Tabitha having let their estranged son stay.

With the bedrooms, bathroom and kitchen done, she was plumping up cushions in the living room when there was a knock on the glass.

Startled, Tabitha looked up. Julie was standing by the side of the open bifold doors, Fudge already on his way over to her, tail wagging.

'Hi, Tabitha. I've just got back from taking Raff to Funchal. I wanted to make sure you're okay?'

The emotions that she'd been trying to contain for the best part of the day came bubbling to the surface. She bit her lip and nodded.

'It's just Raff didn't say much, but he seemed upset. I hear Cordelia and Rufus are coming home early?'

'Yep,' Tabitha said, 'and despite me trying to convince him it would be a good thing to speak to them after so long, he thought otherwise, so left.'

Julie walked over, nodding slowly. 'Old wounds, they're hard to fix. If it's any consolation, it's difficult for him to open up and tell them how he feels.'

'I get that, I do. It's just...' Tabitha rubbed her forehead. 'Everything's ended so suddenly and not in the way I wanted it to. I know it sounds crazy because we've only known each other a short time, but it honestly feels as if he's walked out on me.'

'Oh Tabitha.' Julie tentatively put her arms around her. 'I'm so sorry. It was obvious how much you two liked each other.'

Tabitha breathed deeply, comforted by Julie, her hug as gentle as she was. 'It was inevitable that we'd go our own separate ways, I just wasn't prepared for it to be so soon.'

33

A car pulling into the drive a couple of hours later set Tabitha's heart racing. Bailey and Fudge lifted their heads and looked at Tabitha, then towards the garden. At the sound of the front door opening, they scrambled to their feet barking. With tails wagging, they raced to the door. There was scuffling, cries of 'hello you two' before Cordelia entered the living room, Bailey and Fudge chasing at her heels. She dumped her shoulder bag on the floor and crouched down, both dogs jumping into her outstretched arms as they tried to lick her face.

Rufus hobbled in on crutches with a pained expression.

Cordelia stood up and glanced around before looking coolly at Tabitha. 'He's gone, hasn't he?'

'Yes, he has. He thought it was for the best.'

Tabitha's stomach felt as tightly clenched as her fists as she tried her hardest to hold it together. Part of her wanted to rage at Rufus and Cordelia on Raff's behalf, but with Cordelia's stony face and Rufus's obvious distress, she needed to remain calm.

Tension bristled; there was none of the relaxed and happy banter of her first evening. Only the dogs were behaving normally, excited to see their owners return, eager for the attention.

Leaning on crutches, Rufus looked drained, his usual chattiness dampened, his tanned face tired and washed out. The long journey with three connections had obviously taken it out of him. He smiled weakly at Tabitha and put a hand on his wife's shoulder as she emptied her shoulder bag on the coffee table. 'If you don't mind, I'm going to lie down.'

'Of course,' Cordelia said, although her tone was still clipped.

'Do you need help with your luggage?' Tabitha asked, at a loss for how else to break the tension.

'It can stay in the hallway for the time being.' Rufus made his way towards the bedroom.

Now what? How soon could she make herself scarce? From loving being here, all she wanted to do was flee, a feeling that kept following her around, never seeming to let up.

'There's, um, food in the fridge if you're hungry,' Tabitha said to fill the silence. 'Fresh bread and fruit too.'

'How dare he stay here without our knowledge.' Cordelia turned on Tabitha, anger blazing in her eyes.

Tabitha sighed, resigned that an easy escape wasn't going to be possible.

'How could you allow this to happen?'

Tabitha tried to control the churning in her stomach, wanting to answer with calmness to counteract Cordelia's rage. 'It wasn't as simple as allowing it to happen,' Tabitha said, keeping her voice low and neutral. 'He turned up in the middle of the night – I wasn't even aware you had a son; there are no photos. You never once mentioned him—'

'So it's our fault?'

'I didn't say that. I just want you to understand why he took me by surprise and because I didn't know about him, there was a hell of a lot of explaining to do. Taking into account it was midnight and he had nowhere else to go, what did you expect me to do? Kick him out?'

Cordelia bristled. 'You had no right.'

'I didn't feel I had a choice!' Tabitha's calmness vanished.

'You should have asked us.'

'Hindsight's wonderful, isn't it? He didn't know I was going to be here and at the time it was for one night.'

'Then how on earth did he end up staying?'

The events of the past couple of weeks flashed through Tabitha's mind; a snapshot of moments that kept drawing them together, from first locking eyes in the hallway to tequila-fuelled laughter and tumbling into the pool; standing together on the path beneath the waterfall and dancing in the club in Funchal; kissing him that night after the wedding then waking up in his arms.

'It's complicated,' Tabitha said, holding Cordelia's cool gaze.

'That doesn't answer anything.' Cordelia folded her arms. 'He had no right to be here and you had no right to let him stay without our express permission.'

'Which you wouldn't have given.' Anger flared inside Tabitha, her calmness erupting into contempt. 'You've cut him off and constantly pushed him away. Can you blame him for sneaking around?'

'But why?' Cordelia said with an edge to her voice somewhere between upset and anger. 'If he hates us so much, why bother coming back at all? Unless of course it's because he wants to use us and our house. Take what he feels he's owed.'

'You don't get it at all, do you? He doesn't hate you. He loves you. Both of you.' Tabitha echoed the very words she'd said to Raff the evening before about his parents loving him. 'All he's ever wanted is for you to see him for who he is.'

'And who is he, Tabitha? Huh? Because I sure as hell don't

know. He's done his very best to distance himself from us through his behaviour and actions.'

'He's kind, intelligent, troubled, confident, mischievous – lots of things. I do know he's desperate for your approval. He's lived his life never thinking he's good enough.'

'And yet, he's continued to fight us despite everything we've done for him.'

'What? You mean pay for his education?'

Cordelia pursed her lips.

'He was just a child when you sent him away.' Tabitha couldn't bite her tongue any longer. 'What did you expect would happen? You put the whole thing in motion because it suited you. Then you go and accuse him of stealing.'

Cordelia snapped her head round, her demeanour changing from anger to shock. 'He told you about that?'

'He's talked to me a lot.' The dogs had settled down in their usual spots, but Tabitha noticed Fudge's eye kept twitching open as their voices rose. She was sure Rufus would be able to hear them too, and was probably relieved to be well out of the way. Even if she ended up regretting speaking her mind, she wanted to stand up for Raff. 'Why would you believe the cleaner over your own son?'

They were standing at opposite ends of the coffee table, squaring up to each other like they were in a boxing ring.

'He was troubled. There was a lot going on with him back then. He'd got in with a bad crowd, was doing drugs. He may have been living in London but we found out stuff. He spent quite a bit of time with Rufus's parents in Surrey; Raff at least talked to his grandma. And on the occasions he was back here, it was obvious what he was in to.'

'Yet you didn't talk to him.'

'It all blew up – there was no chance to. He stormed out; called us all manner of things under the sun. And, of course, when the truth came out about our cleaner having been caught stealing from other clients, the damage was done.'

'So you knew it wasn't him yet you've continued to let him believe that you think he stole from you? That's low,' Tabitha said. 'You need to put him straight.'

'I don't need to do anything. You have no right to... to...' Cordelia faltered, shook her head and breathed deeply. She looked as if she was on the verge of tears and Tabitha steeled herself for the inevitable torrent of abuse she was sure was about to come her way, because she'd overstepped.

The heightened emotions of the past few days, from the absolute joy of being with Raff to the sudden reality of him running away and leaving her to deal with his parents, was all too much. 'I'm sorry,' Tabitha spluttered, knowing she needed to put an end to this and walk away. Raff's problems weren't hers to fight, however much she felt for him. 'I don't think I should stay here tonight. You need time to yourselves and I've most definitely outstayed my welcome.'

Cordelia didn't argue; she didn't say anything. Her perfectly made up face looked older; her bubbly spark from their initial meeting two and a half weeks earlier had evaporated. Her eyes were red and tired, and the fight had seemingly gone out of her.

Tabitha escaped to the guest room, which was empty except for her luggage. The sheets had been washed, the bed was made, all evidence of Raff erased. Tabitha packed her washbag and the clothes she'd left out, heaved her rucksack onto her back, her guitar over her shoulder and thumped her way down the stairs with the suitcase.

Cordelia was standing on the villa's threshold, gazing out at the shadowed garden. She turned as Tabitha dragged the suitcase across the tiles.

'Where will you go?' The coolness in her voice remained, yet her face had softened a little. 'Do you need to call a taxi?'

Tabitha shook her head. 'I'll see if Julie can put me up for the night.'

'Julie?'

'She's been really good to us.'

'Us?' The sternness returned in Cordelia's frown and clenched jaw. Tabitha instantly knew she'd made a mistake in mentioning her. '*She* knew Raff was here?'

'Only by chance; none of this is her fault...'

But Cordelia was already pacing to the front door.

Shit.

Fudge jumped down from the sofa, padding after Cordelia. Tabitha left her luggage in the middle of the room and shut the bifold doors to ensure the dogs stayed in.

By the time Tabitha had made it out of the front door, Cordelia was almost out of sight. Tabitha closed the gate behind her and ran to catch up with Cordelia storming along the lane towards Julie and Anton's house.

'Julie has done nothing wrong.' Tabitha tried to catch her breath as she kept pace with Cordelia, ashamed and horrified that she'd managed to get Julie into trouble.

'She's always interfered,' Cordelia snapped, not slowing in the slightest despite wearing heeled sandals. 'She's always looked down on me when it comes to my parenting. She's taken Raff in like he's some kind of stray animal that needs looking after. How can she understand my position when she doesn't even have children of her own?'

'Perhaps there's a reason for that...' Tabitha trailed off. It wasn't her place to tell Cordelia about Julie's struggles.

Tabitha thought of Raff, on a plane somewhere over the Atlantic, escaping this whole messy situation; she wanted to hate him for leaving her to confront his parents on her own and yet, every time she thought about him, her heart ached.

Cordelia reached the house and battered her fist on the front door. 'Julie!'

There was no point in attempting to say anything else; Cordelia was headstrong and determined, much like her son.

The door opened a crack and Julie's usually passive face appeared furrowed with worry.

'We need to talk.' Cordelia was firm and unwavering as she glared at poor Julie.

Julie stood back and opened the door.

Cordelia stormed in.

Tabitha looked at Julie apologetically. 'I'm so sorry.'

'This was bound to happen sometime,' Julie said under her breath as she closed the door behind her.

'How dare you meddle in my family's business; how dare you not tell me that Raff was back!' Cordelia exploded the second Julie and Tabitha joined her in the open-plan living area. She was rooted to the spot, standing rigidly with her hands on her hips, her expression as furious as her tone. If Anton was home, he was making himself scarce.

It was as if all of Cordelia's pent-up anger and upset needed to go somewhere and as it couldn't be directed at Raff, Julie was the next best thing.

Tabitha suddenly felt like the outsider she was, looking in on the situation. The 'nosy' neighbours thing ran deeper than that – there was real resentment on Cordelia's part, with Julie having a far closer relationship with Raff than she'd ever had. Without intending to, Tabitha had managed to give Cordelia the perfect excuse to confront her.

Words flew between the two women about the last couple of weeks and what Julie did or didn't know. Cordelia dominated in both her tone and presence, making Julie seem more vulnerable than ever.

'You've always interfered with Raff,' Cordelia said coldly. 'You've always stuck your nose where it doesn't belong!'

'No,' Julie said calmly. 'I've been there for Raff; that's called caring, not interfering.'

'You have no idea how hard it is to be a parent.' Cordelia's voice cracked. 'No idea at all.'

Julie looked on the verge of tears. Tabitha's heart went out to her, knowing that having a child would have meant the world to her, while Cordelia was throwing all the love and care she'd given Raff over the years right back in her face.

'Maybe I don't, but that's only because I couldn't have children of my own,' Julie said quietly, her voice wobbling as tears ran freely down her cheeks. 'My love had nowhere to go, besides our beloved Jasper and your Raff. *Your* Raff,' she repeated. 'I understand that. I tried to be a friend to him. The last thing I wanted was to steal him away from you; that was never my intention. What I saw was a young man who was struggling emotionally and I decided to be there for him. Don't forget, it was you who asked me to babysit him in the first place. And when you were away, I was here. Raff chose to come over to have dinner and spend time with us. It was a pleasure getting to know him.'

Tabitha had no idea how Julie remained so calm, but she did. But then she was a very different person to Cordelia. Life had a habit of not being fair – Julie had been childless despite being desperate to be a mother, while everything about Cordelia suggested that motherhood hadn't ever been her priority.

'I didn't know how to love him,' Tabitha heard Cordelia say to Julie as she quietly backed away. 'I'm from a family of high achievers. I went to Cambridge – it was expected of me and I didn't defy my parents. Rightly or wrongly, I expected the same of Raff.'

Tabitha wasn't a part of this; the conversation was between the two women. She may have unwittingly instigated it, but she needed to give them the space to talk. She slipped out of the patio door and closed it behind her, relieved to escape into the night, the large garden shadowed and invitingly peaceful after the tension inside. She took the time to reflect, not just on the last couple of weeks, but the past few months that had led her to this moment. Would she change anything if she could do it all again?

Fifteen minutes later, the patio door clicked open and footsteps tapped across the paving. Cordelia stood next to Tabitha, smudged eyeliner accentuating the puffiness from crying. Tabitha glanced back and caught sight of Julie in the doorway. Despite looking wrung out, Julie gave her a weak smile and nodded, before slipping inside.

Cordelia stared ahead across the dark garden. Tabitha did the same. The night was only broken by the moon glimmering silver on the velvet black ocean and the specks of lights from the other houses clinging to the hillside mirrored the stars.

'You like Raff?' Cordelia's voice cracked as it filled the stillness.

'Yes, I do.'

Tabitha looked at Cordelia, whose eyes were brimming with tears, a tissue clutched in her hand, shoulders tense as she stared out.

'I'm sorry he didn't stay,' Tabitha said quietly. 'I asked him to.'

Cordelia nodded and scrunched the tissue tighter. 'Julie explained a lot of things. Things I had no idea about.' She sniffed and dabbed her eyes. 'And I'm sorry our actions forced you into this situation to begin with. Please come back and stay tonight. Let's not leave things this way.'

'Julie's been nothing but kind to me, to Raff...' Tabitha motioned towards the house. 'She only wants what's best for him. I think she'd be happy if you managed to repair your relationship. It would benefit everyone.'

Cordelia nodded. 'I think I have an apology to make before we go home.' She breathed deeply and turned to her. 'I hope you'll come back?'

She didn't wait for an answer. With determination, Cordelia headed into the house. Tabitha could just make out Julie's gentle voice asking if everything was all right.

Tabitha took one last look at the ocean, cool and dark, glittering in the moonlight. The endless space begged the question: where would she go next? Where was she drawn to? Back to the comfort and familiarity of her family, or perhaps she should head across the ocean on an adventure? As Cordelia's and Julie's voices drifted into the night, she realised she hadn't yet replied to Ollie. But, for now, with the island bathed in darkness and feeling drained after a day filled with emotion, she only had the energy to make one decision. She turned towards the warm light spilling from the house and took a deep breath in readiness of joining Julie and Cordelia. What was one more night?

34

Tabitha woke up alone, in the guest bed she'd shared with Raff just the night before. So much had changed in such a short time. Her anger at him for leaving had dissipated to the extent that she wished he was here with her, but then, wouldn't that make it all the harder to leave for good later? She was leaving the villa, but was she leaving the island?

She grabbed her phone and clicked on to Ollie's message. Writing together and touring the world, wasn't that once the dream? Perhaps this was the opportunity she'd been waiting for. She'd buried all the past hurt and misunderstanding and he was offering her a chance for things to go back to the way they used to be and an even bigger platform for her songwriting career.

She made a snap decision and thumbed a quick reply.

Sorry for taking a while to get back to you. Things have changed, meaning I'll be leaving Madeira sooner than expected. I should be flying out later today, but I can come over to yours first and chat more about the tour if you're around? I'm definitely interested...

By the time she'd showered, Ollie had replied with a simple 'yes, come on over' along with his address. Tabitha sent a thumbs up emoji back and dressed for comfort in trainers, black dungarees and a fitted white T-shirt. She slicked on red lipstick and gathered her washbag and the rest of her belongings. If things worked out with Ollie, she could always change her flight again...

Cordelia was already up, sitting on the terrace next to the pool, her back to the house, the dogs lying by her feet. Tabitha packed her washbag in her suitcase, took a deep breath and went outside.

'Morning,' she said, joining Cordelia at the table laid with fruit, yogurt, toast and coffee.

'Morning.' Cordelia offered her a weak smile. 'I hope you managed to sleep okay in the end.'

Although pristinely dressed with flawless make-up, she looked tired, as if the oomph had been taken out of her. Not that Tabitha was surprised after the events of last night.

She was thankful when Rufus hobbled onto the terrace and joined them with a beaming smile. Sitting outside having breakfast reminded Tabitha of her and Raff doing the same that first morning together. How easily they'd fitted into each other's lives. Despite the ups and downs, he'd made quite the impression, which left her feeling uncertain, conflicted, sad... So many emotions were swirling around her head.

Rufus broke any lingering tension. A good sleep had energised him and he was as chatty as he'd been when he'd picked Tabitha up from the airport, filling the silence with anecdotes from their holiday, all of the incredible experiences they'd had before his accident, from a boat safari on the Rufiji River, to a wine tour in the Stellenbosch region of South Africa. Both Tabitha and Cordelia were happy to listen and eat.

With breakfast polished off and coffee drunk, Rufus started to gather together the empty plates and bowls.

Cordelia dabbed her lips with her napkin, dropped it on her empty plate and looked at Tabitha. 'Walk with me.'

Tabitha glanced at Rufus, who gave her an encouraging smile but grabbed her arm before she could follow Cordelia. He waited until his wife was out of earshot. 'I just want you to know, I should have been there for Raff more.' His jaw clenched and the upbeat bravado that had been on display over breakfast evaporated. 'Although it was my wife's idea to send him to boarding school, I went along with it, even though I knew he wasn't happy. I didn't do anything about it. I was busy and never had the time; it's not an excuse, just the truth. I told myself he'd be better off back in England getting a good education with lots of friends his own age.' He looked at her with tight lips and sorrow in his eyes. 'That's not all I'm sorry for. I should have fought his corner too. Cordelia was adamant he'd stolen from us. Too often I've turned a blind eye in exchange for an easy life when I shouldn't have done.' He shrugged and gestured down the garden. 'She's waiting; you'd better go and join her.'

Tabitha watched him hobble away, the dogs padding after him as she digested his words. Revelations like this were all well and good, but it wasn't her who needed to hear them. Sadness clenched her heart at the thought that Raff had missed out on his father's apology.

With a sigh, she wandered down the garden, taking strength from the warmth of the morning sun and the calming green of the surroundings. Cordelia was by the hammock, her hand resting on the trunk of the palm tree. She turned when Tabitha reached her.

'I owe you an apology.'

Tabitha shook her head. 'You really don't.'

Cordelia held up her hand. 'I owe Julie one too, and Raff.' She sighed. 'I did apologise to Julie last night.' She paused and fiddled with the rings stacked on her fingers. 'The thing is, I've always envied Julie, at least her ability to connect with Raff when I couldn't. She's been there for him when I wasn't and I didn't really understand why until last night. I guess what I'm trying to say is I've never given her the time of day, never actually talked to her, just made assumptions. I honestly thought because she and Anton didn't have children it was because they'd chosen not to, while I've struggled juggling my career with motherhood.'

Tabitha didn't know what to say so she went with nothing, giving Cordelia the opportunity to unload.

'I didn't want to have children.' Cordelia twisted the bangle on her wrist. She didn't meet Tabitha's eyes, staring instead across the bottom of the garden glimmering in the heat haze of the morning. 'That's the absolute truth.' She swiped angrily at her eyes and gave a hollow laugh. 'I don't think I've admitted that to anyone apart from my husband.'

'You didn't feel differently when you found out you were pregnant?' Tabitha thought back on the all-consuming feeling of love that she hadn't anticipated once she'd come to terms with her own unexpected pregnancy.

'No. I wanted to, desperately so, because despite not wanting to be a mother, I never once contemplated not going through with it.' She took a shuddery breath. 'Actually, that's a lie, I did contemplate it, I just knew that wasn't an option.'

'What about Rufus? How did he feel?'

'Shocked, then worried about how much our comfortable life would change. He got me through a difficult pregnancy and birth, though. We made the best of it, but it was easier for him. I had to take time off, while he continued his career. It was my life that was hugely disrupted and I was incredibly envious of him being able to escape to the City for work. He got to meet people and carry on with his life. I loathed being a stay-at-home mum and wife and being supported by him. I went back to work after just a few months. We were lucky Rufus's parents weren't too far away, plus we had a nanny. I'll openly admit I wasn't a hands-on mum. My focus was always on my work and then building our business. I honestly thought Raff would be better off spending holidays in a place like this,' she swept her hands towards the garden and ocean view, 'yet still having the education we felt he deserved back in England.'

'He needed you, though. Both of you. It's obvious from the time I've spent with him, he's always craved your love, however much he's tried to push you away.'

Cordelia nodded and bit her lip, her cheeks flushing. 'I know; Julie said. I appreciate that I didn't consider the impact it would have on him being away from our home, family and friends. I also understand that her openness and maternal spirit was exactly what Raff needed.' She looked at Tabitha with red-rimmed eyes. 'I didn't know what Julie had gone through. Anton too. Trying and failing to have a family of their own. Such heartache.'

This softer, empathetic side to Cordelia took Tabitha by surprise. It made her hopeful that there was a way Cordelia and Rufus would be able to rebuild a relationship with Raff. If only he'd stayed.

Cordelia finished talking and they strolled back up the garden together. Perhaps a newly created openness and understanding between Cordelia and Julie would help to heal the hurt; their mutual love for Raff bringing them together. They just needed Raff now to finish the healing process.

* * *

Tabitha was heartbroken to say goodbye to Bailey, Fudge and Misty. The dogs knew something was up as she dragged her luggage outside before crouching down to give them one last stroke and tickle beneath their chins.

Cordelia and Rufus came out with her, shutting the dogs safely inside. Julie was waiting in her car on the lane.

Tabitha turned to Rufus and Cordelia. 'I don't quite know what to say. I guess sorry and thank you seem appropriate.'

Cordelia nodded. 'This pet sit will certainly be a memorable one for you.'

You don't know the half of it, Tabitha thought.

The coldness from last night had gone from Cordelia's voice. She looked smaller somehow, washed out, the events of the past few days having taken their toll. It certainly wasn't how Tabitha had imagined her time on Madeira would end, but at least the animosity had gone. The smile Cordelia gave as they shook hands seemed genuine.

Rufus clamped his hand on Tabitha's shoulder. He looked far more refreshed than his wife did, having had a restful night while missing out on all the commotion. 'You take care and have a safe flight.'

'I will, thank you.' She glanced down at Bailey and Fudge sitting by the window, their big eyes looking at her lovingly. She swallowed back the lump in her throat; this was the worst part, leaving the pets, yet here her emotions were amplified more than anywhere else she'd been.

She adjusted the guitar strap where it was digging into her shoulder and, with one last glance at the dogs, she walked across the driveway, giving Cordelia and Rufus a wave just as a taxi pulled up outside the gate. For a second, she thought it had been booked by mistake until a door opened and a tall figure emerged.

Tabitha squinted in the mid-morning sun. 'Raff?'

Hoisting his rucksack on his back, he opened the gate and strode towards her, a determined look on his face.

A mix of surprise and joy twisted through her. 'What are you doing back?'

'I made a mistake walking out yesterday the way I did,' he said as he reached her, his blue eyes focused on her and only her, ignoring his parents hovering by the front door. 'It wasn't fair on you. However much I don't want to face up to things and have a difficult conversation with my parents, it was completely wrong to let you deal with them on your own.'

As they stood together in the blissful September heat, a flood of warmth seeped through her. 'To be fair, after a shaky start and a bit of a thing at Julie's last night with your mum, they've been really decent. It's you they want to bollock.' She allowed herself a slight smile. 'But they were also devastated that you weren't here. Whatever's happened in the past, it's not too late for you all to make amends.'

'I kinda realised that when I got to Funchal. I was killing time, trying to get my head straight and couldn't figure out what the hell to do, but I knew I couldn't leave, so I didn't get on the plane. You were totally right; I do need to talk my shit through with them. They need to hear me out and perhaps it's about time I gave them a chance to explain their side of things. I've made assumptions for years, driven by anger, and they've only ever seen a side to me that they don't like – a side that, to be honest, I don't like either. It's no wonder they've thought badly of me. You faced up to Ollie and had a difficult conversation, I figured why the hell can't I.'

'I'm glad you're doing this.'

'And I'm glad you told them.' Raff's cheeks clenched as if he was fighting his emotions. 'You're leaving now?'

Tabitha swallowed back tears and nodded. Despite how hard it was to walk away from him, she felt better knowing that he had the chance to make peace with his parents and begin to heal his long held hurt.

'Where are you headed?'

'Um, Funchal. To see Ollie. He, er, wants us to write and possibly tour together.'

Raff frowned. 'I thought you were planning on going to Lisbon and then your sister's?'

'That's what I thought too.' She shrugged and held his gaze. 'Things never work out quite the way I hope.' She glanced away from him. 'I don't know. I have lots to think about and decisions to make.'

Raff glanced towards the villa. Cordelia and Rufus were standing on the shadowed porch together, their arms around each other's waists, waiting and watching.

Raff turned back to Tabitha, closed the distance between them and took her in his arms. She remained rigid for a moment, her hand clamped on the suitcase handle, before she melted into him, sliding her arms around his waist, not wanting to let go. He kissed her deeply and she kissed him back, not caring that his parents were watching, Julie too from the car.

He pulled away, his eyes damp.

'You understand Ollie wants more than just to write with you.' His jaw clenched, his eyes steely as if trying to stop his own emotions from wavering.

Tabitha sighed. 'That's really not the case.'

'You'll see I'm right.' His eyes roved across her face. 'But you need to do whatever makes you happy.'

Tabitha swallowed and placed a hand on his chest. 'Go make peace with your parents. And, um, perhaps I'll see you around.' She echoed the words she'd uttered with anger the day before, but she meant them this time, desperately hoping that this wouldn't be the last time they'd see each other.

With eyes blurred with tears, Tabitha dragged her suitcase across the driveway to where Julie was waiting, ready to take her to

Funchal. To Ollie. Or perhaps onwards somewhere completely different, where she could start over. Or she could return to the comfort and love of her family, to Elspeth and her beautiful nieces. Decisions bubbled like molten lava, her insides a jumbled mess of emotions, uncertainty twisting through her.

Tabitha loaded her suitcase, rucksack and guitar into the boot and slid on to the passenger seat.

'Are you ready?' Julie asked gently.

'No, not really, but let's go anyway.'

35

Although Tabitha had seen pictures of Ollie's Funchal villa, she'd never been there before. It was the place he'd bought when he'd found fame and fortune after winning *The Star*. He'd upgraded his London pad too. Long gone were the days of roughing it in a damp shared flat.

He greeted her with warmth and his stubble tickled as he brushed her cheek with a kiss. His arm remained around her waist as he led her inside. If Rufus and Cordelia's place had reminded her of a show home, Ollie's pad was positively palatial.

He gave her a tour of the four-bedroomed villa, with its gleaming walnut wood floors and expensive art decorating the white walls. The whole of the living area had floor-to-ceiling windows looking out over the infinity pool. There were views to the ocean and the green terraced hillside punctuated by red roofs and white villa walls, occasional blue pools and swathes of palm trees. He had his own gym, an enclosed garden and various outdoor terraces for entertaining, including the most impressive one with the pool where you could see for miles.

The villa was empty of other people. Tabitha hadn't expected it to be. She thought his PA, who'd been at his birthday party, would at least be there, but she wasn't. As they wandered around, she realised how different it felt in his company to seven years ago; there was a strange expectation and uncertainty. More expectation on his part; her uncertainty came from wondering what he actually wanted from her. Worries scrambled her thoughts about how they would work together, her own commitments to the record label she freelanced for and what going on tour with Ollie would actually entail. Yes, she wanted to embrace life and all its opportunities, but was this the right decision? Her head flashed with a possible future. Ollie's fame was epic and he was offering her a chance to work with him and be back in his life.

As Ollie grabbed a bottle of wine from the fridge and led her out on to the largest terrace, Raff's comment about Ollie danced around her head. Had she been naïve to think a platonic relationship was all Ollie had ever wanted? The distance of years had given her a new perspective. And it wasn't a case of *who* she wanted; it was *what* she wanted. As Raff had said, she needed to do whatever would make her happy.

She tuned back in to what Ollie was saying as they reached oversized beanbag loungers by the pool.

'It's a bloody lush place for parties; stick around and we can have one before the tour kicks off.' He opened the wine, poured it into two glasses and handed her one. 'I'm going back to London after the tour finishes. Need time in the studio to work on the next album.'

He swigged the wine, set it down on the table between the beanbags and peeled off his T-shirt.

Tabitha sat down on the closest beanbag and took a large gulp of the chilled wine, feeling the need for it as her eyes trailed Ollie. His confidence hadn't changed, but she had. She felt differently about him; it wasn't that she was uncomfortable around him, it was just the comfortable familiarity had been lost.

He dived into the pool, his muscled shoulders and arms slicing through the water. He was showing off, like he'd always done, but she had a strong sense that he was doing it on purpose, enticing her with his home, with the opportunities he could offer, with himself...

He swam over and rested his arms on the tiled side, close enough to reach out and touch her. The sun sparkled on the turquoise pool, making Ollie's tanned muscled shoulders gleam, the ink decorating them streaked with water. Was it a mistake to have come here?

During the drive to Funchal with Julie, she'd felt so muddled as they'd talked about Raff turning up and what that meant. Julie had been filled with worry for him, while the surprise and delight Tabitha had felt at Raff's return had been overshadowed by sorrow at leaving. Their conversation had moved on and it was a fond and tearful farewell when they'd reached Funchal. Thinking clearly about it now, perhaps it would have been wise if she'd asked Julie to drop her off at the airport instead. That would have been sensible. A clean break, from the island, from Ollie, from Raff...

'Have you got a bikini with you?' Ollie's eyes traced her face, lingering as they dropped downwards. 'Come and join me.'

She knew then, without a doubt, that everything had changed. If Ollie had suggested something like that eight or nine years ago, it wouldn't have been as loaded as it was now.

What was she doing? Flirting with the idea that this could be her second chance at a big break? She was doing absolutely fine. She'd found her own success; she was making her living doing what she loved. What more did she want?

It was then it hit her; everything she'd been running away from and trying to figure out slotted into place, the puzzle pieces of her life finally coming together. She needed to move forward and find her own place in the world; there was no point in attempting to recapture something from the past that would be messy and a mistake, or settle for something she wasn't 100 per cent sure about, like she'd almost done with Lewis.

Ollie heaved himself out of the pool and swaggered over, bare-chested and grinning, his swim shorts clinging to him, leaving little to the imagination.

Tabitha scrambled out of the beanbag lounger. 'I think I'm going to go.'

Ollie frowned and ran his hand through his wet hair. 'Why? You've only just got here.'

His smooth, toned chest ran with rivulets of water. How jealous would those girls who'd drooled over him in the rooftop bar be at the idea of her alone with their idol. Their newly single idol.

But none of this was what Tabitha wanted.

'I've got a flight booked for later today,' she said.

'Then cancel it.'

Tabitha shook her head. 'I think I need to head back to the UK, see my family for a bit.'

He scooped up a towel and dabbed his chest dry. 'Okay, so see your family, then join me on tour in a couple of weeks. The best of both, that way.'

Tabitha studied him, wondering if he really did want her back in his life as just a friend. 'Can I ask you something?'

'Anything.'

'Remember way back in our third year in Cardiff, we had a party at our student house one night and you ended up crashing in my bed?'

He held her gaze, his eyes narrowing ever so slightly.

'It was the night we kissed,' she prompted, 'the one and only time.'

He nodded, a hint of a smile beginning to form. 'Yeah, I remember.'

'How did you feel about it?'

'About us kissing?' He laughed, dropped the towel on the beanbag and moved closer. 'Let me remind you.'

Before she could react, his lips were on hers, his damp hands dipping under the edge of her dungarees and beneath her T-shirt, finding bare skin. He kissed her harder, his tongue probing, his hands caressing. She closed her eyes and kissed him back.

He pulled away and grinned. 'Does that answer your question?'

She met his familiar blue eyes. 'It certainly does.'

36

Ollie kissing her was the deciding factor for Tabitha. She'd kissed him back to give him a second chance, to see if this time she'd feel any differently. She hadn't. She appreciated his good looks, admired what he had achieved and was glad of his friendship, but he did nothing for her, not compared to the way she felt with Raff... She'd never seen the attraction Ollie had for her because she'd never felt that way about him. Ollie welcoming her back into his life wasn't about repairing their friendship, that was long gone. Time and distance had allowed Ollie to believe the possibility of romance was there, while for Tabitha his kiss had had the same effect as the first time. Yes, she could have used him, gone along with it, furthered her career, written and toured with him, but she didn't want to wind up in bed with him, she didn't want to be a focus of the media circus that surrounded him. She still thought of him as the Ollie she'd met at eighteen and a relationship beyond friends just didn't feel right.

Tabitha considered letting him down gently, but she decided he needed to hear the truth. 'You mistook me reaching out after all this time for feelings that just aren't there. You were my best friend and, despite everything, I hope we can remain friends, but I don't want to be with you. You broke my heart through your actions and I can never be with someone I don't trust. Not to mention you've just split up with your girlfriend. I'm not going to be a rebound to make you feel better.'

Ollie folded his arms. 'Tabs, you know that's not what this is.'

'Maybe, maybe not, but try thinking about me for once and what *I* might want. There's nothing more than friendship between us, of that I'm sure.'

He laughed off the rejection and called her a taxi. They said goodbye and it felt good to walk away. This time she wasn't running away from a difficult situation and confusing feelings like she'd done a year ago with Lewis. She was choosing a new and exciting path for herself, which she realised was exactly what she'd been doing since the night Ollie had claimed her song as his own. She'd stood on her own two feet and carved out a successful career for herself, by herself. She didn't need the likes of Ollie Pereira back then and she certainly didn't now.

* * *

Tabitha caught her flight to Lisbon, messaged her sister about her decision and stayed the night in a hotel at the airport before flying to Bristol early the next morning. After a taxi ride and a train journey, she made it to Cardiff Central Station.

Elspeth's beaming smile and welcome familiarity was everything she needed and Tabitha couldn't help but laugh and cry as they hugged each other.

They chatted all the way back in the car about the girls and the first wedding in the newly renovated barn, about Gethin being left at home looking after the kids and their glampers while cooking dinner. It was as if Elspeth understood that Tabitha wasn't ready to talk about herself, to relive the events and the emotions that had led her to being back in the UK, and Tabitha was grateful for her sister's sensitivity. It was only when they turned off the main road and bumped down the track to The Wildflower Hideaway that Elspeth turned the conversation round to Tabitha.

'I had hoped you'd turn up here with Raff,' Elspeth said gently as she pulled up in front of the whitewashed cottage with honeysuckle and ivy on either side of the front door.

Tabitha sighed. 'He came back, you know, to make amends with his parents. Your advice helped and it was the best outcome.'

'For him, maybe.' Elspeth gave her a knowing look.

'Yes, for him.' She found it hard to talk about Raff without feeling a knot tightening in her chest. 'I hope he manages to piece together their relationship.'

Elspeth switched off the engine. 'You didn't think to invite him here?'

'He took me so much by surprise, turning up just as I was leaving. Anyway, it was all a bit of a muddle as I was about to see Ollie...'

Before either of them could say anything else, the front door opened and Olivia and Nancy streamed out, all long strawberry-blonde hair and beaming faces as they danced about in front of the cottage, peering through the car window with massive grins.

Tabitha's anxiety melted away and her thoughts about Raff dispersed as she got out of the car to a chorus of 'Auntie Tabitha! Auntie Tabitha!' before being enveloped in the warm squishy hugs she'd been longing for.

'Let poor Auntie Tabitha at least get in the house!' Elspeth laughed as she slammed the car door shut.

The girls' chatter was at a hundred miles an hour as they led her towards the cottage.

Gethin stood in the doorway, an amused smile on his face as

Olivia and Nancy clung to her, squealing and laughing. 'Leave the luggage,' Gethin said in his lilting Welsh accent. 'I'll bring it in in a bit. Dinner's ready and the girls are *starving*.' He raised his eyebrows and hugged Tabitha. 'They've only told me a million times already.'

As they tucked into Gethin's homemade chilli con carne, the laughter and love flying around the kitchen table was effortless. Although she'd often felt like an outsider, even around her own family, Tabitha couldn't help but be drawn into their undiluted happiness. Her nieces' chatter was joyous, with Olivia talking about school – lots of which she hadn't even told her mum and dad – while Nancy explained in great detail about the bug hotel she was building in the garden.

Tabitha was aware that everything in Elspeth and Gethin's life wasn't as perfect as it seemed on the outside; there had been plenty of tears and stress over the years, from Elspeth's heartache at not being able to get pregnant, their joy of finally conceiving, followed by their surprise at getting pregnant with Nancy not long after having Olivia, to the hard work of recent years moving to Wales and building their glamping business while raising two young children. They'd argued, they'd made up, then argued some more while getting the Hideaway up and running, and yet their love for each other had seen them through the highs and lows. Ultimately, what Elspeth and Gethin had was what Tabitha strived for. Was a love like that written in the stars? For her, she hoped so,

After dinner, and before it got dark, Olivia and Nancy gave her a tour of the Hideaway. Elspeth came with them, hooking her arm in Tabitha's as they walked away from the cottage along a grassy path. The girls ran ahead in their wellies, skirts and jumpers, their wavy hair flying behind them.

Despite Olivia's and Nancy's giggles and chatter, Tabitha couldn't help but notice the peace and stillness as they strolled in the cool of the September evening, with just the coo coo of a woodpigeon hidden in the trees. Tabitha imagined the wildflower meadows would be stunning in spring, but in early autumn and with a breeze billowing across the landscape, the long grass rippled green in the silvery light of dusk. Woodland clustered at the edges, while the view to the Black Mountains was uninterrupted, the blue-grey sky still bright on the horizon, pale sunlight just reaching the mountaintops. After all the vistas she'd seen on her travels, this was as idyllic as any.

The girls chatted together, yet Elspeth allowed Tabitha to soak up the beauty of their surroundings in peace, only occasionally breaking the quiet to point out the barn and the glamping places tucked away in their own private areas, each with their own hot tub, firepit and veranda that made the most of the view.

'The woodland cabin will be free from next week,' Elspeth said as they neared a wood-clad building half hidden in a clearing beyond the trees. It reminded Tabitha a little of the garden office in Madeira. 'I've booked it out for you so you have somewhere private to stay and work.'

Tabitha squeezed her sister's arm tighter, overwhelmed by the sense of peace and love flooding through her. The endless space was soothing and it felt a little like home after moving from housesit to housesit for months on end. She'd absolutely made the right decision saying no to Ollie, of that she was sure, yet she couldn't help but think just how much she'd like to share this place with Raff.

A bat, dark against the clear midnight-blue sky, flew between the shadowed trees as they started to head back. Pools of light from the treehouse, the woodland cabin and the streamside lodge pierced the dusk, and although there were other people staying, it didn't feel as if there was anyone else for miles.

When it got dark, they retreated into the warmth of the cottage and Tabitha helped Elspeth get the girls to bed. They crashed on the sofa in the snug with Gethin for an hour, drinking wine and chatting effortlessly, as they always did.

It was later, when she was alone in bed in the spare room, exhausted after a long day travelling and the emotion of being enveloped in the love of her family, that Tabitha messaged Raff. Even here, miles from Madeira and in a place that she knew for the time being was right for her, he still consumed her thoughts and her heart ached. She didn't want to let the silence between them grow, so she decided to reach out.

Hey there, you were right about Ollie. He definitely thought about that kiss differently than I did. Decided not to stay and headed to my sister's in Wales instead. Hope things have gone okay with your parents. Miss you. Tabs, xx

She spent twenty minutes reading, rewriting, then rereading the message, deleting 'miss you' three or four times before she got the courage to leave it in. After all, that was honestly how she felt and she wanted him to know that.

Of course she hoped for a reply, but after hearing nothing back despite him having seen the message, she realised whatever it was they'd had on Madeira was over. Pushing her upset away, she allowed herself to be swept up in family life. With Olivia at school and Elspeth and Gethin juggling looking after Nancy, the glampers, the acres of woodland and meadows during the day, Tabitha took the opportunity to work. The late afternoon and early evenings were spent playing with the girls, exploring the woods and building dams in the stream before dinner and adult conversation took over once the girls were asleep.

It was a few days later, early on the Sunday evening as Tabitha had popped up to her room to charge her laptop, when a message pinged on to her phone.

Her heart skipped when she realised it was from Raff.

Hey, don't suppose you fancy some pastéis de maracuja? I remember how much you like them…

Tabitha stared at the message, confusion crawling through her, while her heart fluttered at the crazy thought of what she hoped it meant. She held the phone in her lap, debating how to respond when she heard muffled voices downstairs and a door slam shut.

Footsteps clattered up the stairs and Elspeth appeared in the doorway out of breath.

'You have a visitor,' she said as the biggest grin spread across her face. 'And he's even hotter in real life.'

EPILOGUE

EIGHT MONTHS LATER

Porto glittered in the sunshine with the wide meandering river flowing to the ocean, its northern bank lined with restaurants and cafes, while on the other side of the Douro, the port houses clustered. Tabitha sat at an outside table in Ribeira Square, her hands clasped around a coffee, relishing a peaceful start to the spring day. Behind her, the stone buildings with their wrought-iron balconies and walls painted either a red wine, peach or lavender colour led deeper into the old town. It was a myriad of winding lanes and beautiful old buildings, many with crumbling plasterwork, looming over narrow streets.

This spot, with its uninterrupted view to the river, had fast become her favourite during the two-week pet sit looking after a friendly tortoiseshell cat. From her table, she could see the Dom Luís I Bridge spanning the wide river to the cream, white and grey buildings on the south bank. Interspersed with pockets of trees and washed by watery sunlight, they studded the hillside. Tabitha sipped her coffee with a satisfied smile.

A tall figure striding along the wide riverside pavement caught her eye, pulling her attention from the view. Catching sight of Raff walking towards her always reminded her of their first shock meeting nearly nine months before. So much had changed since then, but her heart still skipped when she laid eyes on him, although for different reasons now.

'Morning.' Raff leaned down and kissed her. He settled himself opposite and ran a hand through his hair. He looked as if he hadn't long been awake and was deliciously sexy with it.

'You saw my note then.' Tabitha smiled.

'Sorry, yeah, I was dead to the world this morning.'

'You managed to meet your deadline?'

'Yep, book two is delivered and you have my undivided attention for the rest of the weekend, I promise.'

A waiter came over and Raff ordered a coffee. He leaned back in his chair with a contented sigh and gazed out at the river sparkling in the morning sun.

Raff showing up at her sister's had shocked and elated Tabitha. The timing was perfect and the two of them had moved in to the cabin in the woods for the next couple of weeks, working during the day, eating with Tabitha's family in the evening and spending the nights alone. They kissed in the hot tub to the sound of owls hooting and the sight of bats flying, then headed to bed to continue exploring the feelings that had been ignited on Madeira.

On the weekends, the girls would come and find them, although Elspeth didn't allow them to be disturbed until late morning, conscious of how much Tabitha and Raff craved alone time. Saturday and Sunday mornings were spent in bed having lazy morning sex and talking about everything, before the girls' laughter filtered from beyond the trees, dragging them out of bed to explore the woods rather than each other. The girls couldn't get enough of Raff, taking him into their hearts as much as he had with them. For Tabitha, those couple of weeks at the Hideaway were some of the best she'd ever had.

As Tabitha and Raff began to fall for each other, the landscape had begun to change. The leaves turned golden yellow, bronze and red, while a chill wind blustered autumn in. With an occasional frost in the morning and the cooler nights, they were glad of the wood burner and the cosy cabin with its bed up in the eaves. Outside, crunchy leaves carpeted the grassy clearing and the firepit was a necessity when they sat out in the evening. The view from the wildflower meadow changed too; the woodland was ablaze with autumn colour, while the distant mountains took on an ethereal silver hue. The sunshine was weaker, the colours more muted now summer was over.

Just as the puzzle pieces had slotted into place when Tabitha had last seen Ollie on Madeira, living with Raff cemented all the feelings that had been swirling during her time on the island. The possibility of what could be was slowly turning into reality.

Raff's relationship with his parents was in no way fixed, but they'd talked and had begun to heal the hurt after years of misunderstanding. The difficult and revealing conversations that Tabitha had been party to with Cordelia and Rufus after Raff had left were continued when he returned, along with heartfelt apologies from Raff's parents for accusing him of stealing when, deep down, they knew he hadn't.

There was communication between Cordelia and Rufus and Julie and Anton as well after Raff had impressed upon his parents just how much Julie, in particular, had supported him over the years. There'd been tears on all sides. Raff had confided in Tabitha how hard it had been to dig up the past he'd run away from, but cathartic too. It had been freeing for them both to revisit difficult periods in their lives, to try to come to terms with their sadness. Raff being brave enough to face his parents and their chequered past had made Tabitha do the same with hers. Opening up to Julie and then Raff on Madeira had been the start of her own healing process. At the Hideaway, Elspeth was there for her and they talked, as they'd always done, but Tabitha shared everything, and when Raff arrived, there was no topic off limits between them. She'd never been in a relationship with anyone she'd felt so free and comfortable with.

Raff had no ties and had been desperate to escape London and a past that was plagued with bad choices and regret. Travelling with Tabitha offered a clean slate and, for her, after weeks of living together and delving deeper into their lives and their feelings for each other, she didn't want to go anywhere without him. He was open to new places but had the independence that had always been missing with Lewis. So, at the end of October, amid tears, laughter and the promise of visiting again soon, Tabitha and Raff said goodbye to Elspeth, Gethin, Olivia and Nancy and, after a flying visit to Devon so Raff could meet her parents, they headed to the US. During the three weeks Tabitha spent in Nashville writing with an up-and-coming new star for the record label, Raff worked from their apartment. They slotted together perfectly, both of them relishing their independence while making the most of their evenings and the weekends together. Tabitha's desire to be on her own had evaporated as her love for Raff had grown and they'd both embraced a social life in Nashville, with Tabitha saying yes to invites to parties or meals out with her producer and drinks with the singer, which only a few months before she would have turned down. Raff never once held her back. He encouraged her and had been by her side when she'd wanted him to be without ever leaving her feeling stifled.

Ollie's US tour had kicked off and a video of Ollie standing on stage in front of thousands of fans dedicating the final song of the night to Tabitha went viral.

'I'm making good on a promise – something I should have done a long time ago. "A Star Like You" was actually written by my good friend, talented songwriter Tabitha Callahan. I'm sorry for all the hurt I caused. This is just the start of making it up to you, Tabs.' After only sporadic messages from Ollie since she'd last seen him on Madeira, this public apology surprised her, making it clear that he really was intent on trying to put things right.

Her social media followers shot up and both she and Ollie were a hot topic for a few days, to the point that she got a taste of his life in the public eye and didn't like it one bit. It cemented her opinion of fame being the last thing she craved. Ollie was welcome to it, but she appreciated the gesture and the public apology more than anything.

As well as the video, his Instagram was filled with images of him on stage and at parties, but Tabitha didn't regret her decision to not join him and was mightily relieved when the media fuss surrounding her inevitably died down. She had the career she'd always craved, the satisfaction of working on her own terms, someone she loved by her side, along with the ability to travel and follow her dreams. It was everything she'd wanted and more.

The first time Raff had told her he loved her was when they'd gone back to Madeira for a week in February, chasing the sun after a few weeks in the gloomy, cold and wet UK. They'd stayed with Raff's parents for a couple of nights and had dinner with Julie and Anton too, before spending the remainder of the week on their own at an Airbnb cottage nestled among banana plantations by the ocean in Calheta. On their penultimate day, they'd left behind the sunshine at sea level, picked up Bailey and Fudge and driven to Fanal Forest in the northwest for a walk in one of the most stunning areas of the island. The temperature had dropped and the ancient laurel forest had been shrouded in fog. They'd wandered hand in hand among the twisted trunks of the trees with the dogs, the fog drifting like white smoke, blanketing the landscape. It was otherworldly and magical, a complete contrast to the warmth and sunshine they'd left behind. They'd taken a selfie, two shadowed figures with beaming smiles surrounded by white apart from the dark entwining branches reaching out as if to embrace them. They'd kissed and then he'd said he loved her. Wrapped in his arms, Tabitha hadn't hesitated in her reply, her feelings for him as clear as the mornings on Madeira where you could see for miles out into the vast Atlantic.

'I love you too.'

* * *

Tabitha and Raff finished their coffee, just as the tables surrounding them began to fill with tourists. It was a Saturday and they had a couple more days until their house sit in Porto ended and, with a free weekend, she was determined to make the best of it and revisit the places they'd come to love. So that's what they did, strolling hand in hand across the bridge, their thighs protesting as they navigated their way up the hill to Taylor's Port House and sat in the library tasting thirty-year-old tawny port. They headed back across the river for grilled spatchcock chicken at a small family-run restaurant where they only spoke Portuguese.

With aching feet, they got back to the apartment and flopped together on the sofa. Early-evening sunshine streamed through the windows. Dust motes twirled in the light. Much like the apartment in Paris and the log cabin in Canada she'd stayed in, Tabitha didn't want to leave their Porto apartment with its large shuttered windows, exposed stone walls and gleaming wooden floors marrying effortlessly with the modern kitchen, bathroom and queen-sized bed. In the heart of Porto's heritage centre, they were walking distance from everywhere and even had the use of the tiny but beautiful courtyard garden.

The cat, Luna, slunk past, smoothing her fur against their legs.

Raff curled his arm around Tabitha's shoulders and sighed. 'I'm going to be sad to leave here.'

'Me too,' she said, smiling at how his words echoed her thoughts.

Raff rested his bare feet on the coffee table and tugged her closer. 'What's your dream, Tabs?'

'It doesn't matter about my dream; it has to be our dream for it to work.' She relished being enclosed in his strong arms and the tickle of his fingers brushing against her skin.

'Okay, what's our dream? You start.'

Tabitha gazed out at their little slice of Porto, temporary but somewhere she would desperately miss. What they wanted to do and the places they wanted to go had often been a topic of conversation over the last few months as they'd travelled together. 'I'd like to live somewhere vibrant.'

'Definitely. Somewhere beautiful and full of life,' Raff added, wafting his hand towards the arched windows with the stonework and wrought-iron balcony of the townhouse opposite filling the frame like a painting. 'What about long term, though? Where do you see us?'

Tabitha met his eyes, which were so open and honest. Not long ago, a question like that would have scared her stupid; now it left her open to the possibility of a future filled with not just the thrill of travelling and having a career she adored, but the security and happiness of sharing it with someone she loved.

She slid her hand across his muscled stomach and rested her head on his shoulder. 'I see us finding somewhere we can't bear to leave, somewhere so perfectly wonderful we just know it could be home.'

'But we haven't found it yet?'

Tabitha shook her head. 'I don't think so.'

'Will we be on our own or with someone else?'

She pulled away from his shoulder and looked at him. 'Are you asking me if I want to have kids?'

'I was thinking more about us getting a dog.' Raff grinned as he caressed her waist. 'But do you? Want kids?'

The ache in her heart at the reminder of what she'd lost was duller now, nothing like the raw pain she'd felt last year. Her thoughts drifted to their future. She nodded and slipped her hand in his. 'With you, yes, absolutely. But not yet, there's too much to do and too many places to discover. Eventually though.'

'Well, yes, I'm talking way in the future.' Raff laughed, taking the seriousness of their conversation in his stride. 'So, before we freak each other out completely, what about short term?' He nudged her gently. 'I'm still up for that long-awaited game of strip poker.'

'Oh, you are, are you? Well, maybe I'll oblige tonight, seeing as though there's no pool for you to push me into.'

'I'll hold you to that.'

'Is that a promise?'

'You bet,' he said. 'And after that?'

Tabitha cupped Raff's stubbled face in her hands and gazed into his smiling blue eyes. She leaned in close and kissed him, teasing with her tongue as he kissed her back, their hands smoothing and exploring, the excitement and desire as fresh as the day they'd met. She planted kisses across his stubbled jaw and up to his ear before whispering, 'To be honest, anywhere with you is fine by me.'

Tabitha pulled away and opened her laptop. Raff slipped his arm around her waist as she clicked on the house sitting website and opened up the map showing all of the available house sits around the world. Their future held the possibility of putting down roots and starting a family, but for now the promise of adventure and new experiences was all they needed.

Tabitha turned back to her soulmate and grinned. 'Where next?'